"Leave it alone, Reeve. I know you're trying to help, but if you dig into things you don't understand, you'll only hurt me. The baby, too."

Once again, Reeve took her into his arms, but his feelings were not nearly as tender as before. Something was going on that he did not understand.

"Explain the rest, Polly," he insisted, trying not to become intoxicated by the fragrant silkiness of her hair.

She shook her head. "I can't." Her voice broke.

Where was his sanity? Despite every bit of sense he had, he bent down and captured her mouth with his. For a moment she did not respond. And then she kissed him back, as though this was the only kiss they would ever share. As though there were no tomorrow.

Dear Harlequin Intrigue Reader,

The days are getting cooler, but the romantic suspense is always hot at Harlequin Intrigue! Check out this month's selections.

TEXAS CONFIDENTIAL continues with *The Specialist* (#589) by Dani Sinclair. Rafe Alvarez was the resident playboy agent, until he met his match in Kendra Kincaide. He transformed his new partner into a femme fatale for the sake of a mission, and instantly lost his bachelor's heart for the sake of love....

THE SUTTON BABIES have grown in number by two in *Little Boys Blue* (#590) by Susan Kearney. A custody battle over cowboy M.D. Cameron Sutton's baby boys was brewing. When East Coast socialite Alexa Whitfield agreed to a marriage of convenience, Cam thought his future was settled. Until he fell for his temporary wife— the same wife someone was determined to kill!

Hailed by *Romantic Times Magazine* as an author who writes a "tantalizing read," Gayle Wilson returns with *Midnight Remembered* (#591), which marks the conclusion of her MORE MEN OF MYSTERY series. When ex-CIA agent Joshua Stone couldn't remember his true identity, he became an easy target. But his ex-partner Paige Daniels knew all his secrets, including what was in his heart....

Reeve Snyder had rescued Polly Black from death and delivered her baby girl one fateful night. Polly's vulnerable beauty touched him deep inside, but who was she? And what was she running from? And next time, would Reeve be able to save her and her daughter when danger came calling? Find out in *Alias Mommy* (#592) by Linda O. Johnston.

Don't miss a single exciting moment!

Sincerely,

Denise O'Sullivan
Associate Senior Editor
Harlequin Intrigue

ALIAS MOMMY
LINDA O. JOHNSTON

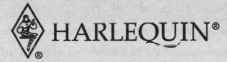

HARLEQUIN®

TORONTO • NEW YORK • LONDON
AMSTERDAM • PARIS • SYDNEY • HAMBURG
STOCKHOLM • ATHENS • TOKYO • MILAN • MADRID
PRAGUE • WARSAW • BUDAPEST • AUCKLAND

ISBN 0-373-22592-X

ALIAS MOMMY

This edition published by arrangement with Harlequin Books S.A.

® and TM are trademarks of the publisher. Trademarks indicated with ® are registered in the United States Patent and Trademark Office, the Canadian Trade Marks Office and in other countries.

Visit us at www.eHarlequin.com

Printed in U.S.A.

ABOUT THE AUTHOR

Linda O. Johnston's first published fiction appeared in *Ellery Queen's Mystery Magazine* and won the Robert L. Fish Memorial Award for *Best First Mystery Short Story of the Year.* Now, several published short stories and four novels later, Linda is recognized for her outstanding work in the romance genre.

A practicing attorney, Linda juggles her busy schedule between mornings of writing briefs, contracts and other legalese, and afternoons of creating memorable tales of the paranormal, time travel, mystery, contemporary and romantic suspense. Armed with an undergraduate degree in journalism with an advertising emphasis from Pennsylvania State University, Linda began her versatile writing career running a small newspaper, then working in advertising and public relations, and later obtaining her J.D. degree from Duquesne University School of Law in Pittsburgh.

Linda belongs to Sisters in Crime and is actively involved with Romance Writers of America, participating in the Los Angeles, Orange County and Western Pennsylvania chapters. She lives near Universal Studios, Hollywood, with her husband, two sons and two cavalier King Charles spaniels.

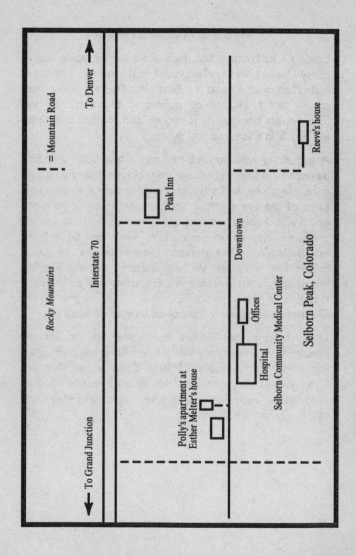

Rocky Mountains

To Grand Junction ◄—— Interstate 70 ——► To Denver

= Mountain Road

Peak Inn

Polly's apartment at Esther Melter's house

Offices

Hospital

Downtown

Selborn Community Medical Center

Selborn Peak, Colorado

Reeve's house

CAST OF CHARACTERS

Polly Black—While on the run from her stepfamily, she gave birth to her baby girl—with the help of a handsome stranger.

Reeve Snyder—A doctor dedicated to saving lives without getting involved in them—but all that changed the night he delivered mysterious and beautiful Polly Black's baby.

Alicia Frost—The ruthless reporter senses a scandal surrounding the new mom in town.

Lou Jenson—A corrupt politician with his career at stake, Lou is determined to find his missing stepdaughter.

Victor and Gene Jenson—Both brothers believe the best place for their stepsister and her child is home with the family.

Al Crackauer—The private investigator is hot on Catherine's trail. He'll let nothing stand in his way.

Ava Calvert Jenson—Has her beloved daughter's disappearance driven this mother mad?

Chapter One

Catherine Calvert Elkins leaned as close to the unyielding steering wheel as she could. Her fingers had nearly become attached to the wheel over the past long, long hours, and her cramped hand ached from clutching the leatherlike surface.

The car took curves well, thank heavens, as she forced it to career through the night. Sheets of rain threw the glare of her headlights back into her face, stabbing her moist, smarting eyes. She blinked, trying to keep them open.

She was exhausted. She had barely stopped to rest over the last what—four days? Five? She had not slept more than a couple of stolen hours at a time along her circuitous route.

"And now, the local weather report," said a disembodied male voice. She'd turned the radio up to blare over the rain's pounding and the rushing air of the defogger, which failed to clear the windshield. Only local news was on now. She had no interest in local news—except for the weather report. More thunderstorms coming, the man informed her cheerily.

Of course.

She hated driving in the rain, especially in the dark.

It was one of many newly discovered dislikes. As with the rest, she had never experienced this one before. There had always been someone....

No. She didn't dare think of that now. She had to concentrate on...what?

Oh, yes. Driving.

But she was tired. So tired.

And numb. The debilitating terror she had felt when starting out had dissipated. For now.

There weren't many cars out this night, not here among the dark mountains along the curving highway. Smart people didn't go out in this weather.

Smart people had a choice.

She had pushed herself nearly to the limit. She knew that. And she was hurting more than herself.

She reached down and lifted the large paper cup from the holder on the console. Making a face, she forced herself to take a swig of the cold coffee she had bought a few hours back. It smelled like brackish water. But she needed the caffeine.

Okay, she promised herself. First cheap motel she spotted off the interstate after daylight, she'd get a room.

It would be a long time till daylight, she knew. And still the rain smashed down on the road, her car, isolating her from the rest of the world.

That was fine. She needed to be alone. She...

Had to...

Stay awake...

She blinked suddenly, alert, as the headlights caught a metal railing dead in front of her. She slammed on the brakes, spun the steering wheel.

Screamed as the car plunged through the rail, ''No...please, no!''

Her last conscious action was to curve into a protective curl.

NEITHER RAIN NOR HEAT nor gloom of night stayed the Selborn Peak, Colorado, city council from its regular Thursday night meeting, Reeve Snyder thought ironically as he carefully guided his Volvo through the blinding torrent.

Nor thunderstorms.

It wasn't as if the business just conducted was so earthshaking that it couldn't have waited a week. But he wasn't the only one who had another demanding job, or a dislike of being out in awful weather. And this wasn't as bad as winter's snowstorms, which he abhorred for good reason. Still, if he had complained, his fellow councilpersons would—

His cellular phone rang. "Yes?" he answered tersely. He knew what the call was likely to be about at this hour, and on such a night: a medical emergency.

"Doc?" The voice was shaking. "This is Ernie Pride."

Reeve had just left Ernie at the council meeting. "Yes, Ernie. What's up?"

"I just saw a car go off the interstate in front of me. I called 911 and help's on the way, but I figured you'd be closer than anyone. Can you come?"

"Sure." Reeve got the particulars and in moments was heading toward the spot, his heart pounding. He was one of a few doctors who lived in this small town, so he was summoned frequently in emergencies. No matter how many times he responded, he couldn't help feeling the rush of anticipation—and dread.

He never knew how bad it would be till he got there.

It didn't take long. Half a mile after pulling onto the

interstate at the entrance Ernie had named, Reeve thought he saw stationary red lights ahead through the still-pouring rain. Sure enough, as he drew closer, he noticed Ernie's Land Rover on the shoulder of the road. He pulled behind, tugged off the jacket and necktie he'd worn to the meeting and, grabbing a flashlight, leaped from his car. Drenched as quickly as if he had jumped into a cold shower with his clothes on, he snatched his medical bag from the trunk and looked around. The shoulder was narrow, and the fence that was supposed to protect drivers from the steep slope below was broken by a large gap. Looking down the hillside, Reeve soon spotted another light. "Ernie?" he called.

"Here, Doc!" The response was muffled by the pounding rain.

Reeve slid through scratchy brush and oozing mud down to the scene of the accident—fortunately, not far below the road. The car was small; it must have been traveling too fast, since it had severed the fence so completely. It rested on the passenger side, the driver's side up in the air. The front was caved in.

Reeve found Ernie perched on the upper edge, prying open the driver's door with a tire iron. It opened with a shriek of metal. "Too smashed to open regular," Ernie said, hopping down. A building contractor, Ernie was a short, wiry man, and Reeve had no doubt he'd have opened the car door with his bare hands if it had been possible.

"Who's inside?" Reeve began climbing up to the opening.

"One person, far as I can tell. There."

Ernie held his hand up to shine his light inside, and Reeve peered in, increasing the illumination with his own light. A woman lay in a crumpled heap at the bottom, against the passenger door. She seemed unconscious, strewn with glass from the smashed windshield, and what he could see of her head and arms was bloody.

His professionalism keeping him calm, Reeve climbed in and lowered himself to where she lay, careful not to step on her. The car reeked of gasoline, plus a hint of spice, as though of rich perfume—and the metallic stench of blood.

Finally kneeling beside her, he turned her over, automatically reaching for her wrist to check her pulse.

A pain so sharp that it might as well have been physical pierced Reeve's heart.

The woman was visibly near term pregnant.

"Damn it," he swore shakily.

He would not lose either one. This time.

KNUCKLES WHITE as he steered his Volvo, Reeve followed the shrieking ambulance to the emergency room door, then parked behind it. As he jumped out of his car, the ambulance's flashing red light swept over him and reflected on the wet pavement. The rain was slower now but had not completely stopped.

The emergency medical technicians responding to Ernie's 911 call had arrived not long after Reeve did. He had already stanched the flow of blood from a severe laceration on the woman's arm, and together they had stabilized her. Her baby was alive but in distress.

Holding an intravenous bag in the air, the EMTs wheeled the woman into the medical center on a gurney. The staff had been alerted to expect the emergency, and Larry Fletcher, a fine obstetrician and a friend of Reeve's, was waiting.

"What do you think?" he asked Reeve without looking at him. He was already checking over the woman.

"Was she conscious at all? Do we know how close the baby is to term?"

"No. She looks pretty far along, though." A wave of helplessness washed over Reeve, but he quickly set it aside. "The baby's heartbeat is weak and thready," he told the obstetrician. "The trauma may have caused a separated placenta."

"If so, emergency C-section's the way to go," Larry stated. "Nurse!" He called to one of the emergency room team and began issuing orders.

For the first time, Reeve got a good look at the injured woman. Her short, dark hair, still containing shards of glass, was a stark contrast to the color of her pale skin. Her long, thick eyelashes were a lighter shade than her hair. There were bloody scratches on her face and arms in addition to the deep cut that had bled so profusely, and she had a large bump on her forehead. She wore a loose maternity dress that bulged out in front. She seemed a pretty woman, and she looked utterly fragile.

Her pallor was deathlike.

Anguish he'd thought he had forgotten threatened to swamp Reeve, but then he noticed her eyelids flutter. Her lips parted, and she seemed to be trying to talk. He leaned toward her. "What did you say?" he asked gently, though a voice inside screamed for him to lift this woman, hold her, force her baby and her to be immediately healed.

Her eyes opened just a slit. He couldn't tell what color they were, and he doubted that they were focused on him. Her brow was furrowed as though she was in pain.

He saw her hand rise slightly from where it rested beside her on the gurney, and he clasped it in his. It was cool and damp and seemed as limp as a shroud.

This time, when she spoke in a quiet rasp, he made out the words. "Help me. Please."

"I'll do all I can. I promise." His blood pounded in his ears. What if—

No, that was another mother, another baby. He had no business thinking about them now. He was the only physician with pediatric experience at the hospital at this hour. He had work to do.

CATHERINE'S EYELIDS WERE heavy. She struggled to open them. They fluttered first. With concentrated effort, she managed to raise them just a little.

She saw only a blur of white. "You *are* awake," said a deep, soothing voice. A familiar male voice. It made her feel relaxed. Safe.

"I thought so. Can you tell me your name?"

She didn't want to talk. Too tired. But she had to respond to the calming voice. "Ca—" she started to say. She stopped, trying to remember why she didn't dare mention that name. "Polly," she finally said. The word came out as a croak. That was the answer she had to give. She had to think of herself as Polly, not Catherine. But as muzzy as her mind felt, she was not sure why.

"Polly what?"

"Black," she managed to answer. Why did she hurt so badly? She felt as though she had been run over by a truck.

Truck? No. The car. She had been so tired, and then…and then…

She came fully awake as suddenly as if she had been pinched. "The accident," she gasped. Why didn't her head clear? She was in a bed in a strange room. A man wearing a white jacket hovered over her. Did she know him? He wore a name tag. She struggled to focus on it. Dr. R. Snyder, it read. A doctor? Where was she?

She looked around. She lay in a narrow bed with railings on the sides. Her sore left arm was hooked up to a long tube that led to a bottle hanging upside down: an IV. Her right arm was swathed in bandages. The place smelled of something sweet and antiseptic. Obviously, she was in a hospital. White sheets were tucked over her nearly flat belly.

Flat?

Everything came back to her suddenly. "My baby!" she screamed, struggling to sit up despite arrows of pain stabbing through her. "What happened to—?"

"Shh." The doctor pushed her back gently onto the bed. "It's all right. You have a beautiful little girl. She's fine." His baritone voice was tranquil and familiar, though she didn't recall ever meeting him. But he sounded as if he cared about her. "Sleep now, and when you're feeling a little better I'll make sure someone brings her in to see you."

"Now." Her heart pounded unmercifully, magnifying each pain.

Nothing alarmed her as much as the fear that the doctor, despite his kind, calming voice, had lied to her. That something was wrong with her baby.

Or that someone had stolen her away.

She searched the man's eyes. They were a golden brown beneath thick ginger brows, and like any good doctor's, they were filled with compassion. But she couldn't trust him.

She couldn't trust anyone.

"Please," she said, making her voice as forceful as she could. "Let me see my baby."

"I think we can arrange that. She was small, you

know. And we were worried about her condition after the accident. That's why we delivered her right away. She's doing well, but she's been under observation since she was born.''

''When was that?'' Polly was almost afraid to ask. How long had she been unconscious?

''About—'' the doctor pushed the sleeve of his lab coat up from a broad, hair-dusted wrist and looked at his watch ''—ten hours ago.''

Ten hours. Her baby had been born that long ago, and she hadn't been awake to see her. To hold her. Polly felt tears rise to her eyes. ''You're sure she's all right?''

''I'm certain, though we're keeping close tabs. I'll have someone bring her soon.''

She tried to watch him leave the room, but instead her head fell back onto the pillow. She felt miserably dizzy, and there was a fierce ache at her forehead. She lifted her hand to put pressure on the spot and felt a large lump. Oh, my. She must have hit something hard.

If only the seat belt hadn't been so uncomfortable around her large abdomen—but who knew what condition she and the baby would have been in if she *had* been strapped to the seat?

Then there was the pain that burned from beneath the bandage on her arm.

She felt awful. And confused. Where was she? In a hospital, of course, but where? She looked around the small, sterile room, but it gave no clue.

She tried to stay awake. She was aware that she dozed off, then awakened again. That was all right, as long as she did not fall into a deep sleep. She had to be sure....

''Here you are,'' said a high, cheerful voice, startling Polly fully awake. A uniformed nurse stood beside the bed, smiling. ''Doc Snyder examined this little darling again. He's a careful one. And then he had to check with Dr. Fletcher to make sure it was all right for *you* to have a little visitor. Dr. Fletcher is your attending physician.'' In moments, Polly felt a soft bundle being snuggled against her right side. She heard a small squeaky sound and looked down.

There, swaddled in a white receiving blanket, was the most beautiful sight she had ever seen: a tiny pink face, with just a smattering of light brown hair. The eyes were closed.

''Oh,'' Polly said wonderingly, suddenly engulfed in a wave of deep emotion that was a conglomeration of relief, tenderness and fierce protectiveness. Ignoring the fuzziness in her head, she maneuvered with care to pull the baby into her arms, mindful of the IV still attached to her, and the pain when she moved. Nuzzling the little head, Polly smelled the soft sweetness of baby powder.

Uncertainly, she unwrapped the baby. She'd had little experience with infants, but she would learn. Quickly. And right now, she had to be certain that this little one was truly all right.

Exposed to the coolness of the hospital air, the baby made little gasps of protest. Her blue eyes opened, though they didn't focus on Polly, and her dimpled little hands punched unevenly at the air. She had the right numbers of tiny fingers and toes, and the little dark stump of her umbilical cord was a contrast against her pink skin. A disposable diaper was fastened over her, and rather than removing it, Polly pulled it away from the baby's tiny tummy and peered inside.

''Perfect,'' she sighed as she wrapped the baby back into the blanket. She held the small form protectively against her side. *I won't let any of this touch you,* she thought.

"How are you doing?" asked a deep, male voice.

Startled, Polly looked up. It was the same doctor who had come in earlier: R. Snyder. The one who looked and sounded familiar. Standing beside her, he seemed tall, though it was hard to tell how tall while she was lying in a hospital bed. His gingery hair, lighter than his brows, was tousled, as though he had just gotten out of bed. There was a shadow beneath his deep-set eyes and a gauntness in his cheeks that also indicated he could be tired. But the boyish smile he aimed at her with his wide mouth was contagious, and she found the corners of her lips twitching in return.

"I think they're fine," said the nurse. "Both of them." She was much shorter than the doctor, and her platinum hair formed a mass of short waves about her round face. Her chin was just a little too shallow, but she beamed at Polly and the baby as though she had something to do with everything being perfect.

Maybe she did. "How did I get here?" Polly asked. "And the baby... I mean the delivery... Were either of you here? I don't remember anything about it." She felt sore all over.

"You were in good hands for the delivery," the doctor said. "Dr. Larry Fletcher is Selborn Community Medical Center's obstetrician. The baby's heartbeat was a little weak, so he delivered her by cesarean section nearly as soon as you were brought in."

"Don't be so modest, Doc," the nurse ordered. "I'm Nurse Frannie Meltzer, Polly. This is Dr. Reeve Snyder. He stopped you from bleeding to death from that lacerated arm of yours at the accident site. And then, soon as she was born, he took care of the baby. Right, Doc?"

"Well, more or less." The man sounded nonplussed.

Polly had to be reading that wrong. Doctors were like politicians, weren't they? Egotistical? Never wrong?

She shuddered, and the movement enhanced the pain in her head, her arm. "Thank you," she said stiffly. She noticed that his expression froze. Had she sounded aloof? She didn't have to trust him, but neither did she need to be rude. "Thank you," she repeated more fervently, gently hugging the baby to her. "For everything."

"You're very welcome." He smiled once more—not with the same warmth as before, though. She felt suddenly sorry, as though she had somehow lost a friend.

She shook her head a little. He wasn't her friend. No one here was her friend.

No one anywhere, except for her former roommate, Lorelei.

"So where am I?" she asked. The doctor had mentioned the name of the medical center, but Polly couldn't recall it.

"Selborn Peak, Colorado," the nurse said, arranging a blanket around the baby. "It's a ways west of Denver, but much, much smaller."

"Our medical center serves half a dozen communities around here," Dr. Snyder told her, crossing his arms in his lab jacket. Even when he spoke about trivialities, his voice was low pitched and soothing. Polly enjoyed listening to it. "If you had to be injured at all, you were fortunate," he continued. "You were closest to Selborn Peak, even though we're several miles off the interstate. But when I first saw you in the car..." A haunted expression that she couldn't interpret crossed his face but it made her suddenly want to offer him words of comfort. Strange. He was the doctor, she the patient.

And she was hardly in a position to comfort anyone.

"I'll stop in later," he said, "if that's all right."

The baby began to cry, a gaspy, sad sound, and Polly rocked her gently. "Please come back," she said to the doctor, realizing she meant it. Maybe she could pretend, at least, that she had a friend here.

"Okay," said Nurse Meltzer after Dr. Snyder had left. "We've been taking care of this little one, but I know she's been waiting for you."

She discussed with Polly how to breast-feed, then showed her how to hold the infant, who quieted immediately.

Then they were alone—Polly and the baby, whom she moved again, into a position that didn't put so much pressure on her aching side. Laurel. That was what she would call her, after Lorelei. Laurel Black, just as her ID showed *her* to be Polly Black.

Polly reveled in the tiny, uneven tugging as the newborn suckled at her left breast. She hugged her warm, sweet baby to her, watching her in wonder.

Her baby. Hers alone.

"We're going to be just fine, Laurel," Polly whispered. "Just you and me." She began to hum a soft, soothing song to the nursing infant, moving again slightly to ease her pain.

This hadn't happened the way she had planned: to give birth by C-section in a hospital in some small Colorado Rockies town while running away from everything she had ever known. Or *not* known, which was closer to the truth.

To have an aching, mixed-up head, an arm that burned when she moved.

To have been so banged up that she had to postpone the rest of her flight for…how long? She didn't yet know.

But nothing in her life was the way she had planned. She, of all people, would never have pictured herself a single mother thousands of miles from the town where she had grown up. A fugitive. All by herself, with Laurel, being cared for by the kindness of strangers.

She had learned, so abruptly, to count on no one's kindness.

Still, she thought of Reeve Snyder. His profession was to help people. But he'd done more than just help. He had saved her life, hers and Laurel's. Maybe that was why he seemed so familiar. Perhaps she had been conscious of him, somehow, as he took care of her.

A kind man? It certainly seemed that way. Good-looking, too; despite how frightened and miserable she had felt, she couldn't help noticing his handsome features, youthfully pleasant yet maturely masculine.

Even those golden-brown eyes of his looked sincere. Concerned. Kind.

But why had he suddenly appeared so troubled?

It didn't matter. She would never know him well enough to find out. The only thing that counted now was survival.

Survival for Polly and Laurel Black.

LATE THAT AFTERNOON, sitting on the stiff, ancient leather chair in his medical center office, Reeve tried to go over some of his insurance billings. But his mind wasn't on preferred providers and allowed amounts and deductibles.

It was on the woman in the building next door, whom he had last seen that morning. Polly Black.

From what he had heard, the records office hadn't been able to find her family from the scanty information on her ID. Had she contacted her husband yet? Even now, a frantic man could be on his way here from some unknown town, scared to death about the condition of his wife and baby.

Reeve could identify with him.

So much so, in fact, that he had to know. "Donna!" he called to his receptionist as he hurried down the hall. "I'll be back in a few minutes."

"But—"

He didn't stay to hear her objection.

The door to Polly's room was partly closed. He knocked.

"Come in." Her voice was stronger now, healthy. Feminine, yet not too high or shrill. A pretty voice. Reeve wondered how it would sound singing lullabies to her baby.

He pushed the door open. "Hello, Polly. I—" He stopped.

The hospital bed had been mechanically cranked up to support her back as she sat. She held the baby at her side, its tiny head against her small, firm breast as it suckled.

Though he took care of both adults and children, this kind of scene was one he seldom viewed. He felt embarrassed at interrupting such a private, intimate moment. But only for a second, for then a rush of tenderness and something else Reeve could not immediately identify swept through him, and he found himself clutching the door frame for support.

Loss. Sorrow. He realized anew that this woman, her accident and her baby evoked emotions he thought he had put behind him long ago.

"Hi, Dr. Snyder." Thankfully, Polly's words interrupted his bleak musings. Apparently flustered, she quickly maneuvered a blanket over the baby's head to cover herself. Chewing her bottom lip with small, even teeth, she looked at Reeve expectantly, as though waiting for him to take her pulse or ask how she was feeling.

Of course she would consider him just another of the hospital crew parading through her room to check on her welfare. "Hi, Polly. I'm here to see how the baby is doing."

For a moment, a hurt look passed over Polly's pretty but bruised face. "She's doing fine." Her tone was bright, but she didn't meet his eyes.

Had she hoped he was here to see *her?* The idea pleased him, and he felt his lips twitch toward a grin. He *was* here to see her as well as her child. He cared about her welfare, too.

Professionally, of course. That was all.

"I'm a primary care doctor, Polly," he said gently. "You've been assigned Dr. Fletcher as your obstetrician. If it is all right with you, I'll be your baby's doctor while you're here."

"Oh. Of course. I'd like that." She smiled then. Though Polly was still pale enough for her complexion to contrast starkly with her short, black hair, her color had improved. Her eyes were the soft gray of dove feathers, and they regarded him with a warmth that stirred ashes cooled long ago deep inside him. "I can't imagine a better doctor for Laurel. That's her name, you know. You've done so much for us already, Dr. Snyder."

"Reeve," he said. "This is a small town, and we go by first names here." Not always, of course. But he somehow didn't like the distance that "doctor" put between them.

"Reeve," she repeated softly. The melodic sound of the single syllable tripping off her tongue made him want to request an encore. He took an involuntary step toward the bed, and his eyes met Polly's soft, gray stare for an infinite, exquisite instant. He felt his pulse pound in his veins, wondered if he should grab a cuff to see how elevated his blood pressure had become.

The baby began to cry. Reeve welcomed—and cursed—the interruption.

"Shh," Polly crooned softly. She cradled little Laurel, maneuvering the blanket over the flimsy hospital gown—but not before Reeve got another glimpse of an exposed curve of breast. The sight sent a wave of heat immediately to his groin.

What was wrong with him? Even if he hadn't been here as her doctor, he was a professional.

Polly cuddled the tiny, swaddled body close. "Hush, Laurel," she pleaded. "You're all right, little one." As the baby's wails grew more frantic, Polly looked helplessly at Reeve. This was probably her first baby, and the new mother was still a neophyte. She didn't look very old, after all—maybe midtwenties. Her complexion was nearly as smooth as her daughter's, and despite the bump on her forehead she didn't need any makeup to appear beautiful. Her nose was narrow and perfect, her eyes large with a thick fringe of lashes, her mouth just a little too wide.

"Here," Reeve said. He repositioned the infant on Polly's shoulder, then patted the baby's back gently. The receiving blanket was a soft spun acrylic, warm from being against Polly and her daughter. In a moment, Laurel gave a small burp.

Polly laughed. It was a relieved, merry sound that made Reeve's heart fill. "I should have figured that out."

"You will the next time." Reeve hesitated. "I imagine one of the staff has already gone over this with you, but I understand they weren't able to locate your family. Can we call someone for you?'' *Your husband,* he wanted to ask. *Where is he, and why did he let you travel alone when you were so close to term?*

She blanched as white as the sheet behind her, and her gray eyes grew as round and frightened as a captive doe's. "You can't.'' She sounded almost frantic. Then her lips curled in an unsuccessful attempt at a smile. Her voice was much calmer. Even. *Too* even, as though she were reciting a memorized line. "Actually, I don't have any family to notify. I was orphaned as a child, and my husband and I were divorced months ago because of my pregnancy.''

It didn't take a psychiatrist's credentials to know she was lying.

Reeve couldn't breathe suddenly, as though someone had put a tourniquet around his windpipe. He felt his own color deepen. "I see. Well, good luck to you, Ms. Black.'' He turned and strode toward the door. He had to get out of there.

It wasn't his problem. Not this time. But he still felt as though he had been gut punched.

He heard a soft noise behind him, like someone crying.

None of his business, he told himself. But he found himself turning back as he reached the door.

Polly held her squirming baby against her. Tears ran down her cheeks beneath tightly shut eyes, and she was shuddering.

Reeve had to stop himself from taking a step toward her. He wouldn't comfort her. He didn't want to.

If she were keeping this baby away from her husband, Reeve could only despise her.

Unless she had a damned good reason.

Chapter Two

She was free. That was all that mattered.

Then why had Dr. Snyder's snapping at her for no apparent reason caused her to break down? He meant nothing to her.

Except that he was her hero. He had saved her life— hers and Laurel's. His had been the first kind voice she had heard in ages. And now he had turned against her. The knot in her stomach tightened more at the thought.

She shouldn't feel particularly bad about *him*. That had happened a lot lately—people turning out to be quite different from what they had seemed. Her husband. Her own family.

Tears brimmed again in her eyes, but she refused to cry anymore.

She was all alone. Unless she could get to Lorelei, and even that possibility was fraught with danger, for anyone hunting her might recall Lorelei as her college roommate and realize she was heading there.

Polly sighed raggedly and hugged Laurel closer, inhaling her sweet-sour baby aroma. The movement reminded her of her injuries, since she still ached all over. Laurel made a soft protesting noise, and Polly rearranged her more comfortably, stroking the perfect, pudgy smoothness of the skin of her arm.

Polly. Polly Black. Thank heavens she had remembered to call herself that even when she had been most confused.

"Hi. How are we doing here?" The nurse with short platinum hair and a happy demeanor stood in the doorway. Nurse Meltzer.

Polly forced herself to smile. "Just fine."

"Great!" The nurse bustled into the room and arranged the bedclothes around mother and baby. "She's a tiny one, but she's doing wonderfully. I know she was delivered early because of the accident. When was she really due?"

Polly hesitated. In case the news was out, she didn't want anyone to associate her with the woman she had been. "Oh, right around now. My mother told me she gave birth to small babies, too. My sister and me." She didn't have a sister, of course. Just two stepbrothers, and both of them had— Well, never mind that.

"I see," said Nurse Meltzer. "Lunch will be wheeled around in about an hour, and the TV's remote control is on that little table beside you. Need anything for pain?"

Polly considered the idea. Her aches were bearable, and she needed to stay as alert as possible. "No, thanks."

"Then can I get you anything else?"

A new life, Polly thought. No, she was taking care of that herself. But she knew what she really wanted. "Does anyone have copies of newspapers for the last few days?" She sought a plausible explanation. "I'm a comics addict, and I want to catch up on my favorites for the time I've been traveling." Flimsy. She knew it.

Her mind groped for names of famous comic strips in case the nurse asked which she liked.

Fortunately, she didn't ask, didn't even look suspicious. "Housekeeping's usually good at tossing stuff like that," she said. "But I'll check."

"Thanks, Nurse Meltzer," said Polly.

"Frannie," said the nurse. "I don't like formalities. As long as you don't mind me calling you Polly."

"I don't mind at all." *As long as you don't call me—* No, she wasn't even going to let herself think that other name. It belonged in the past.

"We'll take little Laurel into the nursery soon, too, so you can get some rest."

Polly hugged the baby closer. "I want her to stay."

"But after a C-section and your accident…well, we'll see how you do. We usually get new C-section mothers up to walk by now, but because of your other injuries, we've left you alone. That's why you got a private room, too, by the way. A little place like this doesn't have many singles. But we'll have you up and about soon. I'll check with Dr. Fletcher."

"Okay." But Polly half wished Reeve Snyder was *her* doctor, not just Laurel's. They'd been having such a friendly conversation, and then…

"But Dr. Snyder is concerned about you, too," Frannie continued, as though reading her mind. "Not only did he help you on the road, but since he last checked on you, he's been asking a lot of questions."

Polly's heart leaped into her throat and sat there pounding. She didn't want *anyone* to ask questions about her, not even the kind and handsome doctor. *Especially* not Reeve Snyder, who had noticed her. She wanted to be an ant on the counter, a crumb on the floor. Totally inconspicuous. "Oh," she said as calmly as she could, even mustering a smile she hoped looked nonchalant. "What kind of questions?"

"About your family, whether anyone had been able to tell them about your accident."

Then he didn't believe her. Polly's muscles tensed, hurting her, and she started to shake. What was she going to do?

"One of the ladies in the office tried to find a phone number to go along with the address on your driver's license," Frannie continued, "but she didn't come up with anything." Her tone was quizzical.

Polly made herself take a deep, calming breath. She tried to sound nonchalant. "It's an old address. I lived temporarily in an apartment after the divorce." Funny how easily the lies poured out. Not long ago, she had been the kind of person who almost always told the truth. "I was on my way west to stay with a friend while I had the baby." That, at least, was accurate.

"I see. Do you want us to call your friend?"

Polly shook her head. "No. She wasn't expecting me at any particular time, and I wouldn't want her to worry." *She wasn't expecting me at all,* Polly thought.

"Okay. Here, let's make you more comfortable." The nurse took Laurel from Polly and laid her gently in a bassinet beside the bed. "I'll go check on those newspapers. If you need anything else, just ring." She gestured toward the call button on the stand beside the bed.

"Thanks."

As the nurse left the room, Polly sighed heavily, letting her head sink as she finally relaxed. Then she glanced at the baby. Laurel was napping peacefully, sucking a little in her sleep. Polly smiled tenderly at the tiny form. Her baby. A small, but gigantic miracle.

She would do anything to keep Laurel from harm.

She had already done much more than she'd ever imagined herself capable of.

Maybe it was time to go.

She looked around. A door and window were the only means of escape. She didn't know what floor this room was on. And she was still hooked up to an IV. There was no easy flight from here. And she still felt rotten.

She supposed this was a typical hospital room, small and starkly white, with the bed in the center. At least the antiseptic smell wasn't overpowering. Polly heard voices and footsteps as people walked down the hall— other mothers with new babies?

Someone looking for her?

She shuddered. No, no one would know she was here.

But Reeve had been asking questions, even though she'd told him she had no family. He might give her away.

Not intentionally. He had saved her. He had, for the most part, acted sympathetic. Surely he was just curious. Trying to help. He wouldn't put her in jeopardy now, if he knew better.

Unless... She shook her head so sharply that pain shot behind her injured forehead, and she groaned softly. Reeve Snyder couldn't know her family. Not way out here.

She couldn't let paranoia get the better of her.

She didn't dare forget she was always in danger.

For the moment, she was trapped. But as soon as she was well enough, she would leave this place.

Awkwardly, despite her soreness and the IV in her arm, she reached out to pick up the TV remote. It was midafternoon, between most news broadcasts. Fortunately, the hospital had cable. Keeping the volume low, she channel surfed till she found a cable news channel, where two commentators discussed the latest Middle East peace talks. Polly pressed the mute button and settled back in the bed.

She awoke a short while later when the nurse returned, arms filled with newspapers. "Couldn't find them all," she said. "But I think most of the comic sections are here."

Comic...oh, yes. That had been her excuse. "Thanks."

"In case you want to know more about the area, I brought the community paper, too—the *Selborn Peak Standard*. It's got mostly store ads and classifieds, but it's trying to get a reputation for local news stories."

For the next half hour, Polly poured through the papers, focusing on the *Denver Post*. One issue was dated the day after the event that had made her flee her home. None of them carried anything about it.

Maybe that wasn't surprising. Colorado was a long way from Connecticut. Still, what had happened, and to whom, could easily have made national news—if her family had so chosen. The way they decided to play things would be a message to her—provided that she could figure out the right interpretation.

If nothing got into the news, that would mean they had determined to keep it as much of a nonevent as they could. They would want her to return home as though nothing had happened. As long as she stayed quiet and became a good little girl once more, everything would be fine.

If the story were publicized, though, she would have to see how it was handled to determine the message. And if—

A knock sounded on the door, and she jumped a little,

startled. She looked up to find Dr. Reeve Snyder standing there.

His tall form filled the doorway. He was again dressed in a lab coat that did nothing to hide the width of his shoulders. Its bright whiteness set off the gingery color of his thick, neatly combed hair.

For a physician who wasn't *her* doctor, he certainly showed up a lot.

And for a woman who didn't want any connection with anyone, who wanted no questions asked about her, she certainly was glad to see him. Polly found herself smiling warmly despite the way he had left earlier.

"Mind if we come in?" he asked. "I want to introduce you to someone."

"Sure, Dr.—uh, Reeve."

She tried to interpret the look on his face as he stood at the door. The steep angles of his dark ginger eyebrows seemed to signify anger, yet there was a longing in his eyes.

Strange, Polly thought. And wrong.

She of all people shouldn't try to read others' minds from their faces. She had been so mistaken before.

Their eyes met then, his a deep, golden brown. The shadows disappeared for a moment. There was something in his expression that seemed to toss a silken line between Polly and him, connecting them.

No. That couldn't be. She made herself blink, and the connection was gone. She looked down at the newspapers beside her. How ridiculous she was being! He was the doctor who had saved Laurel and her. He probably saved a life every morning before breakfast, two more on Sundays. If he looked or sounded familiar, it didn't mean anything. She was nothing special to him.

When she dared to glance up again, he had turned to

say something to the person behind him. Her heart skipped a beat. What if whomever he brought was...

Silly. She was way off in the wilds of Colorado, for heaven's sake. And Reeve's presence would be a buffer, no matter who he was talking to.

Keeping her voice low so as not to wake the baby, Polly tried to put her nervousness aside. "Sorry things are such a mess, but I've just been reading." She pushed aside some newspapers and smoothed the sheet over her awkwardly short hospital gown, wishing she had a long robe on instead.

Not that it mattered, of course. Nothing had passed between them before. Yet, for that one moment, his gaze had seemed to wrap around and hug her.

How absurd she was being!

"Glad you're feeling up to a little reading." Reeve finally strode into the room, an appealing sureness to his walk.

The man accompanying him was much shorter than him, and his T-shirt and tight, stained blue jeans revealed a wiry build. "This is Ernie Pride," Reeve said. "He's the one who saw you go off the road and called me."

Polly offered her hand to Ernie, ignoring the soreness the motion caused. His grip was strong, and she thought she smelled a whiff of paint. "Thanks," she said sincerely. "From both of us." She gestured toward the bassinet where Laurel slept.

"You're welcome." Ernie bent to look at the baby. "She's a little beauty, isn't she?"

Polly beamed.

"Bet her daddy's going to be right proud of her," Ernie continued.

Polly felt her smile freeze, and she darted a glance at Reeve. His expression remained blank, but she could sense disapproval radiating from him like heat from a sun-baked sidewalk. Why should that bother her so much? She didn't care what he thought.

She forced herself to shrug. "Oh, her daddy divorced me when I became pregnant. She's just *my* baby." And that would be the way it would stay, Reeve Snyder and his unexplained displeasure with her notwithstanding.

No matter how badly—and incongruously—that displeasure hurt her.

"I'd be surprised at any father who wouldn't want to know about the birth of his child," Reeve said. His tone was mild, but his eyes had narrowed, and a shadow again darkened them. "Don't you think someone ought to inform him?"

Like you? Polly thought, beginning to panic. This angry, curious man might be trying to find the baby's father—and in the process he could learn something about her. And that could only end in disaster.

She made herself shrug again, praying she looked nonchalant. "Well, Dr. Snyder," she improvised, "not that it's any of your business, but just guess why a man would dump his wife because she's pregnant." He looked suddenly discomfited, and she pressed her advantage without waiting for him to reply. "Because there's some doubt whether this baby was his." Polly smiled snidely, though she was cringing inside. As though *she,* of all people, could have been unfaithful—even after all her husband had put her through.

And the thought of Reeve thinking she could do such a thing sent a stab of misery shooting through her.

But her comments had had the effect she'd desired—sort of. Something inside twisted and began to shrivel as Reeve looked at her with distaste. "You were right in the first place, Ms. Black," he said. "It was none of my business."

Ernie shifted his weight from one leg to the other, inserting a thumb into the waistband of his jeans and hiking them up. "Glad I could be of help," he said. "But I'd best be leaving. Ms. Black, you be careful driving when they let you out of here. City council may not be letting out next time."

"I'll be careful," Polly said fervently, wondering what he meant by "city council." But he had already turned away.

So had Reeve. The sight of him leaving made her want to cry again. She watched the stiffness in his broad shoulders beneath his white doctor's coat as he followed Ernie toward the door.

Polly closed her eyes, wishing she could call him back, could tell the truth—or enough of it so he wouldn't despise her.

But this was better. He would keep his distance. Just because he'd been her hero didn't mean she could make him her friend.

And certainly didn't mean she could harbor thoughts of something even closer between them. It was too soon after Carl's death to think of *any* man that way. And the way Carl had been... Polly doubted she would ever dare trust a man again.

She let herself collapse back onto the raised bed, but before Reeve left, another man shouldered by him into the room. "Ms. Black?" he asked. His small glasses had the thick black frames that Polly believed had been popular in the 1960s. The man looked as though he might have been a throwback to the era of hippies. Although his hair was thin and wispy, it nearly reached to his shoulders, and he wore a suit that appeared to be polyester.

"Yes, I'm Polly Black," she replied warily. She needed a nap, and she had an idea this visit would not be as pleasant as the one from Ernie.

Reeve followed the man back into the room. Polly felt her pulse quicken in pleasure.

Cut it out, she told herself. Whatever his reason for returning, it wasn't because he was glad to be with her.

Again, Reeve made the introductions. "Ms. Black, this is Clifford, from the medical center's administration department." She wasn't sure whether Clifford was his first or last name.

"Exactly." Clifford's voice was high and nasal, and he sniffled as he talked. "We need some information. I've forms for you to fill out, and we need to talk about your insurance."

Polly drew in her breath. She had been too relieved that she and Laurel were all right to consider the practicalities, but of course their hospital stay would be expensive. She had even had surgery; she was sure cesarean sections were not cheap.

She had money—some. But her flight had been spontaneous, and she hadn't had time to grab much cash. She'd already charged gas on her credit card. She doubted the card's limit was high, and eventually someone would realize it was a fake.

And if she used it again here, someone might be able to track her down.

What could she do? She had no one to ask for a loan. Not even Lorelei; a struggling actress in Hollywood would not be able to scrounge up the money this hospital stay was likely to require. Even if Polly dared to call her. She'd planned to get there first, then figure out some way to meet up with her friend short of telephoning her.

She wouldn't be surprised if Lorelei had already been contacted. Her phone might even be tapped.

But Polly had no place else to go. And now she didn't know if she had a drivable car. She hadn't enough money for another clunker.

"Ms. Black?" Clifford's nasal voice cut into her thoughts.

"Sorry," she said. "I'm afraid a hospital visit wasn't in my plans. I was going to a friend's, and I was planning to have natural birth with a midwife. I...I have no money or insurance."

"I see." Clifford's pale eyes squinted behind his glasses, and he did not look at all happy.

He glanced at Reeve, who stood impassively near the doorway, watching the scene. Polly cringed inside. Now, on top of everything else, he would think of her as a deadbeat.

"It's not that we're not compassionate here at Selborn Community Medical Center," said Clifford. "But these things must be dealt with promptly, and—"

"I don't think Ms. Black's precarious state of health allows for a discussion of finances now, Clifford," Reeve interrupted.

Polly glanced at him in relieved surprise. Moments ago, he had acted as though he found her as despicable as a cockroach on a hospital lunch tray. Now he seemed to be protecting her.

"Thanks," she said. "You're probably right. I feel awfully tired now. But Mr. Clifford—" she lifted her chin toward the scowling little man "—I don't welsh on debts."

An idea suddenly struck her. Here she was, in a tiny

town in the middle of nowhere. No one here knew she wasn't Polly Black, and any people her family had out searching for her would believe she was still pregnant; Laurel actually hadn't been due for a month.

Selborn Peak, Colorado, just might be the haven Polly—and Laurel—needed.

"I don't have to be where I was going for some time," she continued, excitement making her heart flutter. "Once I'm feeling better, if I could find a job here at your hospital, one where I would still be able to take care of Laurel, I could hang around till my bill is paid."

The corners of Clifford's pinched mouth curved up as though he attempted a return smile. "That might work. The center has a good child care facility for the doctors and staff, though your baby's much too young—their minimum age's six months, I think. I'll keep my ears open to see what kind of job might be available. Though in your condition, and with a new baby..."

"I've always been healthy," Polly said eagerly. "I'm sure I'll bounce back just fine." A child care facility, right where she worked! If she stayed here long enough to take advantage of it, she could drop in all the time, be near her baby, even while on the job.

But what would she do in the meantime?

A sudden wave of helplessness washed over her. She knew no one here. Whom could she ask for advice?

And hadn't she determined she would never again depend on anyone else's assistance?

She closed her eyes for just a moment, then opened them again as she fought to regain her resolve.

She would find a way.

"Thank you, Mr. Clifford," she said, meaning it. Thanks to the sour little man, everything would work out fine. She was certain of it.

She looked toward the door, to find Reeve Snyder still just inside. He was staring at her. Once again, she could not read the cool expression on his face—but although it might be wishful thinking on her part, he did not look as though the idea of her staying for a while upset him.

And that somehow made her feel much better.

"Here you are!" A throaty feminine voice projected from the doorway, and in marched a woman Polly hadn't seen before. She was nearly as tall as Reeve, with a flowing broomstick skirt and peasant blouse that dipped nearly to her ample cleavage. "I've been looking all over for you." She took Reeve's chin in one hand and gave him a kiss on the cheek.

"Hi, Alicia," he said. Stepping back, he looked a little embarrassed as he glanced toward Polly. Or maybe that was just her imagination. In any event, Polly felt strangely disappointed, as though a present she had dreamed about for years had suddenly been snatched out of her hands.

"Who's this?" Alicia asked, her long strides swishing her skirt as she approached the bed. Her jaw was strong and her nose just a little too long, but combined with her broad cheekbones and large, probing brown eyes, made a striking effect. Her wavy hair, held back by a pair of narrow reading glasses, was deep russet. The shade didn't look natural, but then, neither was Polly's. "Is this our little accident victim?" the woman pressed.

Polly tensed. How did this woman know about her?

As though reading her mind, Alicia said, "I know everything that goes on around here, but I'm always eager to learn more."

"Alicia's a reporter," Clifford said.

That explained it. It also made Polly's blood begin to freeze in her veins.

"That's right. I'm with the *Selborn Peak Standard.*" Alicia lifted one of the papers from Polly's bed and pointed to an article on the first page. "I do features, news, anything. So tell me about your accident." With a flourish, she pulled a small tape recorder from a pocket in her skirt.

Oh, Lord, Polly thought. The last thing she needed was publicity. She had knowledge that could put her family—those she had thought of as her family—away for years. If they didn't stop her first.

Then there was what she had done to Carl.

No, she had vowed to stay silent. It was safer. "I…I'm sorry," she said. "There's nothing much to tell, and I'm so tired…." She let her voice trail off, sending a pleading glance toward Reeve.

His return look seemed a combination of puzzlement, amusement and compassion. "My patient needs rest," he said. Polly glanced at him in surprise. She wasn't his patient; Laurel was. But she wasn't going to argue with him.

"All right," Alicia said, popping the recorder back in her pocket. "I'll let you take me to dinner then."

Reeve's dark ginger brows knit as he opened his mouth. Polly had a sense he was about to refuse the invitation. She was incongruously *hoping* he would refuse the invitation. But with a sympathetic glance toward her that seemed to tell her his refusal might mean Alicia's continued probing, he said, "Good idea. Let's go."

Clifford left the room first, followed by Alicia. Polly sighed and leaned back into her pillow as she watched Reeve trail behind. He turned back to her at the door. She thought he was going to say something. But with a shrug of those broad shoulders, he left.

After all the visitors, all the nervousness of Alicia's visit, Polly felt unbearably sore and exhausted.

That had to explain why she felt so bad about knowing Reeve Snyder was having dinner with that dazzling reporter.

IT WAS LATE EVENING. The door was ajar.

The first time Reeve had entered Polly Black's hospital room unannounced, he had come upon her nursing the baby. The sight had been utterly tender, yet even now he throbbed in recollection, as he recalled its erotic effect on him.

But even more unnerving had been the connection he'd felt between them later that day, when he'd arrived with Ernie. Reeve had felt tied to her even more strongly than when he had held her hand in the emergency room. It was as though he were linked in some indescribable, immutable way with the lovely young woman who seemed to represent all he despised.

Not that she was Annette. His deceased wife hadn't even had the decency to act embarrassed when she lied.

After dinner with Alicia, Reeve had taken her home, then had come back to the hospital. He had some paperwork to do, he'd told himself.

But he knew that wasn't the only reason he was there.

Taking a deep breath to steel himself, he tapped gently on the door.

He thought he heard a reply, but when he walked into the dimly lit room he found her asleep. Her bed had been lowered, and the baby wasn't in the room. Quietly, he began to slip out again.

"Reeve?" Her voice was soft and husky, strangely seductive in this stark, sterile setting. It reminded him of waking up beside a woman after a night of passionate lovemaking. It had been a long time since he had experienced that. He knew Polly's tone was the result of her sleepiness and nothing else, yet he felt his stirring libido awaken even more.

"Sorry," he whispered. "Go back to sleep."

"I was awake." She pulled the sheet about her neck and maneuvered herself awkwardly into a sitting position. The IV was no longer in her hand, but she clearly still felt sore. Her mussed, dark hair formed a soft, wavy cap that framed her face, and her eyes were only half-open, reminding Reeve of sweet seduction.

What was the matter with him? He was a doctor, used to seeing patients in all states of undress, and yet this woman was making him forget every ounce of detachment he'd ever possessed.

"Well, in any event you're awake now." His voice sounded more gruff than he had intended, and he saw her wince. He knew she was fragile; he had seen tears in her eyes before. Now he felt like even more of a louse.

"How was dinner?" she asked. He couldn't quite identify the emotion in her tone: curiosity? Irritation? Jealousy?

Unlikely, though the thought somehow appealed to him. More likely, she was simply still sleepy.

"Fine," he replied noncommittally. "Guess what?"

"What?" Her gaze was wary, as though she thought he would load on her the straw that would break her back.

"After we spoke with Clifford, I made sure he looked for a part-time job for you here at the center, to start when you're recuperated enough. I called after dinner. He's found something."

"Really?" Her smile lit up her entire lovely face, and

Reeve found himself wanting to return it. "What is it?" She propped her weight on one hand resting on the bed.

"Wait." He hated seeing her look so uncomfortable, so he drew closer and pushed the button that adjusted the back of the bed. It rose with a whir, and she leaned back as soon as it stopped. This close, he could smell her soft spicy scent, the one he had been aware of even when he'd discovered her in her wrecked car, except now the scent was incongruously interspersed with her infant's baby powder. He pulled up a metal chair from beneath the window and sat near the bed. "How are you at convincing delinquent accounts to cough up what they owe?"

She gave a small laugh. "Like me?"

He laughed, too. "Well, at least you're willing to pay. Some people who owe the center ignore their debts."

"I'll pay, I promise. And if I have to do it by strong-arming others into paying, too, I'll manage." She sounded so serious that he wanted to squeeze the small hand that lay on top of the white bedclothes. Strong-arm? She seemed too delicate for that. And yet her offer to stay and work here, while still recuperating from an accident and surgery, told him that she had a powerful determination that was inconsistent with her vulnerable demeanor.

"Great. As soon as you're feeling up to it, I'll have Clifford fill you in more about the job. Oh, and Frannie Meltzer has an idea about child care."

"Thank you," Polly said. "I really appreciate this. I can't tell you how much." Her face glowed, her small chin tipped up and he had a sudden urge to bend and kiss those full, tempting lips.

He stood in a hurry. "I'd better go." He walked

briskly toward the door, but remembered something and turned back to her.

She was staring after him. There was a longing expression on her face, as though she had wanted him to kiss her.

He shook his head. Fool. He was imagining it. Even if he weren't, such an act would be utterly inappropriate. She was a patient at the medical center. *His* medical center. She was nearly his patient, for he had treated her before anyone else.

And, he reminded himself, she had a husband somewhere. Maybe a divorced husband, but one who just might want to know about this baby, despite what Polly had claimed about sleeping around—a claim Reeve couldn't bring himself to believe.

"I almost forgot," he said. "Clifford said someone called, asking after you."

She didn't move, yet seemed suddenly to cringe. Her face drained of the little color it held. "Who?"

"I'm not sure, but I had the impression it was the guy from the gas station where they towed your car. Clifford said something about selling it for scrap parts."

"Oh." Her voice sounded weak, but it grew stronger. "Well, sure. Though I'll want to talk to him about it first, just in case it can be fixed."

Reeve gave a brief, ironic laugh. "Not the car I saw. But I'll tell Clifford to have the guy speak with you."

He said his goodbyes, then left the room. He paused outside the door in bemusement. Was Polly Black a runaway wife? That would explain a lot. Her reactions were not those of a woman simply traveling to stay with a friend. She had seemed afraid when he'd mentioned that someone was asking after her. She had seemed terrified when she'd learned Alicia was a reporter.

And if she were hiding from her husband, then what? If it came to a choice between helping her hide and revealing her whereabouts to the poor bastard whose kid was being kept from him, which would Reeve do?

Maybe it was his attraction to this woman that made Reeve unsure whose side he would take.

Chapter Three

"So what do you think?" asked Frannie Meltzer. An unbuttoned blue raincoat flapped open over her nurse's uniform. Her platinum hair was more mussed than usual from the chilly fall breeze outside.

Polly stood in the living room of a furnished one-bedroom apartment two blocks from the medical center, holding Laurel, now nine days old, against her shoulder. The place smelled of pine cleaner, and patches of brighter white paint on the walls indicated where pictures had hung. The green overstuffed sofa and matching chair appeared to have been thrift store issue. But a rich walnut wainscoting lined one wall, and a delightful stone fireplace dominated another. And there was a small TV—the better to keep her vigil over the news.

The apartment was on the top floor of a garage behind the house owned by Frannie's great-aunt Esther, and the rent was cheap, making Polly's decision easy. "It's wonderful!" she told Frannie. "Don't you think so, Laurel?" she said, rubbing her daughter's back reassuringly.

Never mind that the entire apartment would nearly have fit inside the master bathroom of the house she had just left. Her former residence had never been her home. It had never really *felt* like her home.

When Polly and he had married, Carl had bought it to please her mother and stepfather.

Well, this place would be all hers—hers and Laurel's.

She walked into the tiny kitchenette, remembering the house she'd shared with Carl. It had been in the kitchen of the large house that Carl had first confronted her. He had brandished a gun to scare her.

She had been wearing a flowing maternity dress, a little designer number. It had been blue....

But that was all behind her. Now, Polly wore inexpensive stretch slacks and a plaid maternity top, the tie in back cinched tight since she had nearly regained her figure. The clothes had been salvaged from her wrecked car. Her toiletries, too, had been there, including a small bottle of the costly perfume she had loved—and probably never could afford again. Surprisingly, no one had stolen her bag, as would have happened in a large city. Not that there was much worth taking—except for one small item of importance to her. It was still there.

She would need a new, nonpregnant wardrobe here— all the better to prevent discovery, at least for the next three weeks, until Laurel's actual due date. Polly would also have to dye her hair again soon. She had noticed in a mirror at the hospital that its lighter roots had begun to show. She had darkened her eyebrows and lashes, too, and these would eventually need touching up.

She glanced out the kitchen window, which overlooked the driveway. The yard was fenced, and it was beautiful. In the center was a magnificent aspen, its fall leaves brilliant gold.

More important, the place looked secure.

Frannie had followed her into the kitchen. "Do you think you'll take the apartment?" she asked.

"Absolutely." Polly knew she sounded enthused. She *was* enthused.

She had almost said no when Frannie first told her about the place. Polly had not wanted help from anyone. But she had been acting helpless. What else did she expect but that someone would offer help?

"It's perfect," she said. "I don't know how to thank you, Frannie."

"You just did." She touched Polly's shoulder and smiled, revealing her prominent front teeth.

"Everyone here has been so nice." Polly thought of Reeve Snyder, and a warmth unfurled inside her. During the past days in the hospital, she had seen a lot of him—as he checked on Laurel, of course. He had been kind. Helpful. He never criticized her fumblings as a new mother. In fact, he encouraged her.

And he had helped her get the part-time job that was so important to her. She planned to start soon, since her responsibilities at first would only be to make phone calls from her own home. She could work around her soreness and exhaustion, and be able to care for Laurel by placing calls only when her daughter napped.

Polly would increase her time and responsibilities gradually. And her pay. At her starting rate, it would take her years to work off her debt, especially since Laurel and she needed money to live on.

Employed by the medical center, which was so close to this place, she would be around doctors if she needed help.

Around Reeve Snyder. The idea pleased—and troubled—her.

Despite the occasional, confusing times he stomped out of her room with no explanation, she liked him. But she didn't dare get close to anyone.

And he had a preexisting relationship with Alicia Frost. The reporter.

"What are you thinking about?" Frannie asked, startling Polly.

Polly realized she had been staring sightlessly toward the tiny breakfast nook. She made herself smile. "Just how nice everyone has been, especially you, and Clifford, and—"

"Dr. Snyder," finished Frannie. "He certainly has taken you on as a mission. It's like he's from one of those old cultures in which if you save someone's life, you're responsible for her forever."

"That's impossible!" Polly took a step backward so abruptly that she startled Laurel, who began to cry. "Oh, Laurel, I'm sorry. Everything's okay, sweetheart." Polly danced around the living room, but the motion didn't settle the baby in her arms. "Maybe she's hungry," Polly said to Frannie. She sat on the sofa, arranged a blanket over her shoulder and began nursing the baby. She loved the warm, loving bond nursing created between Laurel and her.

But she couldn't concentrate on it now. She didn't look at Frannie. She didn't know what to say.

The last thing she wanted was for Reeve Snyder to feel responsible for her. Only *she* had responsibility for Laurel and herself.

No matter how unnerving that responsibility was.

Taking a chair across from Polly, Frannie returned to the subject as though Laurel hadn't interrupted. "Don't worry that Reeve will continue to feel responsible for you. It's not in his nature, believe me. He can be charming. But it's an act. Ask any nurse at Selborn Community. Or even Alicia—I know she came to see you when he was in your room. After what happened to him, he isn't interested in attachments to any woman.''

Polly should have been reassured. Instead, she felt worse. "What happened to him?"

"He lost his wife and baby in a horrible accident."

A knot twisted deep in Polly's stomach. "Oh, no! How?"

Frannie glanced at her watch. "It's a long story and I'd better get back to the hospital." The abrupt change in subject told Polly she wouldn't hear more from Frannie now about Reeve Snyder's loss.

But her mind was spinning. He had been married. He had suffered unbearable heartache. Poor man. He had helped her, even if his moods shifted as swiftly as a sudden snow squall. Maybe that was a result, somehow, of his grief. How recent had it been? If only she could—

But she could do nothing to ease his loss. She couldn't even deal with her own.

"Now you just get settled in here," Frannie said as she stood to leave. "My aunt Esther—"

"Did I hear my name?"

A large woman in a loose, flowered caftan stood in the doorway. She had a wide nose on which wire-rimmed glasses perched, and her hair was a soft mop of brown waves in which silver was beginning to take over.

Frannie smiled. "Aunt Esther, I'd like you to meet your new tenant, Polly Black."

"Welcome," the woman said in her booming voice, but her gaze was on Laurel, who had finished eating and was squirming on Polly's lap. Esther held out her arms. With just a moment's hesitation Polly handed her the baby.

"Oh, you adorable thing," Esther crooned. Only after she had nestled Laurel over her shoulder and begun to sway gently on her thick legs did she turn her blue eyes, magnified by her glasses, on Polly. "Frannie tells me you're settling here and that you'll be working part-time for the medical center. Any time you want a baby-sitter, day or night, even while you're working, you tell me. I adore babies."

Polly froze. Someone else was acting as though she were helpless. But this was help she really needed.

She would pay Esther. It would be a business transaction.

"Thanks," she said graciously. She let her body relax. It was good to know she had alternatives.

And, perhaps, friends.

STIFLING A YAWN as he walked down the corridor after doing his hospital rounds, Reeve inhaled the ubiquitous odor of disinfectant. The yellow walls of the medical center's office annex reminded him of sunshine, but their brightness failed to perk him up this afternoon. He'd had a late night; an elderly patient had slipped in his shower, and Reeve had come in to handle his treatment.

Reeve stopped at his office door, hand poised on the knob, as a squeak from down the hall caught his attention.

Polly Black pushed a stroller toward him, one that had seen better days. In it was the baby, Laurel, propped up with blankets. She was wide awake, her large blue eyes staring merrily ahead, tiny arms waving.

They stopped in the middle of the hall, and the squeak ceased. Reeve found himself grinning. "Hi. I thought you were discharged from the center this morning."

"I was. But I wasn't allowed to explore as a patient, and I wanted to see where I'll eventually be working.

It's windy out, so I cut through the office building. Didn't want Laurel to get too blown.''

"Of course. Frannie told me you're staying at her aunt's place down the block. Are you okay to walk around like this? You look a little tired."

"I'm taking it slow and easy. We won't be out long."

Polly's bruises and cuts had faded, and the bump on her forehead had nearly disappeared. She looked slender in her cinched plaid top and slacks. Her cap of dark curls framed a face with perfect bone structure. Her full, pink lips, smiling in what seemed like a perfectly innocent and friendly manner, nevertheless reminded Reeve of his too-frequent urge to kiss her. The thought, as usual, caused a chain reaction—warmth that crept up his body, a tightening in his groin....

Alicia had attempted to get him interested since his wife had died. She had tried too hard. But Polly...

"Your stroller makes a lot of noise," he said, to change the direction of his thoughts.

She looked abashed, and that made him feel ashamed of his criticism. "Sorry," she said. "I borrowed it from Frannie's sister and didn't know how to make it stop squeaking."

He stared at her in surprise. The solution seemed elementary to him.

But maybe not to everyone. Certainly not to Polly. "Oil. Or WD-40. I probably have some in my office. Come in, and we'll find out."

The small squeak pursued him into his office as Polly followed with baby and stroller. Sure enough, he had a can of spray. Waiting until Polly picked up the baby, he used the spray liberally on the wheels, then tested it. In moments, the squeal was gone.

"Thanks," Polly said. "You've saved me again." A

flush immediately crept up her lovely face, and her hand went to her mouth. "But that doesn't mean you have any responsibility—" She stopped, reddening even further.

She charmed him, with her sweet blushing. He wanted to take her into his arms, baby and all, and assure her that helping her had been his pleasure.

How ridiculous. What was it about this woman that caused him to forget professionalism and turn into a drooling idiot?

It was the baby, of course. And his memories.

And this woman had a husband somewhere—former or not—who had the right to see his daughter.

"Don't worry about it," he said, keeping his tone level. "My responsibility is to the medical center. You wouldn't want that squeak disturbing the patients, would you?"

"Of course not." She looked even more disconcerted. Reeve silently cursed himself. He seemed to be going out of his way to make this woman feel uncomfortable. And he had no right to judge her for the way she treated her divorced husband...no matter how Annette had treated him.

But the baby—

"Is it all right for me just to wander around the hospital?" Polly sounded concerned. "Frannie said I could, but...well, I don't want to break any rules. She was on duty this afternoon, or she would have taken me."

"I can show you around," Reeve blurted.

Why had he said that?

"I wouldn't want to put you to any trouble." But there was relief in her gray eyes, and he knew he wouldn't back out now, even if he wanted to.

Which, he admitted to himself, he didn't.

You're a thousand kinds of fool, he told himself. *This woman is not Annette. Hanging around her and her baby isn't going to bring Cindy back to you.*

And if her husband—ex-husband, she'd said—was idiot enough to let Polly and her baby go, that was his problem, not Reeve's.

"Okay, ladies, step right up," he said, letting his voice project like an old sideshow barker's. "Follow me to the stupendous, the unequaled, Selborn Community Medical Center."

DAMN IT! thought Polly, following Reeve down the office corridor. She wanted to stamp her foot. Scream. Do something to ingrain the lesson deep in her soul so she wouldn't have to learn it even one more time.

She had done it again, acted helpless. Allowed someone else to fix something for her.

And that someone had been Reeve Snyder. The very handsome man, she reminded herself constantly, who had saved her life, then helped her find a job.

If she weren't careful, she could come to rely on him. And that was the last thing she wanted to do.

Never mind that her latest folly had been as trivial as a squeaky wheel. She stared with dislike at the stroller she pushed, then shook her head. It wasn't the stroller's fault. It was hers.

"Thanks," she said as Reeve held the door open for her, then she exclaimed, "Oh, this is lovely!" The path between the office building and the hospital was a concrete walkway, surrounded on both sides by a large, attractive garden. Fall flowers not only emitted a wonderful fragrance, their gold and orange shades were a bright relief from the sterile sameness of the surrounding buildings. Wooden benches lined the walk.

And towering above them, just like over the rest of the small, quaint town, were the giant, craggy Rockies.

"It is a nice oasis, isn't it?" Reeve brushed a leaf off a bench with a proprietary gesture. "I sometimes come here to eat lunch and get away from the chaos of the center and my office."

"Maybe Laurel and I can, too." She glanced at Reeve and found him staring at her. Was it her imagination, or was there a look of longing in his golden-brown eyes? Surely he didn't want her to invite him to join them.

She wanted to.

She didn't want to.

She stayed silent.

They continued walking, and in moments, they were inside the medical center. It was a much smaller facility than Polly was used to. She always equated hospitals with the big-city facilities in Boston where her mother and stepfather had gone for their minor surgeries. And the one where her father had been taken....

Laurel began to cry. Polly stopped the stroller and unstrapped the baby, taking her into her arms. "It's all right," she crooned, not having the foggiest idea what had upset the sweet, squirming infant. She had fed Laurel not more than half an hour earlier, had changed her diaper. Still... She pulled up the tiny pink dress she had borrowed, like everything else, from Frannie's sister, and stuck her finger inside the diaper. Sure enough, it was wet.

"Oops, you're a quick one, baby," she told her daughter. Placing Laurel carefully on a bench, she managed to change the diaper swiftly. She was getting to be a pro at this.

The idea of her being a pro at anything made her smile.

"What's so funny?" Reeve asked. He didn't snap at her to hurry, hadn't said anything at all when she delayed his progress.

He was so different from—

"Nothing," she said hurriedly. "Now, little one, let Mama know if you get uncomfortable again." She gave Laurel a kiss on her soft, smooth cheek, strapped her in the stroller again and stood. "Not that I've any doubt that she'll tell me next time she's wet. She's not one to keep things to herself." Polly knew she sounded proud, but why not? She would encourage this little one to speak up for herself forever.

"Sounds like you'll be a good mother." Reeve's voice sounded wistful, and Polly glanced at him. He gazed down the hallway with a blank expression on his face, as though he had just commented on the weather.

Polly recalled what Frannie had told her: that Reeve had lost his wife and child. Maybe just being around babies made him uncomfortable.

"Look," she said, "if you have work to do, I'm sure we can find our way ourselves."

Was that an expression of pain that crossed his face? Darn it! She didn't seem to handle anything right with this man. "I'll show you to the patient accounts office, at least," Reeve said. "And maybe the child care center, too, for when Laurel gets older." He took Polly's elbow as they began walking again. She remained utterly conscious of the small contact, as though every nerve in her body had suddenly marched through her to congregate in that one small spot.

She sought a topic of conversation to take her mind off the warmth of Reeve's fingers through her light maternity blouse. "Having a child care facility right in the medical center is a wonderful idea."

"Thanks," he said.

She looked at him in puzzlement.

He chuckled. "It was my idea."

"Really? It sounds like something a woman would dream up."

"I dreamed it up to *attract* women. And men. The best medical personnel that we could lure to such a small, out-of-the-way town to create a community medical center. And it's worked remarkably well."

"Then this medical center was your idea?" Polly was impressed.

They passed a busy cafeteria filled with people in white and green uniforms. The pleasant aroma of spicy tomato sauce wafted out the doorway. "You can always come here for a good bite to eat." Reeve pointed inside. "We also attracted some pretty darned good food service people." He started walking again, and Polly joined him, the stroller rolling before her. "Yes, the center was my brainchild. I grew up around here, saw too many injuries that would not have been life threatening get that way because it took too long to get adequate help. I didn't intend to get into emergency medicine myself, but I wind up helping a lot in crisis situations."

"Laurel and I are glad you do." Polly knew her voice sounded warm. Embarrassed, she glanced at Reeve, to find him looking at her intensely, his golden-brown eyes dark with an emotion she couldn't interpret. A tingling began in her toes and rocketed through her. What if he really was someone she could trust? What if—

Forget that. She couldn't trust anyone, especially not herself. She had been so wrong before. So very wrong.

Pulling her gaze away, she stooped to straighten Laurel in the stroller. When she stood again, she attempted to get the conversation back on a neutral topic. "So, you were the center's founder. Are you involved in its administration?''

''Everyone here is. It's a sort of co-op, where the doctors all have a stake in its success. Right now, I'm in charge of a committee to raise funds for a new rescue helicopter that'll pick up injured people on the slopes and take emergencies to big Denver hospitals. Sometimes I wish my role was more low-key, though. People seem to equate me with organizing, which is why they also elected me to city council.''

Polly halted so fast her head spun. She pretended to study a painting of snow-covered mountains, but she felt suddenly as icy inside as though she were standing on one of the depicted slopes in her underwear. ''You're on city council?'' She heard the choked tone in her voice and cleared her throat.

''That's how I came to be out the night of your accident.'' Reeve must have caught her tone, as he sounded defensive.

There was no reason he should, of course. Just because she had a deep, terrifying aversion to politicians...

She had almost forgotten everything. Why she had fled. Why she was here.

But now she remembered. Only too well. And she needed to get away from Reeve Snyder. To compose herself. Collect her thoughts.

If he had been kind to her, it had been for a reason. He was not just a doctor. He was a politician. Politicians were controlling. Manipulative. Deceptive.

She swallowed a sob.

She recalled only then Ernie Pride's reference to city council when he'd visited her hospital room. If only she had realized—

But it would have made no difference. Except she

wouldn't have believed that she might come to trust Reeve.

Just beyond them was a patients' lounge filled with comfortable-looking upholstered chairs interspersed with tables covered with magazines. The few people in the room watched a television in a corner.

"Excuse me," Polly managed to murmur. "I'm going to sit down for a little while."

"Are you all right?" Reeve's voice sounded as though he were in a cave. No. *She* was in the cave, and the ceiling and floor, covered with stalactites and stalagmites, were closing in on her.

"I'm fine," she insisted. She sat on one of the chairs, then plucked Laurel from the stroller. The baby began crying as Polly held her too tightly.

Cut it out, damn it! she told herself. She was overreacting. It didn't matter to her whether Reeve Snyder was a politician or a polecat. They both smelled equally bad.

It wasn't as though she were involved with him. As though she cared who or what he was.

No, what had gotten to her was her memories. Of *other* politicians.

Of her family.

Reeve sat down beside her. His shining brown eyes were narrowed in question, and she made herself smile weakly at him. She couldn't let on what she thought. She needed the flexible job. Needed to be here.

And if his concern seemed genuine—well, she didn't dare let herself believe it. She knew better.

She had let herself believe before.

"I guess I'm still a little tired after the accident, the baby and all," she said, trying to sound perky. "I'll just sit here for a few minutes, if that's all right."

"Of course." There was a warmth in his voice that

made tears rush to her eyes. What an actor he was! He really sounded as though he cared. "Would you like a drink of water?"

"No. Thank you." She tried to keep her voice even, though she wanted to shriek at him to leave her alone.

At the same time, she wanted him to take her into his strong arms—arms that had rescued Laurel and her—to let her cry on his broad shoulder. She was so alone....

But that would be weakness. Dependency. On the very person who caused her distress.

Just like before.

She would not let that happen again. Ever.

"I...I'm a little dizzy," she said without looking at Reeve. "Do you mind if I just stay here for a few minutes?"

"Of course not."

She expected him to take her words as a dismissal, but he didn't. He was a busy man. A doctor. A politician. Surely he had something to do besides hang around her.

But there he remained. Sitting beside her, he reached over and took Laurel from her.

The sudden emptiness of her arms nearly shattered Polly, and she almost cried out. But she didn't, since she somehow felt relieved, too.

Reeve hadn't abandoned her, even though she had been less than kind to him.

Just because he was a politician did not mean he was as cruel and hypocritical as most she had known. He didn't criticize her, and he didn't tell her he would take care of everything.

He simply cradled the infant against him. He made soft, soothing clucking sounds with his tongue. And, traitorous little creature that Laurel was, she settled down and began to fall asleep.

Polly tried to ignore her awareness of Reeve sitting silently beside her. His presence wasn't comforting, after all, but discomfiting. Yet the heat from his large body warmed her icy insides like nothing had before.

She didn't want to think about him any longer.

Laurel began to fuss, and Reeve got up to walk with her, whispering words Polly couldn't hear. He headed slowly in the direction from which they'd come.

An older couple and child sat at the far end of the lounge, watching television. Polly became aware, suddenly, of the droning of a news commentator.

"And this word just in," came the sincere male voice. "Officials in the Connecticut town of North Calvert have reported the kidnapping two weeks ago of the wife of slain attorney Carl Elkins. It is believed that Mr. Elkins and his wife walked in on burglars ransacking their home, and Mr. Elkins was slain. His pregnant wife, Mrs. Catherine Calvert Elkins, daughter of the town's mayor, was apparently abducted by the suspects."

Oh, God! thought Polly, feeling herself sway in her chair. She caught its arms and squeezed so tightly that her knuckles went skeleton white. She heard her breath come in small gasps.

"Polly. Polly, are you all right?"

She was vaguely aware of Reeve putting Laurel back into the stroller. He started to loosen the neck of Polly's blouse and to push her head between her knees.

"I'm fine," she protested, though she could hardly hear her own voice. "Really." She took a deep breath and pulled away, looking up into Reeve's concerned gray eyes. "Guess I'm not quite as strong yet as I thought."

But she was lying. She *was* strong. She had to be stronger now than she had ever been in her life.

For it had started. Oh, Lord, it had started.

Chapter Four

"Thanks for driving us home," Polly said over her shoulder. Her hands trembled as she fumbled with her key, and not just from the increased chill as a layer of threatening clouds blew over the Rockies. She was glad her back was to Reeve.

"You're welcome," he said. "I'll come in for a minute to make sure you're all right."

"I'm fine," she lied. She should tell him to leave. Now. She needed to be alone. Think things through.

But she stayed silent. Somehow, she managed to open the door. She turned. Behind her, one step down so his sympathetic brown eyes bored directly into hers, Reeve used an arm to hold Laurel firmly against the shoulder of his beige corduroy jacket. It was just as well he had carried the baby. Polly, still aching after her accident and C-section, and unnerved from the news report, had walked upstairs on wobbly legs.

Reeve had apparently noticed. As she ascended, he had pressed one hand steadyingly against her back.

Now, tall and stable and caring, he looked natural carrying Laurel. As though he were her father.

Polly recalled that he once *had* been a father.

And then there was her own father...no, stepfather. She shuddered. What was she going to do?

"I'll take Laurel now." She held out her arms.

"Hang on a minute." Reeve brushed past her.

As he went by, Polly saw that Laurel was wide awake, her big blue eyes taking in everything as Reeve carefully supported her head. She seemed right at home being carried by this stranger.

No. He wasn't a stranger, really. He had probably been one of the first people Laurel had ever seen.

Reeve had certainly been kind to both of them. But that was probably just a consequence of his responsible profession.

In the living room, Reeve unbuttoned Laurel's little pink sweater and took it off, then removed his own jacket to reveal his white shirt, open at the throat. His cheeks, ruddy from the increasing cold, clashed mildly with the gingery hair tousled over his forehead. He sat down, and when he propped Laurel on his knee, she made cheerful baby noises.

"Now," he said to Polly, "why don't you go in the other room and rest? That's my professional advice. Laurel and I will keep each other company."

"Don't you have patients to see? It's still afternoon." She took off her borrowed yellow windbreaker and straightened her plaid blouse, then touched her neck to warm her cold hands.

"I was planning to do charts this afternoon. They'll wait." His gaze swept over her, giving the impression that, in his opinion, her resting could not wait.

It wasn't rest she needed, though. Not with fear still shooting adrenaline through her.

"Sorry if I seemed unsteady, Doctor." She made herself smile. "But whatever you diagnosed as the problem,

I'm over it now. You're busy. I don't want to keep you here.''

But a traitorous voice inside suddenly contradicted her; keeping him here was exactly what she wanted. She liked Reeve Snyder's kind, reassuring presence. A lot. And she feared being alone with her thoughts.

"I've diagnosed that you have one of the most troublesome conditions a doctor can ever run up against." His thick brows knitted in a scowl.

Alarmed, Polly asked, "What's that?"

He grinned. "Stubbornness."

She laughed.

"That's better. Tell you what. You take Laurel, and I'll get us each a glass of water. And though I never trained my fingers to have a surgeon's skills, they're great at punching in phone numbers for take-out food. Do you like Chinese?"

"Yes, but—"

In a moment, Laurel was in her lap, a slight and precious weight that Polly hugged closely to her as Reeve left the room. She was careful, though, not to press the baby against her still-sore incision.

Polly couldn't help it. She picked up the remote control device and turned on the television. She did not find news on any channel. Just as well. But the suspense was unnerving. When would the next report be on? What would it say?

She left the TV on a talk show, but pushed the mute button as Reeve returned, two filled glasses in his hands. He put Polly's down on the elderly, scratched coffee table.

He took the closest chair. "I'll order dinner, but first, tell me what really happened at the center. One moment you were sitting calmly, and the next you were pale and out of breath.''

''You tell me,'' she replied glibly, though she saw again in her mind that horrible TV broadcast. ''You're the doctor. Was that a natural reaction after a C-section?''

His forehead furrowed contemplatively as he shook his head. ''Not to my knowledge, but I'm not an obstetrician.'' He leaned toward her, his large, strong hands clasped between his knees. ''Polly, it's not easy being a new mother in the best of circumstances. You've had a car accident plus major surgery, and…you're alone.''

The same quizzical yet accusatory look was in his eyes that she had seen before, and she wanted to flee it.

''Maybe you should get some help,'' he continued. ''I'll bet Frannie's aunt would be glad to take care of Laurel for you now and then until you're feeling better.''

''She's already offered to baby-sit, and I—''

From the corner of her eye she noticed a picture on the silent television. It was all she could do to keep from gasping.

There were her mother and stepfather, followed by her stepbrothers. What were they saying? She did not dare turn on the sound.

''You know what, Reeve?'' she said, her voice too high. ''You're right. I'm sore and tired, and I need to rest.''

''Fine.'' He reached for Laurel.

''No! Please just go.'' Polly realized she had practically shouted as she drew the baby tightly into her arms. Laurel began to cry, and Polly nearly wept with her. Whatever the news story had been, it was over; a weather map covered the TV screen.

She despised herself for the pain narrowing Reeve's

eyes, but his face soon returned to an emotionless mask. He stood. "All right," he said coolly over Laurel's wails. "Take care of yourself, Polly. Laurel, too."

Standing to rock the baby, Polly said, "Reeve, I…I'm sorry. But I appreciate your bringing us home."

He reached for the doorknob, and Polly had a sudden fear she was losing the only friend she had.

No. Not a friend; a friendly stranger. Still, the thought overwhelmed her. "I'll take a raincheck on that Chinese dinner," she blurted.

"Sure." And then Reeve walked out.

Feeling perversely abandoned, Polly watched the closed door for a long while before returning to the sofa and the TV control.

THAT NIGHT, with Laurel sleeping in the bedroom, Polly sat on the edge of the sofa, heart hammering, an ache in her head although the lump at her brow was receding.

The late news was finally on. Every network had picked up the belated story about the murder of Carl Elkins and the disappearance of his wife.

Polly felt dreadfully alone. How might she have felt if Reeve were still with her? He would lend her strength simply by being there. But would he have recognized her from the old picture they were broadcasting?

She could not have taken the chance. And she had to learn to stand on her own. Quickly.

But for all she knew, Reeve was watching the news, too—and realizing he knew the woman they were seeking. So might Frannie or Esther or Clifford, or anyone else she had met here, including that difficult reporter, Alicia.

"Leave me alone, Lou," she pleaded when a picture of her suave, silver-haired stepfather appeared on one channel. He would not be interviewed, nor would he allow his wife, Polly's mother, to speak. They wanted to grieve privately, he had told reporters.

Not true! Though Polly ached for her poor mother—fragile under the best of circumstances—and what she must be going through, she knew Lou would not be grieving. To grieve, a person had to have a heart. A soul.

She had learned—oh, had she ever!—that Lou had neither.

He had determined when the news would break nationally, and how. She was certain of it. He had the power to twist the arms of local authorities to maintain silence, at least at first, about her disappearance.

And the rest of the story? Not even Lou could have kept Carl's death from the local media, but Polly had seen no national coverage of it as she had fled across the country.

"The news of the kidnapping was initially withheld to protect Mrs. Elkins," intoned the newscaster.

They were playing her disappearance as a kidnapping. The FBI was probably involved. How long could she hide from them?

She had considered, before, going to the feds for help. But they probably wouldn't have believed her story then. And they certainly wouldn't now.

"The public's assistance is being sought," the newscaster continued. "Mrs. Elkins is the daughter of Lou Jenson, the mayor of North Calvert, Connecticut."

"Stepdaughter," spat Polly. "He's not my father."

A glowering Victor Jenson, Catherine's older stepbrother, was interviewed next as family spokesperson. He was taller than his father, though just as slender. She had been so proud of him once, as though he were her real brother. He had dark hair and even features—handsome, in an arrogant kind of way. Beside him stood her other stepbrother, Gene, who resembled Victor in more ways than one.

"We believe our sister Catherine, who is eight months pregnant, was kidnapped by the murderer," Victor said angrily. "We'll never forgive whoever killed Carl Elkins, my brother-in-law. We don't just want Catherine's safe return; we want revenge." He looked into the camera and touched the edge of his right eye, as though wiping a tear. Then he removed his hand from his face and continued, "Of course, we would never want to endanger our sister. And so, we will do all we can to ensure that whoever did this is not harmed, as long as she is allowed to come home."

Polly froze. "Oh, lord," she whispered. He had spoken in code. Quickly, she hunted for a pen and paper, then jotted down what Victor had said.

Long-forgotten memories of her childhood came rushing back. The game...that silly, deceitful, tormenting game.

Her father had died when she was ten, and her mother had married Lou less than a year later. Lou and his sons Victor and Gene had moved into their home. Catherine had felt lost.

Victor and Gene had teased their new little sister at first. They would weave astounding stories, and she would believe them—until they laughed at her, and she would run away crying.

Then, on a day she would never forget, they had let her in on the game. Taught her the code. One brother was designated to lie, the other to tell the truth. The liar always touched the corner of his right eye. It was a secret, they told her, and sacred—never to be revealed to another living soul.

One of her proudest pre-teen experiences was when they had allowed her to make the gesture and stretch the truth in a discussion with a neighborhood kid. She had been accepted.

In retrospect, she realized that they had used the game to dominate her. Once she acknowledged their control, she became the family's pampered princess and the game stopped. Until today.

Now, knowing all the horrors, she wondered if either brother—or her stepfather—had ever told the truth.

Today, Victor Jenson had made that seemingly insignificant gesture that had once meant so much. He had lied on national news, and told her so, wherever she was watching. He said that the family would never forgive whoever killed Carl. That they didn't just want Catherine's safe return; they wanted revenge. Translated, that meant they would forgive her. No recriminations if she came home now.

"Sure, Victor," Polly said bitterly. But she could never forgive *them.*

His last statement, that they'd help the kidnapper go free, was undoubtedly for show. The code was a family secret, and anyone watching would believe that her life would be further endangered if they truly swore revenge.

She did not believe for a moment, knowing what she knew, that she would be safe, back under their control. And now she had someone else to worry about.

She hurried into the bedroom. Laurel lay in the crib, sleeping peacefully in her yellow sleeper. Her little features looked angelic. Polly had an urge to hug her. But she did not want to waken her, allow her to sense her mother's terror.

The phone rang. Polly jumped.

Oh, Lord—had they found her, after all? Had the coded message been meant to put her off guard?

Breathing unevenly, she returned to the living room and lifted the receiver with trepidation.

"Polly? It's Reeve. I hope I didn't wake you, but I've been worried about you. Have you been resting?"

Polly sank onto the overstuffed sofa, almost smiling at the lifeline of his smooth, welcome voice.

"Oh, yes. I'm much better now." *No, I'm not,* she cried out inside. *I tried so hard to leave the horrors behind, but they've followed me.*

"Is there anything I can do?"

Help me! she thought, rubbing her forehead. She desperately needed someone to talk to. But she could talk to no one. "Thanks," she replied. "But don't worry about me."

Don't even think about me, she prayed. *Forget I exist. And in heaven's name, if you happen to watch the news, do not equate me with the missing Catherine Calvert Elkins.*

POLLY SAT AT THE KITCHEN table, which she had been using as her desk, jotting down notes. The phone rang.

In the past two weeks, since the flurry of newscasts about Catherine Elkins's kidnapping, there had been no further reports. Still, even with all the calls she expected returned from people who owed on their hospital bills, she hesitated each time the phone rang—which was nonsense. Someone locating her would just appear on her doorstep...or worse. She glanced toward the apartment door and shuddered.

Her family had probably delayed before letting the news break, presuming that she, alone and pregnant, would slink right back. But she hadn't, so they had taken the next step. Now, with no further word, she assumed they waited to see if she understood their message and returned home, her proverbial hat in hand, to beg forgiveness.

She could do that. She could ease her prickly nerves by giving up and knuckling under, just as she'd always done before.

She would, too—when the beautiful Rockies walked to Connecticut.

The phone rang again and she reached for it determinedly.

"Miss Black, please," said a high male voice.

"Speaking."

"This is Ricky Edwards. You left me a message."

"Oh, yes." Quickly, she thumbed through files in the box beside her chair until she located the right one. "I called on behalf of the Selborn Community Medical Center. According to our records, you owe—"

The receiver slammed in her ear. Sighing, she dialed his number. The phone rang six times before it was answered. "Mr. Edwards?"

"I can't pay," said the disgruntled voice. "Go ahead and sue. It won't do you any good. I've been out of work since the accident that put me in the hospital. I don't have any money."

Polly scanned the sheets on Mr. Edwards's account. He was twenty-three years old, four years younger than she. "Tell me about the accident, Mr. Edwards."

"Well…"

"Maybe there's some way to help you."

"I doubt it. It was terrible!" He described how his motorcycle had been struck by a hit-and-run driver. He'd been in the hospital for six weeks. "My leg's still not right, though I get around. Even lift things. But I'm in construction and need to climb, so I haven't been working.''

"I'm sorry, Mr. Edwards," Polly said, truly sympathetic. "But the medical center took care of you when you needed help. They'll be flexible if you make an effort to pay. I know that from firsthand experience."

"If I could get a job, I'd pay what I could. But—"

"Let me check on something and get back to you." After saying goodbye, Polly hung up. She had an idea. If it worked, Selborn Community would get its money back. And Ricky Edwards—

A tiny cry rose from the other room. "Coming, Laurel," Polly called.

What a good baby she was! She'd slept all morning, allowing Polly to finish her calls. In the bedroom, Polly bent over the crib and picked up her precious daughter, who stopped crying and blinked her adorable blue eyes. Just over three weeks old, Laurel was thriving. She was gaining weight, and sometimes Polly even thought she smiled.

She was perfect. And Polly would do anything to protect her from everything harmful, including her family. *Especially* her family.

Polly watched the news constantly. At first, she'd felt as though she stood in a forest beneath a tree that had been axed. She knew it would fall. She could even guess the direction: straight at her, even if she ran. What she didn't know was when. And how badly she would be injured.

But nothing had happened, except that two weeks had passed. Despite her initial fear, she realized rationally that neither the authorities nor her family must know where she was. In fact, her family's message had told her they didn't.

For the moment, she was safe.

She smiled to herself as she laid Laurel on the changing table and slipped the legs of her sleeper off her. Polly would stay alert. And she had already taken the first steps toward making it on her own.

After she finished changing the baby's diaper, the phone rang again. "Hello, Polly," said the deep, welcome voice of Reeve Snyder. "How's my favorite patient today?"

"Laurel's fine." Polly smiled, balancing the baby on her hip. She held the receiver tightly, as though the soothing touch of Reeve's strong hand radiated from the phone. "She just woke from her morning nap."

"Good. Will you be at the center today? I've a meeting I'd love to postpone, and a lunch engagement is a perfect excuse."

"By all means, use us as an excuse," Polly said, her heart tripping faster. "I was going to stop by anyway. I've an idea you might be able to help with."

Hanging up, Polly smiled. Laurel and she were going to visit with the man who had, so quickly, become a friend.

Abruptly, her smile faded. He was not a friend, she reminded herself. She did not really know him.

And she could not get involved—not again.

Once upon a time, Catherine Elkins had learned to be good and to trust people. But the fairy tale had proved to be a nightmare. And Polly Black knew better than to believe anyone was as he or she seemed.

AS USUAL THAT MORNING, Reeve saw more patients with time-consuming complaints than he'd anticipated.

When he finally walked into his reception room, Polly and Laurel were, thankfully, the only ones there. Polly sat on a hard-backed chair studying a magazine. Laurel slept soundly in her stroller.

Reeve did not interrupt the scene. Instead, he drank it in. Polly, with her short, dark hair, slender frame and full, pink lips pursed in concentration, was a sensuously beautiful woman, a wonderful and caring new mother. She seemed less tired lately, though she still had a certain edginess he did not understand.

He hadn't really needed to postpone his afternoon meeting, but he enjoyed his frequent lunches with Polly enough that he had begun to make up excuses to have them.

"Oh!" She had looked up and seen him. Her hand went to her mouth in a reflexive response.

"Sorry," he said. "Didn't mean to surprise you."

"Were you standing there long?"

"No," he fibbed. "I just got here." He noted the magazine she put down on the table: *Newsweek.* "What's new this week?"

"Another war threatening in the Persian Gulf, drive-by shootings in Los Angeles. The usual."

She always had her nose buried in a news magazine or paper. When he had mentioned it at first, she'd seemed defensive. He still didn't understand why. But now her choice in reading material, and his teasing about it, had become a standing joke between them.

"Ready for lunch?"

"Sure, but it'll have to be inside. I think our days of picnicking in the garden are over already."

"Till spring," he agreed.

He thought he saw dismay in her fleeting glance, then guilt. Did she intend to be gone by spring? As he held the door open so she could wheel Laurel through, a pang of apprehension bolted through him. She had no reason to stay. She could probably get a better job someplace else. Would she leave soon? The thought chilled him more than the blast of cool air that hit him as they reached the office building's side door.

"Brr!" Polly shielded Laurel with her own body as she stooped to tuck a blanket securely about the infant.

"Won't be long till ski weather." Reeve glanced up toward the towering mountains as they strolled along the uneven outdoor walkway toward the hospital. "Some ski areas of the western slope are so close that a lot of winter sports aficionados stay here in Selborn Peak."

He turned back toward Polly. Her eyes were wide, and he thought he saw fear cross her face. "I never thought of that," she murmured.

"What?"

"Skiing," she said with a smile as manufactured as the hospital's endless supply of sterile gloves. "Maybe I'll take up the sport, though not till I've got my strength back."

She was hiding her real thoughts. He knew it. She *always* hid her real thoughts.

Only a damned fool would be attracted to a woman who had probably run away to keep her ex-husband from ever seeing his baby.

A damned fool like him.

OVER LUNCH of flavorful tuna-and-cheese casserole in the crowded cafeteria, Polly had explained her idea to Reeve. "I'm going to ask Clifford if there are any jobs for Mr. Edwards." Ricky Edwards, the man she'd spoken with that morning, had sounded sincerely sorry he wasn't working. Selborn Community Medical Center had hired her under similar circumstances. Maybe there was a job here for Ricky, too—one he could handle despite his injury. "What do you think?"

Reeve raised one gloriously thick eyebrow. "I think you're doing creative things with an otherwise thankless job."

Polly basked in the glow of his compliment. She had a sudden urge to straighten the jumble of pens in the pocket of his white lab coat.

But then he reached over the table and put his hand on hers. A shock went through her at the contact. She had been touched a lot while in the hospital, by the impersonal but caring staff. But not since then, except when Reeve had helped her up the stairs. All the hugs she had experienced since her release had come *from* her, to Laurel.

She liked the sensation of his warm skin on hers. *Foolish,* she told herself. *Very foolish.*

"You realize, though," he said gently, "that Mr. Edwards might have been looking for sympathy so you'd leave him alone."

"I thought of that. I'm not stupid." A little naive, though, she realized with a deep internal sigh, and too eager to try things—like coming up with new ideas to prove to herself that she could succeed at something on her own. She pulled her hand away, ostensibly to scoop a bite of tuna onto her fork. She hadn't needed his touch to soften the blow.

It only made it harder to take.

Despite her mistakes in judging people in the past, she had taken Ricky Edwards at his word. When was she going to learn her lesson?

But wait. What if this time she wasn't wrong? "If he accepts a job, the medical center would benefit," she asserted. "If he doesn't, we're no worse off."

"You're right." There was a twinkle in Reeve's eye, as though he were amused by her determination. "Are you going to ask Clifford?"

"Yes," she said decisively. "I've other ideas for collections, too. And I've thought about fund-raisers for that rescue helicopter you mentioned." She hadn't been one of the busiest volunteers in North Calvert, Connecticut, for nothing. And with volunteering had come fund-raisers for worthwhile causes.

"We could use a little innovation in that area, too." Reeve's wide mouth tipped up in an encouraging grin.

"How about a charity auction? Or a ski event. Or—"

"Is that what you did in your home in Minnesota?"

She blinked at him. "Minnesota? I didn't—" She stopped, aghast. She hadn't intended ever to tell him where she *wasn't* from, let alone where she *was* from.

"North Dakota?" he ventured. "New York?"

He was getting closer. Though his tone was teasing, he dug for an answer she wouldn't give.

"Okay, I'll tell all." Her voice was as light as his. "I'm actually one of Santa's elves from the North Pole."

Reeve burst out laughing. "All right. You win." His face turned serious suddenly, and her heart stopped for an instant. Would he push her further? Get angry that she hadn't caved and told the truth?

But what he said nearly made her cry—from relief and happiness, not fear. "Polly, just tell me if you're in trouble. I'll—"

"Well, hello," interrupted a throaty female voice. Polly looked up to see Alicia Frost approaching. Today, her russet hair was loose, just skimming her shoulders.

Polly inhaled deeply as a myriad of new emotions

washed over her: dismay and distrust. Anxiety. Even fear.

Alicia had written a small article in her newspaper about Polly. Appearing the day Polly was released from the hospital, just as the news broke about Catherine Calvert Elkins, it had described her solo accident along treacherous mountain roads, and her resultant delivery of her baby. It had been a well-written article—but one that could endanger Polly if anyone reading it juxtaposed the stories and put two and two together.

But Polly comforted herself as much as she could; who besides locals read the *Selborn Peak Standard?* Laurel and she would be fine—even when ski season started, and the small town swelled with tourists. More strangers did not necessarily mean more danger. After all, she knew few locals. She couldn't tell them from people who didn't belong here.

"How's the new mama?" Alicia knelt and chucked Laurel under the chin. The baby's eyes opened, and she began to wail. "Sorry."

Polly unstrapped Laurel from the stroller, but her glare went unnoticed as Alicia pulled up a chair and sat beside Reeve. In a stage whisper, she asked, "Are we still on for tonight?"

He looked uncomfortable as he glanced at Polly. He needn't be. Despite their pleasant interchange, despite how just being with him made her feel as uplifted as one of the red-tailed hawks she saw soaring around nearby peaks, there was nothing between them. She knew he was seeing Alicia. The reporter was not the interloper; Polly was, and Reeve didn't owe her a thing.

Still, something inside shriveled at the thought that Reeve was in love with the sophisticated reporter in her form-fitting gray suit, over which she'd carelessly draped her faux fur coat.

Polly got Laurel settled down. She would have to leave soon to feed the baby.

"Sorry, Alicia," Reeve said in a low voice. "I told you I couldn't make dinner. There's a city council meeting, and—"

"I'm covering it. We'll eat before, then afterward you can come to my place for a nightcap." The suggestiveness in her tone made Polly wish she were anywhere but here. It didn't help that Alicia ignored her.

"Excuse us," she said brightly, standing with Laurel in her arms. "Nice seeing you both. Thanks again for lunch, Reeve. It'll be on me next time."

The sudden irritation in Alicia's eyes vanished as quickly as her interest would in a boring story, but it nearly made Polly laugh. Evidently Alicia was displeased by the idea of Polly's lunching with Reeve again, when he had just refused her own dinner invitation.

Reeve stood. "I'll walk you to Clifford's office, Polly. See you at the meeting tonight, Alicia."

"Fine," Alicia muttered. She grabbed her paraphernalia and stalked from the cafeteria.

And Polly wondered if she had added one more enemy to her woefully long list.

Chapter Five

"Okay, sweetheart," Polly told a sleepy Laurel that evening after feeding her. "Bedtime." Since she had already dressed her in a fresh sleeper, she carried her to her crib and laid her carefully on her back, which she had heard was safest. Laurel's eyes drooped.

Polly wished it were her bedtime, too, but it was only eight o'clock. She doubted she'd sleep anyway. Since the afternoon, she had mused about Reeve Snyder and his meeting that night.

He was on city council. He helped to run the local government. Though he was a doctor and seemed as caring as his profession connoted, he had gone into politics.

He must have an affinity for power, as her family did. That, if nothing else, should keep her away from him. Far away.

No matter how unhappy that made her feel.

A knock sounded on her front door. Polly wasn't expecting anyone. She froze, feeling her heart speed crazily against her ribs.

Silly, she told herself. No one who was after her would knock. She hurried toward the door, not wanting whoever it was to rap louder and disturb Laurel. "Who is it?"

"Frannie Meltzer. I just brought Aunt Esther a few things. Can I come in?"

"Sure." With a sigh of relief, Polly opened the door. Frannie's light hair was mussed from the wind. She had on a heavy coat, but as she unbuttoned it Polly saw she still wore her nurse's uniform over her slightly overweight body. "I'll put on some coffee," Polly said.

"Don't go to any bother."

But glad to entertain, Polly put on a pot anyway. She set some cookies on the table while the coffee brewed, then sat across from Frannie. "Thanks," Frannie said, nibbling on a chocolate chip. She looked assessingly at Polly.

"What's wrong?" Polly glanced down to make sure she hadn't spilled something on herself.

"It's Aunt Esther. You've hurt her feelings."

Concerned, Polly considered her recent meetings with Esther Meltzer. She could think of nothing that should have upset the kind older woman. "How?" she asked.

"You haven't asked her to baby-sit. There she stays in her big old house, waiting to take care of little Laurel, and you haven't said a word."

"I haven't needed a baby-sitter."

"Do you mean Reeve hasn't asked you on a date yet?"

"No," Polly said firmly. "And I don't expect him to."

"I've seen you together at lunch in the center."

"I've just been there a few times when he wanted company. And today he needed an excuse to postpone a meeting."

"Right." Frannie was clearly not convinced. "Aunt

Esther and I figured you'd be the one to get him interested in a relationship again.''

"Not me!" Polly forced herself to laugh. That was a complication she didn't need. The idea's appeal, though, sent her insides into a crazy, joyful dance—which she squelched.

"In any event," Frannie continued, "he'd be better off having dinner with you than with Alicia. Did you know that nosy reporter has been asking questions about you?"

Polly's stomach churned. "What kind of questions?"

"Who you are, where you're from, that kind of thing. I overheard her telling Clifford she's checked the usual Internet sources and hasn't found anything on you. She wanted information from him."

Oh, Lord. What was Polly going to do?

"I wouldn't worry about it, though," Frannie said. "Clifford got mad at Alicia, said that the information in hospital records is confidential and that your background was none of her damned business."

"Good old Clifford." Not that the hospital had any accurate information about her, thanks to her fake driver's license and social security card. And not that she expected Alicia to listen to the administrator. Maybe Polly should have nothing else to do with Reeve. The reporter had probably noticed her because she imagined Polly intruded on her relationship. If Polly made it clear she had no interest in Reeve, then Alicia's curiosity about her might wane.

Or would the reporter keep digging nevertheless?

"Anyway," Frannie said as she reached for another cookie, "I saw Reeve and Alicia at the Snow Palace Restaurant downtown tonight. Not that it's my concern.'' She chomped down as she regarded Polly slyly. ''But I suspect it's yours.''

''You have an overactive imagination.'' Like Alicia's. ''Here.'' Polly stood to pour Frannie a cup of the freshly brewed coffee. ''I hope it's not too strong.'' Like everything in her life, she'd had to experiment with making coffee to get it right.

Frannie sniffed the coffee, rolled the cup slightly, then took a small sip as though tasting wine. ''Perfect,'' she proclaimed with a big grin that showed off her large teeth.

Polly smiled and poured herself a cup.

''So,'' the nurse said, ''how are we going to get Dr. Reeve to take you out instead of Miss Frosty the Reporter?''

''We're not.'' Not that it mattered to her, but she had thought Reeve wasn't seeing Alicia that evening. Except at the city council meeting... ''How long has Reeve been a member of city council?'' she blurted.

''Ah, we're not as blasé as we pretend.'' Frannie chortled, then turned pensive. ''About three years. He was elected before the accident.''

''His...wife's accident?''

Frannie nodded. ''His wife's and baby's.''

Polly glanced toward the door, behind which stood Laurel's crib. *Her* baby. Her healthy, living baby.

Reeve had lost a child.

''Poor Reeve.'' Polly shook her head.

''It's even worse than you know.''

Polly stared at Frannie.

''She was running away. At least that's what rumors said.''

''Reeve's wife?''

Frannie nodded and reached for another cookie. "That may be why he hasn't asked you on a date, you know."

Confusion flooded Polly. "I don't follow."

Frannie chewed a bite of cookie, then looked Polly in the eye. "I'll bet he thinks you ran away with another man's baby."

"It's not like that," Polly cried.

Frannie laughed. "I know. I can read people like books. You're running from something, but you'd never intentionally hurt anyone."

Polly bit her lower lip. She was not going to blurt out what had happened. Nor was she going to cry. But she felt like doing both.

Frannie seemed like a nice person, one who could be a friend. But not if she knew the truth.

POLLY WAS KEYED UP after Frannie left, and not just because of the caffeine. She kept thinking about Reeve. His wife. His deceased baby.

No one should ever have to go through that.

Frannie had also revealed that, despite what Reeve had indicated earlier, he was dating Alicia. Well, it was no more Polly's business than Frannie's. Alicia had been asking questions; that was what had pierced Polly's peace of mind. She didn't care what the reporter's relationship with Reeve was, as long as Alicia left her alone.

Then why did the idea of Alicia and Reeve together this evening make her feel so awful?

Polly took a hot shower. Her bruises had faded, and her incision was healing nicely. Much of her soreness had segued into a dull ache.

After drying off, she wrapped herself in the large terry bathrobe with which she had treated herself from her first paycheck. There had been little left for such a luxury after paying her rent and other expenses—including a payment on her hospital bill—but she needed clothes.

She sat in front of the small color television and turned on the news. As usual, she perched at the edge of the sofa, hands clasped. She pushed the mute button when a commercial for mouthwash began. Watching the news had become a habit, but there had been no further messages. She didn't dare to believe her family—or the authorities—had given up. Still, the more time that passed, the colder her trail would become, and the easier she could breathe.

When the commercials were over, she turned the sound back on. A cold front was expected. A convenience store in a nearby town had been robbed. Then her fears were realized. "This just in from New York. A pregnant woman matching the description of missing heiress Catherine Calvert Elkins has been spotted, but police and the FBI are giving no details."

"Oh, Lord!" Polly exclaimed, beginning to shiver. She made herself remain quiet for the rest of the story, though she couldn't catch her breath.

Authorities were not saying where in New York the pregnant woman had allegedly been seen, but she had already disappeared once more. The investigation continued. A description of Ms. Elkins was being circulated—and a picture of her was shown on TV. Fortunately, it was an old one from her perfect-housewife days. It showed her in an expensive designer's suit, one she had worn before her pregnancy, before she had cut and dyed her hair, changed her makeup.

Then there was a local Connecticut reporter who Polly recognized. She was interviewing Catherine's mother. *Her* mother.

Flanked by her husband and stepsons, Ava Calvert Jenson, dressed in black, sat straight in her chair, but her narrow shoulders drooped. Her wrinkle-shrouded eyes darted wildly toward the camera, then stopped on her hands, folded daintily in her lap.

Ava had always been loving and warm, but there was an eternal frailty about her. One of the things Catherine had thought so dear about her stepfather was his protectiveness of his wife. Now Polly knew that had probably been the only good thing about him.

And there had always been the veiled threat of hospitalizing her mother if her melancholy grew worse. That, as much as anything, had driven Catherine to be constantly good, constantly cheerful—until too much had happened, and she could not be perfect any longer.

"Is there anything you would like to say to the kidnapper?" the reporter asked Ava.

For a moment, her mother looked angry. Angry? That didn't seem like Ava. Polly watched carefully. Did she dare hope...?

Ava opened her mouth, then glanced sideways toward where Lou Jenson sat. The camera showed his sad, sympathetic smile at his wife, then focused back on Ava, who suddenly appeared confused.

Polly must have imagined the spark of vitality in her mother, she realized sadly.

In a soft voice choked with emotion, Ava said, "I just want my daughter to be all right."

"I'm fine, Mama," Polly whispered brokenly, touching the cold television screen with her fingers as though it would bring her in contact with her mother. "I'd call you if I could."

Guilt bolted through her. How could she have left her mother that way? But what choice had she had?

Someday, when she was sure Laurel and she were safe, Polly would rescue her mother—even if Ava didn't realize she needed to be rescued. "I promise you, Mama," she asserted solemnly.

The camera zeroed in on her stepfather. She knew Lou was angry, yet he looked at his wife with compassion.

He looked exactly the way he wanted everyone to believe he felt.

Polly shuddered. What was she going to do? Had they actually spotted her when she had passed through New York?

No, or they would have reported it sooner. The claim of sighting her must have been a ploy to get the story back on national news.

But what message were they trying to convey?

She found out when her stepbrothers came into the picture. A microphone was thrust in front of Gene's angry face. "It's getting harder to wait," he said. "Though we appreciate all the authorities are doing, we're taking action ourselves. In fact, we already have. We've hired investigators all over the country. The best. It won't take long. The person who has our sister can be sure of that."

Polly did not see him raise his hand to his face. He therefore did not lie.

The phone rang. Startled, Polly gasped.

She put her fist in her mouth, stifling any other sound. She didn't have to answer.

They had already hired investigators. That didn't surprise her, but now they had told her so. Warned her. They were coming.... Could they already know where she was? What if the person on the phone was *them?*

The phone continued to ring. It would wake Laurel. Polly could always disguise her voice, say it was a wrong number.

She took a deep breath and approached the jangling instrument, her hand outstretched. "H-hello."

"Polly? It's Reeve. Are you all right?"

"Of course." She tried to sound calm, but her words ended in a sob. She shouldn't feel so frantic—not now. She should be relieved. It was Reeve.

"What's wrong? Is it Laurel?"

"N-no." Her voice quavered. She inhaled and tried again to regain control. "Really. I'm…we're—" Despite her efforts, her voice broke once more.

"I'll be right there."

REEVE SLAMMED his car door and ran down the driveway toward the garage.

Something was wrong with Polly. He thought he knew what it was. If he was right, he should butt out. Everything might be just as it should be.

But he had to make certain Polly wasn't in any danger.

He took the steps to the second-floor apartment two at a time and banged on the door. "Polly, it's Reeve."

The door opened quickly. Polly blocked his entrance with her slim body. She tugged at the hem of a sweatshirt as though she had just pulled it on over her jeans, and her short, dark curls looked uncombed.

"What's wrong?" he demanded.

"Nothing." Her voice was hoarse, yet strong. She appeared composed but pale, and her eyes were ringed with red. He wanted to grab her, to hold her tightly in comfort. But that would be stupidly inappropriate. "Let me come in, and we'll discuss 'nothing.'"

"Really, I'm fine now. Thanks for coming, Reeve, but there was no need."

"You're welcome. And I'm not leaving until I'm sure everything is all right."

He saw the uncertainty on her face, then resignation. "Okay. But please stay quiet so you don't wake Laurel."

That puzzled Reeve. If things were as he had anticipated, voices would have been raised enough to waken a dozen babies. But all was silent in Polly's apartment.

He walked toward the small living area. Surprisingly, it was empty. So was the kitchenette. He peered into the bedroom. No one was there, either, except for little Laurel, snug in her crib. The bathroom door was open, and the light was off.

That was the extent of the apartment. Whatever was wrong with Polly, it wasn't what he had thought.

Her ex-husband had not found her. Or if he had, he wasn't here.

Reeve was uncertain how he would have felt had Polly's ex been here. Happy for the man, he supposed, for having located his daughter—as long as the guy behaved in a civilized manner.

"Would you like a cup of coffee?" The frown in Polly's voice indicated she did not appreciate his snooping. "I made some earlier when Frannie stopped by. Or I could make a fresh pot."

"Reheating what you have will be fine."

He sat on the old green sofa. The television was on— a talk show. Polly joined him. She took the overstuffed seat beside the couch, tucking her legs beneath her. Her sinuous, sensual gracefulness stirred him, as it usually did—until he reminded himself how inappropriate that was, especially if what he believed about her past was true.

"Would you care to explain what upset you?" he asked.

"Nothing. Really."

He leaned toward her. "Let me rephrase that. Polly, *tell* me what the problem is."

"No problem." But the strained lines around her gray eyes belied her words.

Reeve fought to hide his exasperation. He needn't have bothered running over here so late. This stubborn woman didn't want his help.

But that did not mean she didn't need it.

He would try another way. "So Laurel was feeling all right before you put her to bed?"

"She's fine." Polly's wan but lovely face brightened like sunlight sweeping away gray skies, the way it always glowed when she discussed her tiny daughter.

If Laurel was all right, maybe Polly's job had gotten to her. "Are Clifford and you getting along all right?"

"Why do you ask?" Nervousness shuttered her expression once more, and Reeve wanted to kick himself.

"No reason." So it wasn't the baby or her job. Everything looked fine here, and Reeve was certain Frannie would have told him if there were a problem between Polly and her landlady.

Reeve couldn't think of anything else, except...

Oh, yes. Alicia. Something inside Reeve glowed at the idea that Polly might be jealous of his relationship with Alicia—though there was no relationship. "I had dinner this evening with Alicia, after all," he began.

"That's nice." The smile on Polly's full, beautiful lips failed to reach her eyes. "Did she ask... I mean, did you have a good time?"

This might be it! But surely it wouldn't have upset Polly to the extent he'd heard over the phone. "She's

working on a story about a big zoning issue at city council. I wanted to be sure she got things right. Dinner was
the only time she was available to discuss it. It was
pretty detailed and she didn't quite understand it, so we
didn't have time to talk about much else. And I didn't
accept her invitation for a nightcap.''

This time, Polly's grin seemed genuine. Did he see a
hint of relief in it? ''Obviously, or you wouldn't be here.
Alicia would have found ways to keep you occupied
long into the night.''

Reeve felt himself redden. ''There's nothing between
us.''

Polly shrugged and stood. ''I suspect she thinks otherwise,'' she said. ''Excuse me. The coffee's warm.''

Though Polly wasn't pleased about his dinner with
Alicia, that clearly wasn't what had upset her so badly.

When she returned with his coffee, he took a sip and
waited till she sat. She appeared more relaxed now. ''So
how was the city council meeting?'' She seemed to spit
out the words *city council* as though they were distasteful.

''Is there something wrong with the council?'' he
asked.

She shook her head quickly. Perhaps he had imagined
her reaction—or she was keeping yet another thing from
him?

''We had a good session,'' he said finally. ''There
were discussions about that zoning issue, some public
works projects for next year, and even assistance with
Selborn Community's drive for funds to get that rescue
helicopter. It's important to the entire area, after all.''

Polly's dark brows raised as though she were amused.
''I can guess who got that subject on the agenda.''

''You'd guess right.'' Reeve grinned in return. ''I

mentioned that a very capable employee at the center was already coming up with outstanding fund-raising ideas.'' The sparkle of pride in her wide gray eyes warmed him like a space heater aimed directly at him. ''Anyway, you'll have to sit in on a council meeting sometime. They're open to the public.''

''Sure,'' she said unconvincingly.

He felt his smile fade. There was so much he did not understand about this woman—what pleased her, what upset her. She was so blasted secretive.

Annette had grown reticent, too, before she had left....

''And your evening?'' His tone was harsher than he had intended. ''Polly, I want to know what upset you that way.''

She stared at him with a wariness in her eyes that, despite his anger, made him want to take her into his arms and reassure her that no one was going to hurt her, least of all him.

Fool! he chastised himself. Of the two of them, *he* was the one who had allowed himself a splinter of vulnerability.

A splinter he was excising. Immediately.

''I'm fine now,'' Polly said softly. ''But I appreciate your dropping everything to check on Laurel and me.''

Enough skirting the subject. ''Was it your ex-husband?''

She blanched. ''What do you mean?''

''I thought I'd find him here. Has he located you?'' Reeve didn't mean for his voice to sound so chilly. But if he were right, she had perpetrated a cruel act against her former husband. And Reeve could not condone it.

She gave a small, unconvincing laugh. ''I told you, my ex will never be interested in Laurel.'' She looked at Reeve so levelly that he half believed her. He'd have sworn she believed it herself.

Putting his cup on the battered coffee table, he rose, set down Polly's cup and grasped her under the elbow. When she was standing only inches from him, he gripped her shoulders. "Then what was it, Polly?"

Her glare was as determined as his. And then she seemed to crumple. "I can't tell you." Despite their proximity, he could barely hear her.

He nearly growled in frustration. "I can't help you unless you're honest with me."

"Oh, Reeve." She sounded small and mournful.

He couldn't help it. Ignoring the warning sirens shrieking in his mind, he pulled her close.

She felt fragile in his arms. The top of her head barely reached his chin. She resisted his embrace, but only for a moment, and then she flung her arms around him.

He could feel her every feminine curve against him. The scent of baby powder was now stronger than the exotic perfume he had smelled before, but the effect of her warm allure on his senses was no less powerful. He buried his fingers in the silkiness of her hair.

"Polly," he finally whispered. "Look, I—"

She looked up, her cheek resting against his chest, and silenced him by putting two elegant and slender fingers against his lips.

He wasn't certain what possessed him, but he touched them with his tongue.

Her flesh tasted salty, as though she had wiped tears away with her fingers. He licked them again, then, reaching for her hand, drew her fingertips into his mouth and sucked on them gently.

He heard her breathing turn erratic—and it was more

than he could bear. He bent down and claimed her mouth with his.

Polly whispered something against his lips even as her own yielded. Hers were warm and pliant, and opened with just the smallest pressure from his tongue.

The kiss rocked him—everywhere. He deepened it. With a moan, he cupped her bottom, pressing her tightly against him.

She gasped. "Please, Reeve, don't. That hurts."

He stopped, horrified. He had forgotten for a moment that she had just given birth by cesarean section, had been in an accident just before. She had had major surgery, and he was touching her as though he were about to make love to her.

"I'm sorry, Polly." He tried to erase the raggedness from his breathing.

Her eyes were confused. "Me, too," she whispered. "I don't know what got into me. But we should never have—"

"No," he agreed with a harsh laugh. "We shouldn't."

"I...you'd better go, Reeve."

He nodded curtly, wondering how this woman had gotten him so aroused that he had forgotten about her baby. Laurel's birth.

Her accident, which had caused their meeting.

It wasn't until he reached his car that he realized the full extent of his distraction. He had never fulfilled his reason for going there.

He still did not know what had upset Polly to the point of tears.

With a frustrated growl, he slammed the car door.

POLLY LEANED ON THE DOOR after Reeve left, her breath coming in small gasps. What had she been thinking of?

She had let Reeve kiss her. She had kissed him back. She had enjoyed it. Reveled in it. She had needed the comfort of being in his arms, but that didn't explain her actions.

If she weren't still so sore from giving birth, who knew what might have happened?

With Carl, lovemaking had been calm and slow and deliberate, at the restrained speed he had set.

Tonight, with Reeve... Her hormones were out of control. Why else would she have noticed so soon after childbirth, so soon after meeting him, the innate sensuality of his proud stride and the lift to his strong jaw? Why else would she have felt drawn to him, connected in some vital yet inexplicable way?

Tonight, his touch had singed her, his kiss had surprisingly stirred her to recall she was a woman, not just a mother... It was all happening too fast, too soon! And even if the timing was right, she could never make love with someone she did not dare trust.

Not that she had any reason to mistrust Reeve—not more than any other man.

"But you want to protect my ex-husband from me, Reeve," she said aloud, hearing an unexpected note of hysteria in her voice. "You want to be sure the poor, wronged man can meet his daughter. Can help bring her up, as you wanted to bring up your own lost baby." She crossed the apartment and sagged onto the couch.

Alicia's questions, then Frannie's visit, had unnerved her earlier this evening.

And then there had been that damned newscast. No wonder she had lost her balance. Investigators had been unleashed to find her. So what? She had known her family would stop at nothing to drag her back.

But after the first flurry of newscasts, when they had clearly not known where she was, when they had asked her to come home, she had dared to hope, dared to relax just a little.

She stared at her hands in her lap. If her stepfather and stepbrothers had wanted to scare her now, they had succeeded. They were pulling out all the stops. They would find her.

But when they did, she had leverage over them. She would use it. She knew what they were.

But they knew what she was, too. And they could hold it over her.

She smiled ironically as her eyes moistened. "Oh, Reeve," she said toward the door. "You wouldn't be so quick to kiss me if you knew. My ex won't come for Laurel or me. I'm certain of it."

She was just as certain that Reeve would despise her if he knew the truth.

For what man could have the slightest interest in a woman who had killed her husband?

Chapter Six

Polly did not attempt going to bed for a long time that night. Her robe tucked around her, she sat on the comfortable sofa and tried to watch an old movie on TV, one filled with sorrow and melodrama. It fitted her mood.

She had acted shamefully—and shamelessly—with Reeve. He would probably avoid her now. It would be better if he stayed away, for he wanted truths she could not give, and she was becoming too dependent on his comforting, if changeable, presence. But she was not sure she could bear his absence now when she was so frightened. Investigators were after her.

Her family would find her. She knew they would—even before the FBI and whoever else was looking for her, since they'd have provided a story to muddy the search. They would want to get to her first.

How could she save herself and Laurel? And her mother, her sweet, fey mother, who had always been there for her during Catherine's childhood—in her own muddled way.

Catherine had had such a wonderful, sheltered upbringing—pretty clothes, the best schools, debutante parties, and then the perfect husband.

And she had never imagined what was really going on.

Her throat dry, Polly went into the small kitchen for a drink of water. She leaned one shoulder against the gold refrigerator, feeling its vibration, her glass in her hand. She did not want to relive what had happened. Not tonight, at least. But she hadn't wanted to all those other nights, or days, either.

She had Warren Daucher to thank—if she could find him. A lawyer and the older brother of a friend, he had run for district attorney when Catherine's stepfather was up for reelection as mayor. Warren had asked Lou for help, and it had been given. Warren had won.

Then, as district attorney, Warren learned that Lou and his sons stole political funds and tax money. Carl got in on the scheme after marrying Catherine.

Catherine learned this when Warren visited one evening to request help. He had sworn to uphold the law, but Lou had warned him he would be crippled—politically and physically—if he didn't keep his knowledge of the Jensons' business quiet.

She hadn't believed Warren at first. But the DA, with access to confidential records, had discovered in a long-inactive file a letter from one of the town's previous mayors alleging the political corruption of the rising city councilman, Lou Jenson. The mayor had feared for his life. Shortly after the date the letter was written, the mayor had been murdered by a mysterious prowler.

Catherine recalled the date well. The mayor had been her own father—her *real* father, John Calvert.

When Warren showed her the letter, a horrified Catherine had threatened to go public to protect her friend and avenge her father. Carl was assigned to stop her. She learned that after she made it clear she would give her stepfather and Carl just one week to come clean. Carl had confronted her that evening...with a gun.

With a thunk, Polly put her glass down in the kitchen sink. Her hands braced against the porcelain rim, she leaned forward toward the window over the sink. It was dark outside, and she saw the stark reflection of her own pale, scared face. She looked away.

Carl did stop her, but not as he had intended. Seven months pregnant, she had struggled for the weapon. It had gone off—leaving Carl dead.

She could claim self-defense. But her stepfather and stepbrothers would only allow such a defense if she returned repentant. They had told Carl to silence her. Now that he was gone, they would do it themselves. That was why she had run.

Warren Daucher had disappeared shortly before her confrontation with Carl. So had the original of the letter that might prove Lou had murdered her father. Warren could not have been paid off, which meant he was dead. Not that she could prove that, either.

If she went to the authorities, the publicity would end her family's political reign of terror—or at least Lou's aspirations for higher office. Otherwise, they might not care whether she returned. They would not take the chance of letting her speak. She would disappear, like Warren. What would become of Laurel?

And if she spoke out now? She hadn't enough proof. They would explain away her ravings. And they would know where she was.

Polly paced the small patch of yellow linoleum that was the kitchen floor. Thank heavens for Lorelei. Polly had not consciously thought of leaving her "perfect" life, yet, she'd been prepared to, thanks to her college roommate. On a lark all those years ago, to see if she could, Lorelei had gotten them each fake IDs, including a driver's license with a photo of Catherine in a short, dark wig, and even a social security card. Catherine had maintained hers over the years. When she'd learned from Warren about her father's murder, she had instinctively applied for a credit card in her fake name, just in case. She had used it to buy her old, now-ruined car.

She doubted it was legal to use a fake identity—but she'd had no choice. She fully intended to pay back the credit card company for her few charges, just as soon as she could.

Warren was gone. Her old life was gone. She had killed Carl.

She went into the bedroom and looked down at Laurel, watching her baby sleep in the shadowed stillness of the tiny room. "It won't touch you, sweetheart. Any of it," she promised. She would make certain of it. All by herself.

Her mind drifted fleetingly—and longingly—to Reeve. *All* by herself, she told herself sternly.

THE NEXT MORNING, Polly walked uneasily into Clifford's office and stopped. The man sat behind his clean desk, staring over black-rimmed glasses. His wispy hair touched the shoulders of a white shirt as starchy as he. He had called earlier and told her to come in, since Ricky Edwards had phoned about a job. For the first time, Polly had asked a delighted Esther to baby-sit.

She had promised herself that, for one day, she would not think of those who were after her. It was her lack of sleep that caused her to be so shaky, not fear.

Clifford wasn't alone. Reeve sat in a chair opposite Clifford's desk. "Good morning." His smile-crinkled brown eyes were as welcoming as the soft tone of his deep voice. Maybe he didn't despise her, after all. She had a perverse urge to throw herself into his arms. Instead, she just grinned foolishly.

"I won't delay your meeting," Reeve continued. He turned back to Clifford. "But we have to make sure something like that never happens again."

"Like what?" Polly removed her gray wool coat and draped it over the back of the empty chair beside Reeve's. Then she sat down.

"We nearly lost a life, that's what," Clifford growled, slamming his hand against his desk.

Jumping at the noise, Polly felt her mouth open in horror. She looked from the furious face of the administrator to the concern written into the crevices of Reeve's broad brow. "What do you mean?" Had someone come after her, injured someone else?

"A bad emergency came in last night," Reeve said gently. "We needed to get the man to Denver right away but had to wait for a helicopter."

"You need that rescue helicopter immediately, don't you?" Polly's hands were cold as much from nerves as from the chill outside, and she rubbed them together. But though she understood the men's concerns about their patient, even shared them, she was relieved. The matter that upset them had nothing to do with her.

"Absolutely," Reeve said. "I was telling Clifford that you had some fund-raising ideas, and—"

"How much will they cost and how long will they take to put together?" Clifford interrupted.

Taken aback, Polly said, "I'd have to do some checking." She glanced at Reeve for support.

His expression was reassuring. "Why don't you fill Clifford in on a few suggestions?" He got to his feet, standing straight and tall. Polly could smell the pleasant scent of the antibacterial soap he used to wash his hands. "Clifford, you listen to Polly so we can put some concrete ideas before the committee. We need to decide quickly how to get that money." The look he turned on the administrator brooked no contradiction. Then he glanced back toward Polly. "I probably have an office full of patients—but stop by when you're through here, okay?" He turned and left.

Clifford shrugged thin shoulders beneath his plaid sport coat. "Dr. Snyder ought to solicit ideas from his own committee—that's what they're there for. As for you, I want to see you get some of those deadbeats to pay—which seems the most likely way of getting the chopper in the foreseeable future."

"They'll pay." Polly made her tone more confident than she felt. "At least some will."

Clifford snorted. "Like Edwards? Did you promise him a job?"

"No, but if there's anything available, hiring him would be a good idea." Though Polly had tried yesterday to tell Clifford her idea, he had not made time to listen. She'd mentioned the idea to Ricky Edwards anyway, to get his reaction. It had been favorable.

Now she laid out her arguments to Clifford. Ricky had expressed a willingness to pay back the medical center. He wanted to work, but he couldn't work in his profession. And he was excited about a job in another field.

"We're not running a charitable institution," Clifford grumbled. "Nor an employment agency."

"It's working for me," Polly argued. She described more of her ideas to Clifford—including some thoughts about fund-raisers.

As tactfully as she could, Polly worked in one of the too-plentiful topics that had kept her anxiety level high.

"I'll bet the center encourages publicity for good community relations. Do you give out information on patients or employees to the media?"

As she anticipated, Clifford glowered at her. "Is this about that reporter, Alicia? If you want her to have information about you, it's up to you to give it. I can't be bothered."

Polly hoped her sigh of relief wasn't obvious. Frannie was right; Clifford hadn't answered Alicia's questions. Polly returned to her fund-raising ideas, and the rest of the time passed quickly, until Ricky Edwards limped in on schedule.

He was a thin young man with doleful eyes. "Do you have a job for me?" he asked, sitting on the chair Clifford pointed to.

"You ever worked as an orderly?" demanded Clifford.

"No, but tell me what to do, and I'll do it."

Ten minutes later, Ricky Edwards stood in the hallway, pumping Polly's hand. His grin revealed a perfect set of teeth. "Thank you, Ms. Black. I can't tell you how much your help means. The hospital isn't the only creditor screaming at me, and now I'll be able to start paying people back."

Polly revealed the outcome to Reeve a short while later in his office. She felt proud enough to burst. "It won't work in all cases, but after Ricky left I suggested to Clifford that Selborn Community start a trial hiring program for people like Ricky and me. He's going to wait and see, but he didn't say no."

"Wonderful, Polly!" Reeve sounded genuinely pleased.

"Ricky was so grateful…. I just know it will work.

And, Reeve, I think Clifford liked my fund-raising ideas despite himself. I was partial to one in particular.''

''What's that?''

''You know the paved walkway between the office and the medical center, in that lovely area where we had our picnics? It's been patched a lot. What if we fixed it up, renamed it the 'Lifesaver Walkway' and provided paving tiles to people who make donations toward the helicopter? We'd put names on tiles of different sizes to acknowledge contributions. When the weather improves, we could do a 'Lifesaver Walk,' where people would have sponsors pay for each mile they walked, and the winner—whoever raised the most contributions—would get a special commemorative tile in the walkway.''

''I like it.'' Reeve grinned. ''I know at least a dozen wealthy locals who'd love to have their generosity recognized that way.''

''That's great! I'll put a plan together. Oh, and Reeve, Clifford thought I was doing so well that he asked me to come in for an hour a day, whenever I can, to discuss payment options with patients. He even lent me an answering machine in case people return calls while I'm here.'' She showed Reeve the box she had set down on the floor.

She was coming up with ideas by herself—good ideas. She was earning a living on her own. What's more, she was making plans as if investigators weren't on her trail.

Of course she was. She had to live until they found her. And when they did— well, she would figure out something.

Her eyes met Reeve's. His were filled with friendship. And then, as their gazes held for a long moment, his expression melted into something warmer. Much warmer. As though he, too, was recalling their embrace last night.

"I'm proud of you, Polly." His low voice was a caress.

Polly wondered where the usual air-conditioned chill of the hospital had gone all of a sudden. Not that she couldn't guess. Reeve had dissipated it with his yearning stare. Or maybe it was the hot, moist glow inside her that his look engendered.

Were her hormones that far out of control, or was it her foolish mind? There was certainly nothing seductive about their surroundings. She forced herself to stand. "I need to go rescue Esther from Laurel," she murmured.

The spell was broken. Reeve's features relaxed. For a moment, she wondered if she had imagined his hungry look.

She hoped not.

"I bet you're the one who needs rescuing, from missing your baby." Reeve's lopsided grin was teasing, though there was still a hoarseness to his voice. "I'll walk you out."

He held the door, and as she passed him her shoulder accidentally brushed against his chest.

She recalled only too well the hard, muscled wall of his chest when he had held her against it. When he had kissed her.

She swallowed, about to tell him a quick goodbye, when Alicia Frost, dressed in a clinging black sweater and slacks, strode into the still-crowded reception room. Her hair was fastened off her face, emphasizing her striking features.

Alicia's eyes lit first on Reeve, wide and pleased. Polly could tell the moment the reporter noticed her; her gaze narrowed. Her momentum didn't slow. "Reeve, glad I caught you. I need a moment to make sure I got the facts from last night's council meeting correct. Hi, Polly. Nice to see you.'' She was a smooth fibber, Polly thought.

"Hi, Alicia," she said. "I'll leave you to interview Reeve. My business with him today is over."

Bending toward Polly, Reeve said, so softly that only she could hear, "I'll call you."

I won't want to answer, she thought. And then she corrected herself. She would want to answer. Very much. *Too* much.

"I'll have to call you about your questions, Alicia." Reeve gestured at the full office. "I'm pretty busy."

"Sure." But Alicia looked quite put out. "Make it this afternoon, please. I'm under a deadline."

To Polly's dismay, Alicia began walking out with her. "Poor fellow has so little time." The reporter's throaty voice was even lower than usual. "I hate to bother him unless it's important." She looked at Polly as though expecting an explanation of the important matter that had brought her here.

Polly chose not to tell her about her anticipated success with Ricky Edwards. And she certainly wasn't going to mention that she'd heard Alicia was asking about her. She tucked the answering machine under her arm and buttoned her coat; the bright sunlight outside the hospital had failed to heat the chilly air. "See you."

Only then did she notice Alicia staring at her.

"Is something wrong?"

"Not at all." But a puzzled expression appeared on the reporter's face. "It's just that there's something familiar about you."

Polly's stomach plummeted. Catherine Elkins's photo had appeared on last night's news and in today's papers.

Surely Alicia wasn't connecting her with her former self. She made herself laugh. "We've met before."

Alicia's echoing laughter sounded nearly as forced as her own. "Of course. Just a fleeting thought I can't put my finger on. Anyway, if I figure it out, I'll know where to find you."

"Sure," Polly said, feeling as though a metal band had tightened inside her.

THE PHONE RANG that evening while Polly was changing Laurel. She let the answering machine pick it up, appreciative of Clifford's kindness in lending it to her. "Nice to have a mechanical maid, isn't it?" she crooned to Laurel.

Was it Reeve? She considered gathering up the baby, soggy diaper and all, to find out. The idea of speaking with him again made her heart sing.

Silly, she told herself. She had no business being so happy just to talk to a man.

She froze a moment later when the caller's voice resounded through the small apartment. "Polly? It's Alicia Frost. I've been kicking around a delightful idea for a feature story for the paper, all about Selborn Peak's two newest residents—Laurel and you. I'd love to do a folksy piece on how you came here, where you're from, what you think of the place, that kind of thing. Please call as soon as you can so we can plan a time and place for the interview." She gave a number, then said, "Don't forget, now. Bye."

Forget? Polly was hardly likely to. This was just what she had been afraid of when she'd learned Alicia was asking about her. Her hands shook as she dusted Laurel's smooth little bottom with talcum powder.

The winter snows of the Rockies would fall in Hades before she would give Alicia an interview.

Had the aggressive reporter recognized that Polly was Catherine Elkins? And would she take no for an answer?

Polly's history was hardly one she would want published in a newspaper, even a local one. It could lead the authorities, and the investigators her family had hired, straight to her.

Polly sat on the sofa with the baby, who wailed in her arms. On top of everything else, she was scaring Laurel with her own fears. "I'm sorry," she whispered quietly, rocking her infant with infinite care. "It'll all be fine." But how could she convince her baby when she could not convince herself?

"OH, HERE YOU ARE."

It was a week after Alicia had first called about the interview when the reporter strode into Polly's cubicle. She sat smoothly on a chair facing Polly, knees together beneath her short suit skirt. "Reeve said you were in today."

Polly looked up from the ledger sheets she had been sorting. Alicia had a predatory smile on her perfectly made up face.

For a moment, Polly wanted to scold Reeve. He knew she dreaded the idea of an interview. Why hadn't he told Alicia she had gone home?

She sighed. It wasn't his fault. He had even offered to tell Alicia to leave her alone. Polly had told him not to; she needed to deal with the situation herself.

With Alicia, though, she had simply avoided the issue.

Nothing had happened in the week since Alicia had asked for an interview, not even any further news reports. No horde of investigators had descended to drag her home. Maybe, just maybe, Selborn Peak was small and remote enough to provide the haven Polly needed—if she stayed out of the news.

She had carefully kept her hair, brows and lashes dark, her makeup light, her contacts with strangers—except for those who owed Selborn Community Medical Center—minimal. But what would happen next?

And she had known she could not put this determined woman off forever. Had Alicia been doing other research about her? The idea of her digging around for information about the fictional "Polly Black" made her shudder.

"You had lunch with Reeve today, didn't you?" Alicia asked.

"Yes," Polly admitted. As she did nearly every day. It had become a wonderful habit. "I needed to talk to him about some of his slow-paying patients."

"No need to be defensive." Alicia rummaged in her oversize bag and pulled out a pad of paper, pen and small tape recorder. "I know Reeve and you are seeing one another. No problem as far as I'm concerned." But when she looked back at Polly, her large brown eyes were narrowed—whether in speculation or pain, Polly couldn't tell. "Anyway, glad I caught up with you. I've space in tomorrow's paper for that feature I mentioned, and I've been dying to interview you. I need to hurry, though. I'm working on a big investigative story I hope to sell to a Denver paper or TV station, and I'm interviewing someone for it this afternoon."

Polly's heart sank. Not only did she have to worry about her whereabouts being divulged in Selborn Peak, but Alicia had connections in Denver, too. "Sorry, I don't have time. My baby-sitter has to be somewhere this afternoon, and—"

"No problem. I'll come with you and leave for my meeting from there."

Drat the woman! She certainly didn't understand subtlety.

"Sorry," Polly repeated. "I don't want to be interviewed." She stood, grabbing papers and her purse. "I've got to run."

Alicia's next words stopped her at the door. "Polly, I'm determined to do a story about you. Wouldn't it be better if you had some input?"

Polly's breathing stopped, making her even more aware of the thundering of her heart. She turned slowly back. "I...I really wish you wouldn't," she said softly.

"Why not?" Alicia's strong jaw tightened stubbornly. For a moment, Polly wished she could pull the woman's russet hair out by its darker roots. Catty, she told herself. Alicia was simply doing her job. Or maybe she was trying to get revenge for her perception, wrong though it was, that Polly had stolen Reeve.

Polly sat again and faced the reporter. She fumbled for words. "Can I tell you something off the record?"

"That depends."

Polly closed her eyes, dejected. She felt tears coming. Was this how it would end? Would her family find her because of a reporter who felt jilted? What would they do to her? To Laurel? If she did not knuckle under to their demands, would they tell the authorities she had murdered Carl? Let her go to prison, while they raised her sweet, defenseless baby?

No. That couldn't happen. But how could Polly stop it?

"I can't prevent you from printing whatever you want." Polly swiped angrily at the tears that rolled down her cheeks. "But I'm scared, Alicia." She looked up to meet the woman's eyes. Shock had registered in them. Whatever Alicia had expected her to say, it wasn't that.

Slightly emboldened, Polly continued, "In a way, you have my life in your hands. Laurel's, too."

"What do you mean?" Though Alicia had paper on her lap and her pen was poised, she wasn't taking notes. Polly didn't see the tape recorder but would not be surprised if it was running in Alicia's bag. Was it legal to tape a conversation without revealing the fact to the other person?

It didn't matter; Polly would not say anything significant. She had been considering plausible stories for her background, but none had seemed workable. Now she would have to improvise.

"I told Reeve that my ex didn't care about Laurel's birth. That I had slept around during our marriage." She grimaced. Saying such a thing even to protect herself was distasteful.

But better than revealing she was a hunted killer.

"And did you?" Alicia asked. There was a small smile on her face, as though she had Polly where she wanted her—where she would reveal something to make Reeve hate her.

"No," Polly replied firmly. "But I didn't want Reeve, or anyone, trying to locate my ex. You see…" She hesitated, then blurted, "He would hurt me if he found me."

No bolt from the blue struck her down for this lie, either.

"Then you were an abused wife?" pressed Alicia. She leaned forward in her chair. Surely that wasn't sympathy in her eyes.

"Yes," Polly asserted. "That's why I ran off while pregnant. It was one thing for him to hit *me,* even after we were divorced, but I was afraid for the baby. If you do an article about me, he might learn where we are. Please, interview someone else for your feature.''

Alicia was silent for a long time. ''Does Reeve know?'' she finally asked.

''No, no one does. I was ashamed. It was only my problem until I had a baby.''

''You poor thing.'' Alicia reached a hand toward Polly. ''I did an article once about a battered women's shelter. A lot of women stay in bad relationships because they blame themselves. But it wasn't you, Polly. It was something in your ex-husband—something horrible and cruel.''

Something her own family had encouraged, Polly thought. With his impatience, his belittling of her ability to think for herself, Carl had, in a way, abused her, though he had never struck her. But he had aimed a gun at her that last night....

She couldn't help it. The tears that had only trickled down her cheeks before came out in a torrent.

Just as Reeve walked in. ''Polly!'' he exclaimed, rushing toward her. ''Damn it, Alicia, what did you do to her?''

''Nothing,'' Polly managed to insist. ''It wasn't her.''

''The poor thing told me about her background, Reeve,'' Alicia explained. ''She was a battered wife. That's why she's hiding out here.''

Reeve folded Polly in his arms.

No, she told herself. *You have to pull away. You can't continue this lie, not with Reeve.*

But his embrace was too comforting to rebuff. And so she stood there, in his arms, in front of another woman who probably loved him, and allowed a sense of solace to wash over her.

This was wrong, she told herself. They would both feel sorry for her now.

All because of another lie.

Chapter Seven

Reeve drove Polly home that afternoon. "Good to see you, Doctor," said Esther when he walked Polly to her door. The woman gave Polly a brief rundown of the baby's welfare, which was excellent, then left.

Laurel lay on her back in the playpen, making pleasant chortling sounds and kicking her feet. Reeve wanted to pick her up, but that could wait.

"Thanks for driving me home," Polly said faintly, obviously trying to dismiss him.

Though Reeve could have strangled Alicia for trying to go forward with the interview that Polly had vetoed, he was also grateful. If she hadn't prodded, he might never have gotten the truth from Polly.

The pallor of Polly's face contrasted starkly with her dark, curly hair. He wanted to take her back into his arms, keep the world from hurting her further.

If only she had admitted it to him right away. There were things they could do. That he could do.

He couldn't fault her for hiding her baby from her ex-husband under these circumstances. Instead, he admired her gutsiness.

"Sit down, Polly." He indicated a spot on the ragged sofa beside him.

Polly had added decorative touches to the small apartment since the last time he had been there—mostly a scattering of dried flowers in colorful pots. They made the place seem more homey, lived-in. As though she could be settling in.

"But Laurel—"

"She's fine," Reeve said. "Please, come here."

Polly looked nervous as she obeyed, as though afraid he would criticize her again for running away without telling her ex about the baby. But now that he knew why, he understood.

Not all runaway wives were like Annette—bored and unfeeling and vindictive. Polly had had a good reason.

"Why didn't you tell me?" he asked gently, gathering her into his arms. She felt small and fragile, and he had a nearly irresistible urge to punch out the man who had hurt her—he, a doctor who spent his life healing people.

In his younger, wilder days, he'd had such thoughts. Had even gotten into his share of down-and-dirty bar fights. But he believed he had driven those feelings out of his system by his youthful stint in the army.

Anyone, though, he thought, could be driven to violence by the right circumstances.

"I...I couldn't tell you," Polly said.

"Sure you could. Polly, it's not your fault. Alicia said she'd explained that to you. She comes on strong sometimes, but she has a good heart. And this time, she was right."

"It's not that simple." Polly struggled in his arms till he loosened them a little. When she looked up at him, there was an earnestness in her dove-gray eyes that made him reel inside.

"Nothing emotional ever is simple," he said, caressing her smooth cheek with his fingertips. "But we can go to the authorities. They can prosecute abusive spouses. He wouldn't be able to bother Laurel or you from prison."

She closed her eyes as if in pain. Did she still love the man? Pain of his own swept through Reeve as though he had been stabbed with the sharpest of scalpels, and he sat back.

"Not all abusers are convicted," she said. "And even if they are, they get out of prison eventually."

"Has your ex located you?" Reeve demanded. If so, he would act immediately, do whatever it took to protect her.

"No," she stated. "And I'm sure he won't."

Reeve wondered how she could be so certain. But for now, she was probably right; it was better that she stay hidden. If there were any sign of trouble, though, he would insist that they go to the authorities. "I knew you were afraid, Polly," he said. "And I wondered why you were so interested in the news. Is your ex a crook, too? Are you expecting to see something about a crime he's committed?"

She stood. Her hands on her hips, she shook her head so vehemently that her dark cap of hair swirled about her head. "Leave it alone, Reeve. I know you're trying to help, but if you dig into things you don't understand, you'll only hurt me. Laurel, too." She stalked into the tiny kitchen as though wanting to get away from him, but he followed. She buried her face in her hands. "I shouldn't have told Alicia what I did. I should just have let her print whatever lies she wanted."

Once again, Reeve took Polly into his arms, but his feelings were not nearly as tender as before. Something was going on that he did not understand. She had not told him everything even yet. And she clearly would not do so. Was she lying? Was she simply hiding her child from a worried ex-husband, after all?

"Explain the rest, Polly," he insisted, trying not to become intoxicated by the fragrant silkiness of her hair.

She shook her head. "I can't." Her voice broke.

Where was his sanity? Despite every bit of sense he had, he bent down and captured her mouth with his. For a moment, she did not respond. And then she kissed him back, as though this was the only kiss they would ever share. As though there were no tomorrow.

His groin tightened almost painfully as he responded to the passionate woman in his arms. Their embrace grew even more heated. Tasting the saltiness of her tears, he thrust his tongue into her mouth, and she responded by taunting him with her own. Her body pressed tightly to his, and he ran his hands on her back, her bottom.

Her full breasts thrusting against his chest nearly drove him crazy. He wanted her. Oh, how he wanted her.

But it was still too soon after childbirth, wasn't it?

"Polly, we can't do this now. I mean, you aren't healed from giving birth—"

She broke away with a gasp. Her breathing was ragged as her gray eyes stared wildly into his. "I can't. It's not just my physical condition…I can't." Tears flowed down her smooth, pale cheeks once more. "I'm sorry. My behavior is inexcusable. I know it. I'm sorry. But please go, Reeve. Now."

"What's going on, Polly?" he growled, no longer attempting to hold back his anger.

Her eyes full of sadness, she remained mute.

"I won't come near you again if I don't get answers," he warned.

She still said nothing.

Grabbing his jacket from the chair where he'd thrown it, he stalked out the door.

SAFETY, POLLY THOUGHT. *That and anonymity.* That was all she wanted, she told herself as she faced Clifford the next day at the center. For her, safety lay in being unknown.

But Clifford had just told her someone was looking for her.

"Who?" she asked, nervously undoing the bottom button of the bulky navy sweater she had splurged on recently then buttoning it again.

The administrator glared over his black-rimmed glasses. He had called her into his office the moment she had walked into the hospital that morning for her hour of work.

"Some guy. I don't know. But he was asking as many questions as that cursed reporter. Get publicity on your own time, Ms. Black," he grumbled, dismissing her with a wave of his hand.

But she didn't want publicity, her mind shouted as she made herself walk slowly and calmly through Clifford's door. Who was asking about her? An investigator? Had she been found?

If only she had someone she could talk to. Someone who could learn the facts. Someone who would help.

The person who came to mind was Reeve

But he had made it clear he wanted nothing to do with her unless she gave him answers. And that she could not do.

So, she would deal with the situation. She needed to collect her thoughts, devise a plan. She would sit somewhere quiet and jot down ideas. If it were an investigator, she would determine exactly how to handle the situation.

She reached the open door to her cubicle—and stopped. She heard low voices inside.

Oh, no! Her cubicle had been a dubious sanctuary at best; now it was no sanctuary at all.

If she were a normal person, she could just walk in and confront whoever had entered her space without permission. But she was not a normal person. She was a fugitive living under an assumed name, and someone was asking questions about her.

Her pulse racing like Class Five river rapids, she pivoted and began to hurry away. She was glad for the indoor-outdoor carpeting in the administration area, but her footsteps, as her low-heeled boots thudded on the floor, sounded to her as though she tap-danced a trail for someone to follow.

"Ms. Black?" called a man's voice behind her. "Wait."

Her legs braced as she considered running. Instead, she made herself stop. Shoulders hunched, she slowly turned to face whoever was behind her.

Two men approached. One was Ricky Edwards, in his green orderly's uniform. His fists were clenched, and his usually sad eyes were wide. Was that fear Polly saw in them?

The other man was a stranger. Appearing to be in his fifties, he had deep creases in his face, all the more pronounced because of his frown. He was much heftier than the thin Ricky, and wore a tweed suit. His lower jaw jutted belligerently. "Just who do you think you are?" he demanded.

The bigger question was, who was he? In any event, she had no intention of telling him anything. She tried to keep her voice cold as she said, "Excuse me." She turned once more and began walking down the hall.

"Wait!" the man called.

"Cut it out," she heard Ricky say. "Leave her alone."

But the man began arguing with Ricky, in tones too low for Polly to hear. She picked up her pace and instinctively headed toward Reeve's office.

No, she told herself. She should not go there. She could not rely on Reeve or anyone. Hadn't she decided to deal with everything that happened to her, from now on, on her own?

But the panic that caused her breath to come out in small, audible gasps trumped her argument with herself. She needed help.

As usual, Reeve's waiting room was full. Donna wasn't at her desk to tell Polly whether Reeve was with anyone. Right now it didn't matter. She had to see him.

She knew the layout of his office, both from visiting him on business and from bringing Laurel in for well-baby checkups. The door to his small administrative office was open, as was the door to one of the rooms in which he saw patients. That meant he was probably in the other room—with a patient.

Polly knocked on the door.

"Yes?" She felt her knees unlock in relief as she heard his voice.

"Dr. Snyder, it's Polly Black. Could I see you?"

"Polly?" His tone was surprised. In a moment, the open doorway was filled with his solid masculine frame. His brows were knit in a puzzled frown. Beyond him, Polly could see a mother dressing an infant; he had apparently just completed another examination.

"Reeve, I'm sorry to bother you," she said, hearing

her own breathlessness. "It's just that someone was asking questions, and he followed me here. I wasn't sure...I mean, I didn't... He wanted—" She stopped herself. Her fear made her babble. She couldn't do this. She should not be here at all.

She took a deep breath and tried to clear the lump that filled her throat. "This is inexcusable," she murmured, looking at a piece of lint on the gray carpeting. "I apologize. I'll deal with this myself." She allowed herself to glance up at his face again. His expression was unreadable.

And then he looked over her shoulder.

"My apologies, Dr. Snyder," said Ricky Edwards, his voice quavering. "I tried to keep him from coming here, but he was insisting on talking to Polly, the meddling old—"

"Cut it out," interrupted the voice of the angry stranger. "No need to disturb you, Doctor. I just need to speak with Ms. Black."

"You don't need to speak with anyone." Ricky's tone sounded like a plea. "This is none of your business."

Polly blinked. Ricky apparently knew the man. What was going on?

"Why don't we all go into my office?" Reeve's voice was soft, but Polly heard the anger in it. Resignedly, she followed. If he was aggravated with her before, now he would be furious.

When everyone was seated, Reeve unbuttoned his lab coat to reveal a white shirt beneath. He leaned forward, his elbows on his desk, and asked the stranger, "Now, who are you?"

"Randall Edwards," he replied. "His uncle." He jerked a thumb toward Ricky.

Polly felt herself go limp in relief. He wasn't an investigator. Whatever he wanted with her, he had not been sent by her family—had he?

She straightened. Maybe this man was a local detective hired by her stepfather.

But, no. Randall explained himself briefly. "Ricky's my sister's kid—hers and her low-life husband's. Ricky didn't go to college, and she wanted him to. It was bad enough he went into construction, though it's at least got some advancement. But then there was that accident. I figured it'd take awhile, but he'd get better, go back to work."

He turned a menacing look toward Polly. After what she had feared, his obvious malice rolled right off her.

"Now, just who do you think you are, Ms. Black, hiring him to do this kind of menial labor for peanuts?"

In her relief, her words poured out in an incensed torrent. "I'm an employee of Selborn Community looking out for the center's best interests, as well as your nephew's. He needed a job and I found him one. If you don't like it, Mr. Edwards, tough. It's Ricky's life, not yours."

"Good going, Polly!" Ricky clapped his hands. He grinned snidely at his uncle, his earlier uneasiness apparently vanquished. "Butt out, Unc," he said.

After explaining things more thoroughly to his uncle, Ricky left the room with him. Polly tried to follow.

"Wait a minute." The command in Reeve's resonant baritone stopped her as much as his strong hand on her shoulder.

She turned and looked up, trying to ignore the shiver that went through her at his touch. It wasn't from fear, but from the delightful recollection of other touches from Reeve, when he had clearly wanted her. Unexpectedly, desire crept through her, deep and hot and—

"More secrets, Polly?" His bitter tone broke the spell.

She chose to misunderstand him. "What do you mean? Mr. Edwards explained the whole thing."

"Why were you so afraid?" Reeve demanded. "He obviously wasn't your abusive husband."

"He could have been sent by him. Or—"

"When," Reeve demanded, "will you trust me enough to tell me the entire truth?"

Was she wrong in keeping secrets from him? This time, she recognized that she had behaved in an absurdly paranoid manner. The guy asking questions, the man she had fled, had only been Ricky Edwards's uncle—a nasty character, to be sure, but not worth her panic.

The next time anything happened, she would remember this. She would not overreact.

For a moment, she met Reeve's exasperated stare. She opened her mouth, trying to think of something more to say to explain herself. To secure his forgiveness, and make him want her once more. It was no use; she turned away.

"WELL, ROSALIND, a woman matching our sister's description was reported to have given birth just over a month ago in Memphis," said Gene Jenson, rubbing the side of his eye. Polly thought he looked concerned, yet utterly relaxed in the chair facing the national TV talk show hostess.

"That's right," Victor agreed, adjusting his suit jacket. "We have a pretty good idea now just where she is." He did not touch his face as he looked into the camera.

Gene was lying. Victor told the truth.

Such a ridiculous game, despite Polly's reverence for it as a child. But then, as now, it was significant. They wanted to unnerve her, make sure she understood they were still in command.

She had to be strong.

"A hospital spokesperson said a man who claimed to be her husband stayed by her side," Rosalind said. "Do you still believe she was kidnapped?"

"Absolutely," said Gene, the liar. "Catherine must have been under duress. The man with her was her kidnapper, who probably also murdered her husband."

"We knew she'd have given birth by now," added Victor. "We want her safe return, hers and the baby's, but we're afraid we'll never see her alive again."

Her heartbeat racing like a jungle drum, Polly sat glued to the small set in her apartment. There was her picture yet again, with her long, blond hair, her expensive preppy clothes. She was smiling and obliviously happy. Could that naive young fool really have been her?

The interview ended, and Polly went through her notes, determining which brother had said what. Her family knew she'd had the baby and that she wasn't in Memphis.

They had a good idea where she was.

Should she still believe in the code? Probably…or at least part of it. After all, they had threatened her.

Victor, designated to tell the truth, claimed he no longer believed she would return safely. That meant they would no longer forgive her so easily. She could end up hurt…or dead.

And the baby…? Polly hurried into the bedroom. Laurel lay in her crib, her small, perfect mouth making sucking motions in her sleep. She was nine weeks old and growing beautifully. Polly had recuperated well from her birth—and the accident.

''It'll be all right, Laurel,'' she whispered. ''They don't really know we're here. They're just trying to trick us.'' But the only one she was trying to reassure was herself.

She had done all she could over the past weeks to ensure their solitude. Even Alicia had cooperated. After learning that ''Polly'' had been an abused wife, she had been solicitous. In fact, she was becoming a friend. Which was fortunate. Polly needed another friend.

Since her ill-fated argument with Reeve nearly a month earlier, followed by her fiasco of a flight from Ricky Edwards's uncle, they had spent a lot less time together.

Polly had taken Laurel to his office for her usual well-baby checkup and watched with bittersweet pride as the man she had begun, so foolishly, to care about fussed over her daughter as he performed the usual examination. She had stopped into his office on business nearly every day. But they shared no more lunches or anything else social, no matter how much that hurt.

He was kind, he was cordial, but he remained distant. As much as her heart ached when she was with him, it was better that way.

Especially now. According to this latest media event, her family was close to finding her. Were they just trying to scare her? Quite possibly. She had seen no sign of their high-powered investigators, after all.

She'd thought often about phoning her mother, even Lorelei, to learn what they knew—or even making an anonymous call to the North Calvert police. But calls could be traced. It didn't matter, anyway. If she had been found, something would happen.

But nothing had happened. With luck, nothing would. The first news stories hadn't convinced her to go home. The second round had told her she was being hunted, but except for the threat of publicity, she had seen no indication of danger, here in Selborn Peak.

But now her family claimed, in the new barrage, that they had found her. Maybe it was a lie, designed to terrify her into running. Until confronted with proof that she had been located, she would stand her ground.

She only hoped she was doing the right thing.

A knock sounded on her apartment door. Polly gasped, her hand rushing to her throat. She smiled wryly at her own nerves; it had to be Esther. It was time for Polly to go to the medical center.

"THANKS FOR STOPPING BY my office, Polly." Forcing himself to stay seated at his desk, Reeve kept his tone more impersonal than he felt. In a form-hugging gray sweater that nearly matched her eyes, and slender black pants, she looked wonderful. Sexy. He was so glad to see her he could have shouted, notwithstanding the voice inside that warned against letting his imagination and libido—both of which were much too active when this woman was around—run away with him.

But Polly looked pale and wore a pinched expression, as though she were in pain. She sat stiffly on the chair facing him. "That's okay, Doctor."

Her formality made him want to draw her into his arms and kiss her till she gasped his name. Until she spilled whatever bothered her, and he could get rid of it for her. Until he could undress her and touch her and —

"Clifford said you wanted a summary of ideas for promoting the 'Lifesaver Walkway.'" Her voice cooled his vividly sensual thoughts.

"That's right." He hoped she did not hear the slight raspiness of his voice. The fund-raising event was the best pretext to get her to stop in these days, even though he had been the one to say he would avoid her.

He was, in fact, irritated that he had been unable to get his committee to move faster on the fund-raiser. But more important, he had missed spending time—*quality* time, with Polly. Not to mention her wonderful baby.

He looked at her haggard, yet lovely face. "Is something wrong?" He shouldn't have asked, but he had to.

Her eyes grew wide, but she thrust her chin out defiantly. "Not at all." She fibbed well. But he believed he now knew when she lied and when she told the truth. He still did not, however, know how to get all the truths out of her.

"How is Laurel?"

That made Polly smile with a sweetly maternal glow that rocked him. He had missed having a family but hadn't realized how much until these two entered his life.

"She's fine. Growing. I've had to buy larger baby clothes for her already."

"You'll bring her in for another checkup soon, right? We'll weigh and measure her then."

"Sure." She glanced at him. When their eyes met, hers turned swiftly away.

"Polly," Reeve said quickly, "I never meant…" He stopped. What could he say?

"Clifford is waiting," she said. "See you." In moments, she was gone, leaving the emptiness in Reeve's heart that had been filled, for a few moments, by her presence.

He tried to concentrate on the charts he had been updating, to no avail. His next patients were not due until that afternoon. Perhaps he could get more information on some of his deadbeat patients or other thoughts on the fund-raiser....

He strode down the carpeted hall toward Clifford's offices. The administrator had designated a small cubicle near him for Polly's use. It was close to lunchtime. Maybe Reeve could talk her, just this once, into eating with him.

Then when they were together, he would tell her... what?

It didn't matter. Her cubicle was empty. He popped his head into Clifford's office. "Is Polly around? I had a question for her."

The administrator peered over his black-rimmed glasses. "She went to see Edwards."

"Ricky? How's that working out?"

Clifford's lips pursed as though he had just taken a bite of rancid grapefruit. "Fine," he said grudgingly. "The guy's not a bad orderly, and he's set a reasonable schedule for repaying the center."

Score one for Polly, Reeve thought. And as far as he knew, Ricky's uncle had made no more waves. "Are you considering Polly's suggestion of hiring more delinquent patients to work off their debts?"

"Yes," Clifford muttered. "Now, if Ms. Black were really clever, she'd jump right in and finish her 'Lifesaver Walkway' plan so your committee would have no choice but to follow through. We need that blasted helicopter!"

Reeve had to laugh as he turned to leave. Clifford would never admit he genuinely liked Polly's overflow of ideas.

Polly was a wonderful, bright and innovative woman. She was beautiful and sexy, and she was an asset to the hospital.

And she was secretive and untrusting and averse to telling the whole truth.

Why couldn't he get her out of his mind? And his heart... He was afraid it was a lost cause.

So as not to make the trip to the administrator's office a total loss, he decided to pick up his mail. One wall in the outer office was covered by a large wooden framework containing shallow slots. Mail for all personnel at the center was sorted in designated pigeonholes. Reeve picked up a stack of envelopes from his, then looked in the trays below, where larger packages were placed.

One hefty one was labeled, "To all doctors and staff, Selborn Community Medical Center." Idly, he tore it open.

It was filled with flyers about a missing woman, a Catherine Calvert Elkins. She had apparently been kidnapped several weeks before, while pregnant. Her husband had been murdered. Information was being sent to hospitals all over the country, since, if she were still alive, she would have given birth a few weeks earlier. Reeve had heard about the kidnapping on the news but hadn't paid much attention—until now.

The flyers had a photo on them. He had barely noticed the picture in the media. But now he looked closely. It resembled Polly.

It couldn't be her, of course. Not this woman with straight, light hair framing a face projecting a confident, sardonic expression. Not this sophisticate with too much makeup, wearing an expensive suit.

Besides, Polly hadn't been kidnapped. No one held her in Selborn Peak against her will.

A chill ran up Reeve's spine. Polly had revealed she had been an abused wife. Could these flyers be a ploy by her ex-husband to find her?

No, this woman's husband was dead. Murdered. Polly had said she was divorced. Still...

Polly had been known to hide the truth. But he couldn't be sure that the statements made on these flyers were factual, either. He didn't know their source. He did know Polly. Just in case this *was* her, he would give her the benefit of the doubt—for now, at least.

Grasping the entire bundle of flyers tightly, he carried them back to his office. At his desk, he tore the sheets once, then again, and shoved them into his wastebasket.

But this would not be the end of it. He would get answers from her. This time, he *would* get answers.

"You're sure you can handle payments this large?" Polly had located Ricky Edwards outside a broom closet on the center's third floor, where he had been organizing cleaning supplies.

The young man's thinness was emphasized by the way his green hospital uniform hung on him. His long hair was caught up under a matching cap. "Sure," he said. "I've moved back with my folks—my mom and my low-life father, as my uncle would say, though my dad's actually pretty cool. Anyway, now I don't have to pay rent. I can't send much yet to my other creditors, since I want to pay off this hospital first to show how much I appreciate the job." He grinned, revealing his gleaming teeth. "I have to tell you, Polly, this is the first time someone has suggested I'm paying them too much."

She laughed. "I just wanted to make sure you're not getting in further over your head."

"Thanks." He turned serious. "And I want to tell you again how grateful I am for this idea. Has that Clifford guy listened? Is he going to hire others like you and me?''

''I'm working on it.''

A few minutes later, Polly was on her way back to her cubicle, Ricky's file still in her hands. Running across his updated account information, she had been surprised at how high his monthly payments were. But her idea was working. It was really working!

Without thinking, she headed for Reeve's office. She had to share her pleasure with him.

His waiting room was empty. Not even Donna was there. It was, after all, lunchtime. She knocked on his inner door and peered in.

''Oh, hi, Polly.'' It wasn't Reeve who answered, but Alicia. She was dressed in a pretty peach pantsuit, a large leather tote over her shoulder. She stuffed something into her bag as she approached the door. ''Reeve must be at lunch. I left him a note. How's Laurel?''

''Fine. And I'm doing well, too.'' Polly described her meeting with Ricky Edwards.

''What a hoot!'' Alicia said. ''There might be a story in it. It'd be great publicity for Selborn Community Medical Center.''

''Oh, but—'' Polly bit her bottom lip.

''I'd leave you out of it. You want to grab some lunch?''

''I'd better get back to Laurel,'' Polly said. ''But I'll leave Reeve a note, too.''

Alicia slipped out past her. ''I'll give you a call later.''

''Good,'' Polly said. She was still surprised at how nice Alicia had turned out to be.

Alone in Reeve's office, she approached his crowded desk, looking for something on which to write. Alicia's note contained a question about a city council issue.

Polly couldn't help shivering. She had nearly forgotten that, on top of everything else, Reeve was a politician. As kind as he often seemed, he had sought, and won, power.

He didn't seem to abuse it. But she hadn't recognized the way her stepfamily abused it until it was shoved into her face.

Her own father had been a politician, too, she reminded herself. And he had been wonderful. Like Reeve...

Perhaps she should just leave. But Alicia might mention her presence.

For her note, Alicia had used a torn scrap of paper— from the wastebasket, it appeared, for it was filled with torn pages. Alicia picked one up. And froze. On it was the name Elkins.

Shaking, she pulled more pieces from the basket. In a few minutes, she was able to piece together one full page.

It was a flyer requesting the help of doctors and others to find the missing Catherine Calvert Elkins.

How had she dared to hope she might hide away here, especially after the messages to her, via the media, from her stepbrothers? Her stepfather had put them up to it. He would find her—if he hadn't already.

"No," she moaned aloud. Had Selborn Community Medical Center been singled out to receive the flyers because they knew she was here? In the last broadcast they had claimed, after all, to know where she was. And even if they didn't—yet—someone would recognize her, reveal her whereabouts.

She could assume, since the papers were in his trash can, that Reeve had seen the flyers. Had he torn them up? If so, why?

Had he recognized her?

And Alicia…she had used a scrap for her note. She had put something into her tote bag as she'd left. Had she pieced together one of the notices? Did she, too, recognize Polly?

Reeve had, for the most part, been friendly. Alicia had become friendly. They believed she had been a victim of abuse. In some ways Polly had. Surely she could trust them both not to give her away if they had recognized her.

She laughed aloud bitterly. Hadn't she learned that the people she believed the most trustworthy were the worst of all?

Keep cool, she told herself. She had promised herself she would not overreact. She would not run unless there was proof she had been found. Above all, she would not panic.

But this time there just might be something to panic about.

Chapter Eight

Polly wanted to be by herself—just Laurel and her—while she pondered whether to stay or flee. But that night, solitude was impossible. Esther had invited her for dinner and made it clear her feelings would be hurt if Polly refused.

Reluctantly, Polly had agreed to go. Maybe having adult company would be better for her nerves.

She bundled up Laurel and braved the cold Rockies weather to come downstairs in a sweatshirt, blue jeans, thick socks and boots. She passed the aspen in the yard, its remaining golden leaves trembling in the breeze. Only when she reached Esther's house did she realize that Laurel and she were not the only guests. Frannie was there. Of course Esther would ask her niece to come.

But Reeve was there, too.

"Thanks for inviting me," he told Esther. He was dressed in the beige sweater that hugged the breadth of his shoulders and set off the ginger shade of his thick hair. As wonderful as he always looked in his customary lab coat, Polly thought him extraordinarily handsome in that sweater. His deceptively youthful features were angular enough to make it clear that he was all adult, all sexy male.

She glanced away. She had no business thinking such thoughts about any man, particularly not one who could ruin her future, and Laurel's, by misusing the knowledge that she feared he now had.

The dining room was redolent with the aromas of delicious-smelling food and tart lemon furniture wax. Polly sighed inwardly as Esther sat Reeve next to her at the table, which was formally set with an elegant lace cloth and silver flatware. "Glad you both could make it," said her landlady, winking at Polly.

What would Esther do if she knew her tenant was a fugitive—and a killer? She would hardly invite her to supper.

Polly set Laurel down on the plush carpeting in her child seat. The baby cooed, and Polly gave her a finger to grasp.

"Frannie, come to the kitchen for a minute." Esther rubbed her hands on the apron covering her customary bright-colored shift. "I need a little help."

"Is there anything I can do?" Polly didn't want to stay with Reeve.

"Sit still," Esther chided. "You and Reeve are guests. Tonight's a special occasion. That's why we're eating in the dining room."

"What occasion?" Reeve asked.

"Polly and Laurel have been my tenants for two months," Esther replied, beaming.

Polly made herself grin. Esther was right. Laurel was nine weeks old now. Already Laurel was lifting her head and smiling and even, sometimes, sleeping through the night.

As far as her family was concerned, Laurel was a month younger. But what difference did that make now?

They sought a woman with a baby. Perhaps they had found her.

Reeve raised a water glass. "Let me propose a toast. To Polly and Laurel—may they remain Esther's tenants for a long, healthy time."

And may we do so anonymously, Polly added silently, lifting her glass as Esther and Frannie stood behind their chairs and held up their glasses in turn.

Reeve gently clinked his against Polly's. "And may all your troubles disappear." He whispered so only she could hear, but there was an edge to his voice. "Whatever they may be."

She stared at him. His eyes were contemplative, his wide mouth quirked at a sardonic angle. "Thank you," she mouthed, pretending not to recognize his toast's ulterior meaning.

Esther motioned to Frannie and both women left the room. Reeve continued to look unwaveringly at Polly. She slumped under his gaze as though her bones had turned to talc.

"Polly, there's something I need to discuss with you later." His tone allowed no contradiction. "It's about some paperwork."

She swallowed hard. Of course he had recognized her. How had she imagined otherwise? More important, what was she going to do? "I don't want to talk shop on this special occasion." She softened her refusal with a weak smile.

Reeve raised his thick brows as though telling her she had no choice. *I can't!* she wanted to scream, bending to straighten the blanket around Laurel. *Don't you understand I'm trying to protect my daughter?*

Or would it be better to talk about it? Could she somehow convince him those flyers had nothing to do with her? Unlikely.

This occasion might commemorate not only two months of living here, but the day she determined to flee. But, oh, how she would hate to go! Despite her best intentions, she had begun to develop ties. She sat up again, daring a surreptitious glance at Reeve—only to find herself still the subject of his unnerving, steadfast stare.

She was relieved when Esther and Frannie trooped back in, hands laden with bowls of steaming mashed potatoes and what looked like a hearty beef stew.

"This is delicious," she said a minute later after sampling the rich and tasty dish. Their hostess beamed.

"You grew up around here, Esther, didn't you?" Reeve asked.

"Of course." For the next few minutes, Esther regaled them with stories of her youth, when Selborn Peak had been a tiny village, before skiing became so popular there.

It was Frannie's turn next to describe how things were during her childhood. There had been more people, but the town had still been remote and quiet.

"And you, Reeve," Frannie finished. "I know you and your parents moved to Denver when you were a teen, but I remember you growing up here."

Reeve related recollections of his youth, spiced with boyish pranks and romps through the mountains in the snow with his brother. His golden-brown eyes glowed as he spoke of his childhood; it had obviously been happy. "I turned out rather wild," he said, "so I took a short detour into the army after high school to get that out of my system." His parents and brother lived in

Denver now, but after becoming a doctor Reeve had moved back to Selborn Peak to start the medical center.

"Selborn Peak was a great place to bring up kids," Esther said. "It still is." She looked straight at Polly, then at Reeve and back again.

Polly flushed. "That's why I'm glad Laurel and I are here," she said lightly.

"Where did you grow up, Polly?" Reeve asked. She inhaled sharply. She had been set up. It would be hard for her not to talk about her own childhood after the others had described theirs. What could she say without giving herself away?

"You know," she said with an attempt at a grin at Reeve. "The North Pole. Or was it the South?"

"How about east?" he asked. "You were driving west when you had your accident." He was not going to play her game.

"You're right," she finally said. "I'm from the east, a small, boring town—you wouldn't have heard of it." She took another bite of stew. "Mmm, Esther, this is delicious. I'd love to have your recipe."

"Tell us about your childhood," Reeve interjected before Esther could reply. Drat the man! He was as tenacious tonight as a cat with a bird between its paws.

What did she dare to say? "My dad died when I was little, and my mom remarried. I came to care for my stepfather and stepbrothers." That was the truth, as far as it went.

"And your husband?"

This man would not quit! In a studiedly careless gesture, Polly waved her hand. "He was from the area, too."

"How long have you been divorced?"

"Leave it alone, Reeve. Please." Polly hadn't meant

her anguish to spill out, but she was unable to stop it. Laurel began to cry. "Come here, sweetheart." Polly picked her up. The baby quieted immediately and even smiled at her mother.

For the rest of the meal, Polly was relieved that no one asked any more questions about her background. The adults took turns fussing over Laurel.

Reeve particularly showered warmth on the infant— though he watched Polly constantly from the corner of his eye. Laurel blinked and batted her chubby little fists at him, as if taking in every word he spoke.

Traitorous baby, Polly thought. She knew Reeve was just biding his time until he could confront her with questions....

When everyone had finished eating, Polly stood hurriedly and began gathering dirty dishes.

"You don't need to do that," Esther chided.

"I want to."

"It's my job," Frannie said. "You two make yourselves at home."

Polly tried to think of a graceful way of grabbing Laurel and leaving. Instead, while Esther and Frannie were out of the room, she insisted on stacking dishes on the table. And then she stayed for coffee and a delicious piece of homemade apple pie.

But all the fruity sweetness in the world could not dispel the sour feeling she got deep inside each time Reeve studied her searchingly, as though trying to figure out who she was, what she had done.

Finally, the meal ended. "Thanks for everything," she said to Esther, "but it's time to go feed Laurel and get her to bed." That was the best excuse of all, and it worked.

But not completely, for Reeve made his goodbyes,

too. And when she prepared herself, in the cold air outside Esther's, to toss a brief good-night at the inquisitive doctor, he thwarted her. "I'll come up with you while you get Laurel settled," he said. "And then we'll talk."

Her breath frozen inside her, Polly stammered, "B-but—"

"I threw away some interesting papers today," he said. "And I think I deserve an explanation."

Defeated, Polly bent her head in acquiescence. Followed by Reeve, she carried her baby upstairs.

THOUGH REEVE RECALLED with tenderness the moving sight of Polly nursing the baby in the hospital, he respected her privacy.

He was in the kitchen when Polly returned from the bedroom. "I'm making coffee," he said. "We can talk while it brews."

He watched Polly sink onto the threadbare sofa, head bowed, her long lashes skimming her cheeks. "I'm tired," she said in a voice he could hardly hear. "Could we do this another time?"

In a moment, he was in the chair beside her. He steeled himself against the sympathy that made him want to enfold her in his arms and shield her from whatever had happened. "No, we can't. Tell me everything... Catherine."

Her head popped up. And then her body sagged in resignation. "I figured you recognized me," she whispered.

"So did Alicia, and when there's a story in the air, she's hard to control. If you want my help, you'd better explain." About your husband first, he wanted to demand. Reeve had to know the truth. Had she even been married? If so, was she still married? Divorced? Or widowed, as the flyers said?

Her marital state mattered to him, though he wanted not to care.

Polly—he could not think of her as Catherine—was silent for a long while. She stared across the room toward the bare wall. He studied her face. Her smooth cheeks were as pale as if struck by moonlight, her fair, clear skin drawn tightly against her elegant bone structure. Her full lips trembled, and the despair that radiated from her eyes stabbed at him. Even her curly dark hair, usually so fresh and youthful, seemed limp.

He saw only a minimal resemblance to the confident, overly made up woman in the flyer—but a resemblance just the same.

"All right," she finally said. "I'll tell you what I can, though not everything." She raised one hand at his protest. "There are things I need to keep to myself as leverage."

Though he did not understand, he nodded slowly. Anything would be better than nothing. And if it weren't enough, he would draw more from her.

"You wanted to know about my childhood." Her smile was a grimace. "It was essentially a good one. Or so I thought then."

Tears puddled in her eyes. He wanted to wipe them away. Instead, he stayed still.

"The worst part was that my father died when I was ten. His name was John Calvert, and he was mayor of our small town, North Calvert, Connecticut, named for his ancestors. Less than a year later, my mother married Lou Jenson, a businessman and city councilman. He was on city council for a long time, until he was elected mayor about eight years ago."

"He's your stepfather?" Reeve prompted.

She nodded. "His two sons, Victor and Gene, were rough on me when they first moved in, but after they finished teasing, we became friends. More. I thought we were...family." The last word came out as a sob. She buried her face in her hands and her shoulders heaved.

This time, Reeve did not resist his impulse. He sat beside her on the sofa, gathering her into his arms.

She felt slight and delicate. He pressed his face against her hair. It smelled like the fragrant scent he had noticed the first time he had seen her.

She pulled away, facing him. Her eyes were wet but determined. "Please, let me get this out the best I can."

He nodded.

She twisted one side of her mouth up in an expression again mocking a smile. "We had to tiptoe around my mother, since she was nervous and had occasional spells that came close to being breakdowns. But I was the family's pampered princess. Whatever I wanted, I got. No teenage rebellion from me, though. Any semblance of independence I showed was squelched. My stepfather would ground me. I'd lose my allowance. Mostly, my stepfather shunned me. I hated it. My mother, when she understood, advised me to obey, so I did. I remained their good little girl. I even went to the college they picked and married the man they chose."

Reeve could not stay quiet at this. "But—"

She put her index finger on his lips. It was warm, its pressure light, and he had an urge to kiss it. But she quickly removed it. "Sounds like another century, doesn't it? Anyway, Carl Elkins was the son of a friend of my stepfather's. I knew him from childhood, since he visited a lot with his father. He came from Boston, was educated at Harvard Law, then moved to little North

Calvert. I didn't know why until he asked me to marry him. It was a foregone conclusion I'd accept. I have to admit, he bowled me over, sending flowers and cards, treating me circumspectly but kissing me enough to make me feel wanted.''

Reeve felt as though she had knifed him in the gut. Ridiculous, he told himself. She had come here pregnant. She was a lovely, sexy woman. Of course her husband had wanted her.

''So, we married.'' Polly pulled away to sit at the far side of the sofa. ''I never learned to do much on my own, but my duty was to perform volunteer work in town like my mother. That was how I learned about fund-raising. My stepfather remained mayor, and my stepbrother Gene was his aide. Victor was elected to city council, and my husband, Carl, became his assistant. Everyone still treated me like a princess. They were all so pleased when I got pregnant. A fairy-tale existence, don't you think?''

This time, she waited for Reeve to answer. ''Obviously, it wasn't.''

''Obviously.'' She gave an ugly little laugh, then took a deep breath. ''I didn't learn how awful things were until the brother of a friend approached me, begging for help.''

''To do what?''

''That's the part I can't tell you,'' she said sadly. ''It might endanger you, and it would cause me to lose whatever bargaining power I have. I will say this much, though—it concerns my family. They're powerful. Very powerful.''

Reeve bit back his frustration. ''Polly, I don't... Would you rather I call you Catherine?''

''No. I'm Polly now. And please don't ask questions.

I won't answer. But you wanted to know about my husband. I can tell you that—or at least part of it.''

"All right.'' Reeve straightened on the sofa. He gripped his knees with his hands, though what he wanted to do was to touch Polly, to shake her until she spilled the rest.

She looked at Reeve, and he saw a myriad of emotions play on her face: fear. Sadness. Horror, anger, despair.

"What?'' he urged gently.

"You saw the flyers.'' Her voice was hoarse. "About Carl.''

"Were you kidnapped?'' Reeve asked. "Did someone kill your husband?''

"No,'' she replied. "And yes. I was not kidnapped, but someone did kill Carl—me.''

POLLY WATCHED Reeve's face, waiting for the disgust she was certain she would see.

Instead, his gaze filled with sympathy.

It was nearly her undoing. She felt tears rush down her cheeks like a flash flood in the desert.

Could she be wrong? Maybe keeping things back, when there was someone whom she just might be able to trust, was not the same as learning to rely on herself.

"Tell me about it,'' he said. "I know you were abused and —''

"I wasn't,'' she interrupted vehemently. That was one lie she had to put right, so he would no longer feel sorry for her. She had been stupid, she had been naive, but she hadn't been physically abused. "Carl never raised his hand against me. At least not...not until that last night.''

"What happened then?'' Reeve asked. He still sounded calm, though she'd just admitted she had lied.

Was this the bedside manner he used with his patients, serene no matter what horrible things were revealed—and no matter what he really felt?

"It…it was about my family, you see. I had gained some knowledge that threatened them. Carl sometimes…well, he married me to become part of my family. I realize it now. He didn't abuse me the way you thought, but he sometimes…belittled me. Made me feel inadequate as a wife of an up-and-coming attorney who was part of such a distinguished family. My family meant everything to him. So, when they told him to take care of me that night, he took them seriously."

"Damn him," Reeve said through gritted teeth.

"I did," Polly replied ruefully.

"Tell me how it happened."

She shrugged, suddenly too exhausted to continue.

Reeve moved closer on the sofa, and his strong hand lifted her chin. She was forced to look into golden-brown eyes that radiated determination as well as sympathy. Reeve had a solidly masculine face, shadowed this late at night by a hint of a dark ginger beard. A handsome face. A wonderful face. "Tell me how you killed him," he insisted, rubbing her skin lightly with callused fingers.

His matter-of-fact acceptance was not what she had expected.

She closed her eyes at the emotion that welled within her. That was a mistake. Behind her eyelids, she saw Carl aiming the gun at her. "It was horrible," she managed to reply hoarsely. "My family had told Carl to convince me to stay quiet. When cajoling didn't work, he said he knew what would. He went into the bedroom for the gun he kept for protection, then came after me in the kitchen. He pointed it toward my abdomen, where the baby grew. My baby…and his. How could he even threaten that way?''

Polly crumpled into tears. In a moment, she felt herself embraced tightly against Reeve. "It's okay," he whispered against her hair.

"But I killed him!" she finally said. "When I told him that he wouldn't dare, that my family would have his hide if he harmed the baby or me, he told me which of us had my family's attention and respect—and it wasn't me. He explained they had sent him with orders to do whatever was necessary. I saw in his eyes that he told the truth. Maybe he would just have killed me so the baby could be saved—I don't know. I was so upset that I flew at him. I must have startled him, for he didn't fire. I grabbed his arm and twisted. We fell. The gun went off…."

"It was self-defense, Polly," Reeve said, his hands cupping her face. Once more she looked into his caring eyes.

"But my family will say——"

"You're among friends here," he said fiercely. "No one will hurt you now. You should go public right away, tell your side."

"I can't prove anything, and I'll lose the only leverage I have against them—the threat of publicity and scandal. But thank you for believing in me."

"You're welcome." There was a new huskiness in his voice, and when she looked into his eyes, they were aglow as though illuminated by an internal blaze.

Slowly, drawn by a force as irresistible as magnetism or gravity, she reached over and stroked the lips he had narrowed in determination. She thought at first that she only wanted to show her gratitude.

But he took her hand and kissed the palm. Not just

sympathetically, but with fervor, with his lips and tongue, as though he were making love to her entire body via that one small, seemingly innocuous site.

Sensual patterns of warmth and need circulated within her, curling deep inside her body. "Oh, Reeve," she whispered.

In moments, she was in his arms. He kissed her mouth, her neck, her eyelids, and then found her lips once more. No games with Reeve. She wanted simply to taste him, deeply and forever. She felt the kiss stoke into a conflagration of stimulating awareness. Her arms around him, she felt the strength of his muscular back, then moved her hands up to caress the softness of the hair at the nape of his neck.

She wanted more. Now.

But he pulled gently away.

"It—it's okay, Reeve," she whispered. "I mean, it's not too soon any longer."

"It's always too soon unless you can assure me that you're not going to leave." His voice was raspy, and as she drew back she could see the anguish that etched deep lines in his forehead and beside his eyes.

"I can't promise," she said sorrowfully.

It was her own turn to hurt as he let her go.

Chapter Nine

Stepping away from a willing, eager Polly was one of the most difficult things Reeve had ever done, he realized as he walked, as though wounded, toward the apartment door. But it was the right thing.

He clenched his fists at his sides, then opened them. She did not intend to stay. That was no surprise. He had known that practically from the moment he had met her.

He also knew the pain of getting close to a woman, then having her leave.

He had already come to care for Polly much more than he ever should have. Making love with her now would only make it worse to see her go.

"Reeve?" Her voice behind him was a husky whisper. "I...I'm sorry."

Fighting the torment of unfulfilled desire, he made himself turn back toward her. She sat on that ragged couch, her presence brightening the drab, threadbare room much more than the homey touches she had added.

What was he doing? He couldn't leave. Not now.

Polly's family was after her. Reeve would take care of Laurel and her, he decided.

Quickly, he recrossed the room and sat on the couch beside her. "Okay," he said in a businesslike tone, "now we'll discuss how to protect you. You can't be alone anymore." The person who should be with her was him. To be certain, though, that he did the best job of safeguarding her, he needed the whole story. "But Polly, I need to know the rest to figure out the best way to help you—"

She rose abruptly and stood beside the sofa. Her arms were crossed, and she looked furious. "What makes you think you're going to figure out anything?"

It was Reeve's turn to get angry. "You've already shown you can't fight your family alone. You should have told me sooner so I could make sure you're protected. And you still won't trust me enough to tell me everything. I'll make arrangements to stay with you, but I'll still need to know—"

"I don't want *anyone* with me all the time, if that's what you're thinking. And you don't need to make arrangements to stay with me. In fact, it's about time for you to leave. I'm doing fine by myself."

"Of course," he said, standing within inches of her. He glowered down, realizing he was attempting to intimidate her. "Meanwhile, flyers appear from nowhere and you get ready to run. Right?"

"Right." She moved away, turning her back.

He could see that her shoulders were shaking, and he reached one hand toward her.

"Look, Reeve. I'm not the only one with secrets. And you don't see me trying to pry yours from you."

He withdrew his hand quickly as he stared at her, shocked. Was he keeping secrets? Not intentionally, but... His pain was irrelevant to this discussion. Wasn't it?

But Polly apparently considered it relevant. She faced him and touched his arm. "I...I heard your wife was leaving you the night she and your baby were killed. I'm sorry, Reeve. Truly sorry. But it has nothing to do with me. You can't shield me from my family. No one can. I won't let you disrupt your life in a misguided effort to take care of me. And if I have to leave, it won't be because I want to. You have to believe that.''

He felt as though a scalpel had been stuck in his gut at this stark reminder of Annette and Cindy. "So you don't want me around. And you'd take off with regrets— but you'd leave anyway.'' Sarcasm oozed from his tone, but he did not let himself react to her wince.

"I've Laurel to think about,'' she said softly. She turned away, and when she continued, her voice was a whisper he almost couldn't hear.

"What was that?'' he demanded.

"Nothing.''

But after he had stalked from the apartment, her whispered words came to him with sudden clarity: *And I have to protect you, too.*

THE NEXT MORNING, clad in a borrowed parka with a good, warm hood, Polly walked briskly toward the medical center along the charming town's quaint Alpine streets. The sky was brilliant blue, with just a scattering of white clouds. Polly had never appreciated Esther and her kindness more; it was much too cold that day to subject Laurel to the frigid air from the snow-capped Rockies that towered above.

Laurel had been fussy all night. That had blessedly prevented Polly from letting her own thoughts wander...much. Despite all her good intentions, they strayed anyway, to Reeve.

"I wish things could be different,'' she said into the glacial wind that scoured her face and numbed her lips.

If only she lived a normal life, she could imagine settling down somewhere. Like here. With someone…like Reeve.

But her life was far from normal.

Self-defense or not, she had killed her husband. She was on the run from her own corrupt family, living under an assumed name. They might have found her. She was in danger.

Despite what she had said to Reeve, she was touched by his offer to take care of her. But she had to stand on her own. And if she ran, it would be because she did not want to endanger him, too.

She felt her skin heat in embarrassment as she recalled how she had thrown herself at him. Had practically asked him to make love with her. She had clearly read him wrong, for she had thought he'd wanted her, too.

But he had been right. Making love would not have changed anything between them, except that she would find it harder—much harder—to leave when the time came. And she had no doubt that it would.

Clifford had asked her to come to the medical center that morning as early as possible for her hour of work. That was fine; she wanted to see Reeve early, too. If he really wanted to help, there were a couple of things she'd thought of that he could do.

One was that he could forbear from making her feel worse that she couldn't tell him everything, to at least act as though he understood why she could get no closer to him.

She was still considering the other thing for him to do; as useful as it might be, it could cause treacherous repercussions.

When she reached the medical center, she pushed the glass door open. She was practically shoved inside by the force of the wind. The heat in the nearly empty lounge at the hospital's entry struck her like a blast from a furnace. She stood still for a moment, soaking in the warmth.

"Hi, Polly." Polly turned at the youthful male voice to find Ricky Edwards pushing a cart laden with hospital charts. "Cold enough for you?" The thin young man grinned widely.

"Never!" she said with a laugh. "And you?"

"Doesn't bother me now I have a warm place to work. That was another problem with construction. Even if I *could* work, I couldn't do much this time of year." Nervously, he touched the hair he had pulled back in a rubber band, and his long face grew serious. "I want to thank you again," he said. "For the job, for standing up to my uncle... If I ever can help you, just let me know."

Polly felt her smile tremble, and she hurriedly looked down at the paperwork on Ricky's cart. "You've already done a lot. Since your job here is working out so well, I've gained a lot of credibility. *I* should be thanking *you.*"

Ricky slapped her arm gently and gave her a thumbs-up, then started off with his cart. She headed down the opposite corridor toward Reeve's office.

It was crowded, as usual. Donna, the receptionist, slid open the glass separator between the patient lounge and her cubicle and peered over her reading glasses. "Dr. Reeve is behind thanks to an emergency," she said apologetically. "I'm not even sure he'll be able to get away for lunch."

"Oh," Polly murmured. She had not allowed herself to think about how much she had wanted to see Reeve that morning.

"Laurel is due for her next well-baby checkup soon," Donna reminded Polly.

"I'll make an appointment later," Polly said. She turned to go, but before she could, Reeve stepped into the office behind Donna. He looked wonderful, though a little harried. His white lab jacket looked uncharacteristically rumpled, his hair in need of a combing.

Yet he looked so normal. So comforting. Polly fought conflicting urges to throw herself into his arms...and to flee.

"Hello, Polly!" His tone was soft but neutral. "Sorry I can't make time for lunch, but I'm really busy today."

He had made time for her on other busy days. But she shouldn't expect more from him after last night. She had practically thrown him out.

"Of course," she acknowledged. "I was just going." She turned, trying to stiffen her slumping shoulders.

"Wait. Is there something I can help you with?"

She pivoted back to face him, a modicum of hope rushing through her. "Yes," she said. "I wanted to ask your advice. But I can come back later."

"No, come in now," he said. "We'll make it quick."

HE DIDN'T WANT TO MAKE IT quick. Reeve knew that even as he said the words. For his own well-being, he had to spend as little time as possible with Polly...whom he refused to think of as Catherine.

For *her* well-being, he wanted to be with her constantly. To make certain she was all right, that her family did not harm her.

But she had made it clear she had no use for his protection.

"I didn't mean to bother you." She sat rigidly on a chair in front of his cluttered desk.

"No bother."

She carried a black parka with fake-fur trim. The weather was growing colder, and Reeve was glad Polly now had something heavier than her borrowed coat. He wished he had seen her wearing her new jacket. It would go well with the silver-gray of her eyes. Her beige sweater hugged the curves that he himself had hugged the night before. Unfulfilled need raced through him, hardening him. He felt his fists clench as he sighed in frustration. "How can I help you?"

"It's about the flyers." Her gaze flicked toward the wastebasket.

"They were gone when I got in. I've no reason to think anyone else saw them except, perhaps, the cleaning crew. And I'm sure they're too busy emptying the wastebaskets to pay attention to the contents."

She relaxed as though she could take his word as gospel.

He curled his lips in a self-directed scowl. But Polly noticed and began to stand. "That's all," she said brightly. "You've made me feel better already."

"That's not all," he contradicted wearily. "Polly, I'm making a hash of things. I know you don't want anything between us. That's fine with me. But you need help, and I really do want to help you."

She looked at him with shining eyes. "Thank you, Reeve," she said softly. "I wish…well, it doesn't matter what I wish. It can't come true."

"Someday—" he began, but she cut him off with her upraised hand.

"I've stopped believing in 'somedays.'" She took a step toward the door. "But thanks for the thought."

"You wanted to ask me something," he reminded her.

She nodded. "I'm not sure it's a good idea, though,"

"What's that?"

She leaned forward, resting her hands on the edge of his desk. "Do you have any trustworthy friends who work at other hospitals? Not locally, but anywhere else?"

He nodded.

"Are there any to whom you could mention the flyers, find out if they're being distributed generally or just around here?" She added hastily, "You'd have to be discreet, and so would your friends. You'd have to ask them not to mention your inquiry, but if someone asked directly, they should call you."

"And I'd need to act casual, as if the answer didn't really matter, right?"

"Exactly!"

His laugh was rueful. "I'd have to pretend no interest at the same time I'm issuing directions as though their responses matter a great deal."

"It's a tall order," Polly acknowledged. "That's why I wasn't sure whether to ask." She rose. "Thanks anyway."

"I didn't say I wouldn't do it." He stood, too. "I've a couple of friends with whom I can be cagey without their needing reasons spelled out."

"Really?" The life returned to her eyes. "Great! That information will help me decide if I need to leave right away."

Before he had time to consider what he was doing, he had her in his arms. She was still, but she did not pull away. "Don't leave without telling me first," he ordered. And then he softened his voice. "And thank you for relying on me this little bit, even if you don't feel you can trust me completely."

"It's not that—" she began to protest.

He bent and gave her a brief kiss. He gently patted her behind as if he were merely hurrying her along, ignoring the desire that nevertheless surged through him. "I need to see my patients, but I'll let you know what I learn."

"I'M GLAD YOU'RE STILL here."

Polly looked up from the stack of files she had been organizing to take home. She had spent more than two hours at the hospital. Though she had checked with Esther, it was way past time for her to return to Laurel.

Reeve stood in the doorway to her small cubicle. His lab coat had given way to a sport jacket over his blue shirt and black trousers. She liked his casual clothing. In fact, there was nothing she had seen this man wear that didn't look good on him.

She couldn't help smiling as she motioned him in. Even if she didn't dare to dream of a future with Reeve, that didn't mean she couldn't feel glad to see him. Glad? She was delighted! "Did you finish with all your patients?"

"A while ago. I even had time to make a few calls."

"Really? To your friends?" She spoke aloud; Clifford was out at a meeting. Otherwise, she couldn't have a conversation in her cubicle that she didn't want the administrator to hear. The walls were paper thin. More than once she had heard him chewing out a patient in arrears on his account, and cringed; she had quickly learned that yelling accomplished nothing.

Also, more than once, Clifford had eavesdropped on her conversations with people whom she was trying to solicit for payment. He often dropped in as she was finishing, to give her advice on how to handle delinquent accounts.

His criticism depressed her. She had thought she'd found something she could do on her own, without much direction. Something she was good at. But her boss obviously did not share her opinion.

Reeve slipped into the chair facing her small desk. "Yes, I've talked with a few other doctors."

"What did they say?"

"You're fine, Polly." His grin seemed relieved, as though he, too, had been holding his breath. "At least as long as you stay here. The flyers apparently were distributed all over. I called a close med school friend from Florida, and he said they were posted everywhere. I didn't speak to too many people for fear of giving you away, but I talked to a guy in Denver and another in Arizona. Same thing."

"Then my family doesn't know I'm here." Polly closed her eyes and reveled in the feeling of relief. "Thank heavens. And you're sure your friends will be discreet?"

"I think so. I made up a story about a friend who thought he saw this woman with her kidnapper—a friend in Albuquerque."

Polly laughed. "That sounds perfect."

"So," Reeve said, "let's celebrate tonight. You go home and get Laurel. Then, you can cash in that raincheck for Chinese or any other cuisine that tempts your palate."

She should have said no. His information, as wonderful as it was, did not change anything between them.

But she wanted to share her happiness—for she was uncertain how long it would last. She could not relax, but for now, at least, she had no reason to believe she had been found out.

And she wanted Reeve's company, selfish as that might be.

"Okay. We'll have to make it an early evening, though. I'm bringing home a lot of work to do tomorrow."

That made it clear, she hoped, that this evening would be strictly platonic, too. She would not make a fool of herself again by attempting to seduce Reeve.

"Fine," he said. "I'll pick you two up at six."

THE NEXT DAY, Polly slipped quickly into her cubicle and dropped her parka on her chair. "I'll be right home, Laurel," she muttered under her breath as she rifled through the paperwork she had left in a pile on the desk.

She hadn't intended to come to the center today, but despite her planning the day before, she had left behind some notes.

Her forgetfulness had nothing to do with how glad she'd been to see Reeve yesterday, she told herself. Though maybe she'd been so dazzled by his news that all sense had left her for the short while it had taken her to gather her files.

Then, later, there had been their dinner. They'd decided on Italian, and Reeve had taken Laurel and her to a charming trattoria in downtown Selborn Peak. Illuminated by candlelight, it had served the most delightful fettuccine Bolognese.

Most delightful had been the company. Reeve had been a perfect gentleman, had not even hinted of their aborted passion the night before…yet she had felt the sparks between them burning brighter than all the flames in the restaurant.

At the end of the evening, Reeve had seen Laurel and

her to the door, made sure she locked it, then left. He hadn't even kissed her good-night.

Perversely, his lack of a kiss, of any response to her, had been what had caused her sleeplessness that night. Now she was exhausted.

There! She spotted the handwritten jottings she had made on several of the accounts, and—

"Mr. Clifford, I'm Al Crackauer," boomed a voice from the office next door. "I called earlier to follow up on the inquiry my employer, Lou Jenson, mayor of North Calvert, Connecticut, is making about his missing stepdaughter, Catherine Calvert Elkins."

Polly sank into her chair. She thrust her fist against her mouth to keep herself from crying out.

"You mentioned something about circulars," grumped Clifford. For once, Polly was glad about his abrasive personality. He was not discriminating with whom he used it. "I never saw them."

"No? How strange. We've sent them to hospitals all over the country. A response to them brought me here."

Reeve? Polly's mind screamed. No. He wouldn't betray her. *Alicia?* But Polly believed Alicia would be discreet, since she thought Polly was an abused wife. Perhaps it was someone Reeve had called. Maybe all of them. Maybe his story had not been believable. Maybe he was not circumspect enough. Maybe—

"In any event, here's a flyer. Have you seen this woman?"

Polly held her breath. She had changed her appearance considerably from the self-confident blond Catherine Elkins had been. Still...

"It's not a clear photo," Clifford stated. "But no, I don't think I know her."

"The woman we're seeking gave birth to a baby about

a month ago. Could I see your hospital records to determine how many births there were around that time, who the parents are, that kind of thing?''

Oh, Lord! What would Clifford say? How could Polly keep from being discovered...? She had to leave, immediately.

She rose from her chair, grabbing at the files she had been working on. Her hands were shaking so much that one of the folders fell. The slight slap of it hitting the floor sounded as loud as a firecracker to Polly. She froze, praying that only she had noticed it.

''Polly? Is that you?'' called Clifford. ''Come in here.''

She swallowed hard. ''I was just leaving, Mr. Clifford.''

''This will only take a minute.''

If she protested too much or simply ran, the investigator would get suspicious. She had no choice.

Her breathing ragged, she threw her oversized parka on over her baggy sweatpants, and rumpled her short, black curls. Thank heavens she hadn't put on any makeup today; she had been in too much of a hurry. But the coloring she had used on her brows and lashes was long-lasting. She jutted her lower jaw forward, not sure how much that might alter her appearance. Maybe the investigator wouldn't recognize her.

''Polly, are you coming?'' Clifford called.

''Right away.'' She pushed open the door to Clifford's office and walked in, hunching over the stack of folders she was carrying. ''I'm on my way home,'' she repeated. ''I just came in to pick up the files I needed. If you call me, I'll give you a rundown of the accounts you asked about.''

''Fine.''

Polly ventured a glance toward the man with Clifford. He was dressed in a blue suit. He had a large nose—the better to pry into others' business, Polly was sure. Otherwise, he appeared to be a perfectly normal person.

A normal person who could squash her like an egg beneath a hammer.

"Crackauer, this is Polly Black. She's one of the women who had a baby about a month ago at Selborn Community."

Trying hard not to swallow in alarm as the man's sharp eyes traveled over her, Polly made herself laugh. "A month? No, Mr. Clifford, my little Laurel's nearly ten weeks old. She was born two days after her due date." Don't let him mention the accident, she prayed inwardly. That could be a giveaway.

"Do you work here, Mrs…Black?" Crackauer asked.

"Oh, yes. Mr. Clifford hired me to do accounting, which is right up my alley. I went to business school before I got married. Good thing I did, now that I'm divorced."

Crackauer turned away. "About those records, Mr. Clifford."

Polly nearly collapsed in relief. He did not seem interested in her. She wasn't out of danger, but perhaps she had directed it elsewhere for the time being.

"Bye," she called over her shoulder as she hurried away, her files still in her arms.

Blindly, without even considering where to go, she headed toward Reeve's office. Fortunately, the waiting room was empty.

"Does he have a patient with him?" Polly asked Donna. The receptionist shook her head but opened her mouth to speak. Polly didn't wait. She knocked on Reeve's door, then burst in.

He sat behind his desk, but he wasn't alone. Alicia was there, and she did not appear pleased by the interruption.

"Sorry," Polly managed to murmur, turning to leave.

"Polly, what's wrong?" Reeve called. She heard his chair creak as he pushed it back, but she didn't wait to see if he followed.

He caught up with her in the hall. "What is it?" He grasped her shoulders. His brown eyes were so wide with alarm that Polly realized she must look as terrified as she felt.

Quickly, in a choked whisper, she related what had happened, what she had done.

"And he bought your story?" Reeve asked.

"I…I think so, but how do I know?" To Polly's dismay, her voice rose in a wail.

"I'll find out what's going on," Reeve said. "Stay here, and I'll be right back."

"I can't. I have to go to Laurel."

"Then go home and lock your doors. I'll come over this evening. Promise you'll be there."

"I can't promise," she answered with a sob. "I don't know what to do."

She broke away and hurried toward her apartment and Laurel—but not, necessarily, toward sanctuary.

Chapter Ten

Reeve wasn't surprised, when he reached Polly's apartment an hour later, to find her in jeans and an oversize work shirt, hurriedly packing. Not surprised, but chilled.

"What did you find out?" She threw a stack of Laurel's clothes on the bed. The baby was awake in her crib, kicking and babbling.

He kept his voice level. "Lou Jenson offered a generous reward for information that helps him find his stepdaughter. Crackauer and other investigators have been following up at hospitals in major cities, spreading word of the reward. One of my so-called friends was raising funds for a new hospital wing in memory of his recently deceased father. Since I tried to be discreet, I didn't explain to anyone why it was important not to mention my inquiry."

"And now your friend will get that hospital wing." Though she made an obvious effort to stop it, a trace of bitterness was audible in her voice.

"Not really."

She stopped fussing with the things she was organizing and looked directly at him for the first time. Her gray eyes were as dull as tarnished silver. "What do you mean?"

"The only way to get the story was to talk to Crack-auer myself—which was fine with him, since I was high on his list of people to question. He was pleased to quiz me about why I'd called to ask my friend about those flyers."

"What did you tell him?" She must have expected his betrayal, for her attention returned to the piles of clothing on the bed. Tension showed in the whiteness of her knuckles as she clutched a stack of blouses.

Hurt beyond all reason, he gripped the wall beside him. He spoke in a monotone. "I told him about my friend Chris in Albuquerque, with whom I correspond by e-mail. I said Chris wrote about a young woman whose baby he'd delivered a month ago. I was curious whether the subject of the flyers could be the same woman, and called some friends to see if they'd gotten the flyers or heard from Chris, too. One of my acquaintances is a big-mouth, but Chris is the soul of discretion. I warned him he might be contacted and told him to say he'd been mistaken, that the woman whose baby he delivered was traveling with her husband and they went home to Podunk."

"Did Crackauer buy it?" Polly, sitting on the bed with her trembling knees stiffly together, regarded him dubiously. Her small upper teeth bit into her lower lip.

"He seemed to. In fact, he seemed downright perturbed that I had an explanation."

For the first time that day, Polly's strained expression relaxed a little.

Maybe this was his opportunity to make her see reason. For her own sake, she should stay where she had friends rather than run. That would be better for Laurel, too. And for Reeve...

Forget it. He would not let himself care whether she stayed or left. Not now.

"I know you're afraid," he said, forcing himself to speak calmly. "But think with me, Polly. I believe you should remain in Selborn Peak."

A small cry of refusal issued from her lips—full, lovely lips he even now longed to kiss—but he held up his hand. "Let me finish."

She remained silent, but her expression turned as stormy as nimbus clouds over a heaving ocean.

"I believe Crackauer is convinced you're not the person he's looking for. If that's true, then he'll report to your family that his quest here was a false lead. They'll search someplace else, and you'll be safe. Do you agree?"

"Yes, but—"

"But what if I'm wrong, that he didn't buy my story?"

Her quick nod caused her dark curls to shake—a hairstyle and color that made her look very different from the self-assured young woman in the photographs Crackauer had passed around.

The woman on the photo was pretty, but she appeared pampered and immature, unlike Polly Black. Polly was a mother, an innovative and caring career woman, and so desirable that even now, enmeshed in a discussion that could result in her disappearing from his life, Reeve felt stirrings inside just being near her.

"If he didn't buy my story," he continued, "he'll tell your family. Something will happen soon. You can be ready to run if there's any sign of trouble, but meantime you can remain among friends who'll take your side. That's what Alicia and I were discussing when you saw us together before—how to help you."

"Alicia?" Polly looked stunned. "She's more friendly now, but...well, she's a reporter. And, Reeve, none of you can protect me if my family lets it be known I killed my husband."

"It was self-defense, Polly."

The smile she gave him was weary. "Not if my stepfather decides it's in his best interests that I'm guilty of murder."

Reeve pulled her to her feet, gripping her shoulders as he stared into her eyes. When she tried to look away, he used his fingers to gently turn her chin so she had no choice but to face him. "Did you attack your husband first? Did you grab that gun and come after him?"

"Of course not." She sounded shocked.

"Then he came after you."

"Yes, but—"

"And he threatened not only you, but your unborn baby?"

She nodded, pulling away forcefully. "But you don't understand my stepfather's political power. He—"

"He wasn't in the room with you and your husband."

"But he told Carl to control me. And—"

"Then your stepfather is guiltier in Carl's death than you are, Polly. Isn't he?"

"Yes!" she shouted. "He's guilty of that and much more. Don't you see?"

"No, I don't, because you haven't told me."

"I can't, damn it, Reeve."

"Why not?" he demanded, frustration with this mule-headed woman making him want to slam something.

"Because I care about you. And if Lou Jenson ever learns that, then you'll die, too!"

Reeve stared at her for a long moment. She was serious. *Dead* serious. "Then you won't tell me what this is all about because you want to protect me?'' His breathing had turned irregular, and he clenched his fists at his sides.

She nodded, looking first at the floor. Then, defiantly, she raised her head until her eyes stared straight into his. ''Yes!'' she whispered.

He took a step toward her the very moment she moved toward him. With no hesitation, he crushed her against him, his mouth plunging down to find that hers was waiting.

Her lips were cold at first, as though the fire inside her had gone out. But no. He was convinced moments later, by the stoking exploration of her tongue, that the sparks remained, just waiting for him to bring them alive once more.

''Polly, I'm not asking anything of you. Nothing you don't want to give. But I want you.''

''Then please, Reeve. Don't stop.''

He lowered her onto the bed, then drew away. With a grin at his own sensibilities, he shook out a blanket and draped it carefully over the side of Laurel's crib. The baby had fallen asleep anyway.

And then he went back to Polly.

THE BED DIPPED at Reeve's return. Polly welcomed him once more into her arms.

Was it wrong to want him now, when neither had promises to give? It didn't matter. She might be gone in an hour, a day. But for now, she needed this one, precious moment with Reeve. She could no more stop herself, or him, than she could give up breathing.

Reeve's fingers slipped beneath her work shirt, up the heated bare skin of her back, moving forward to touch with infinite gentleness her breasts, swollen from nurturing her baby.

Polly strained against him, feeling the hard evidence of his desire at her thigh. Her hand slid down between them, to cup him through his pants. She heard his gasp.

She was hardly aware as their clothes disappeared. She only knew how magnificent his muscular body was as he removed his sweater. And then he was completely bare. She stared languidly at his maleness, feeling the pressure inside her rise.

"You are so beautiful," he said. He cupped her jaw as he kissed her once more, and then his hands, followed by his mouth, took their time exploring her willing flesh.

But soon she could wait no longer. "Now, Reeve, please," she whispered raggedly.

She heard the crackling of cellophane and smiled despite her raging need. He was a doctor, prepared for any kind of precaution, even this.

He was gentle as he entered her. She was still a little sore, but she reveled in his wonderful weight upon her. And then he began a rhythm that started slowly and built until the whole world exploded about her.

"Polly!" Reeve groaned, even as she felt her own release.

A LONG TIME LATER, Polly lay silently against Reeve, simply enjoying the feeling of being so close. She sighed and closed her eyes, a sated, feline smile curling her lips.

She should be packing. Running away.

And yet…maybe he was right. Maybe it would help to stay here, where she had friends. Where she had Reeve.

"You know, Polly," he said after a while, "I can't tell you how much it means to me that you want to protect me, but I'm fully capable of taking care of myself.''

She drew away and glared at him. ''Right, Mr. Macho. You don't have the slightest idea of the danger, but you're ready to throw yourself into it.''

''If it'll help you, I will.'' He tried to bring her close once more, but she resisted…for a moment.

''Oh, Reeve.'' Polly sighed, nestling against him. ''I guess I need to tell you what you'd be up against, to make you understand. I'll trust you not to repeat it, so that, if I have to, I can use it as leverage.''

''You can trust me, Polly.''

''Yes,'' she said, while inside knowing that no one, not even Reeve, could fend off what awaited her when Lou Jenson found her. Not *if,* but *when.*

''I don't need to tell you the details,'' she said. ''But Warren Daucher, a friend who had been threatened by the Jensons, showed me evidence that Lou killed my real father all those years ago, probably to get rid of his political influence in our little town. Then Lou married my mother, and the rest is history. Warren found evidence of how Lou hurt other people, too.''

''I'm sorry, Polly.'' Reeve's tone was sincere as he held her tighter.

''Then Warren disappeared—'' her voice cracked ''—and they sent Carl to hurt me. You see why I can't let them catch me. Or Laurel. And why I don't want you involved…''

''Don't worry about me.'' Reeve sounded gruff. ''And I won't let anything happen to you. But it'll be easier to help you if you stay.''

''I'll think about it…if you'll promise me one thing.''

''What?'' His body stiffened, and she heard the suspicion in his voice.

"Promise that, if anything happens to me, you'll take care of Laurel. That you won't let them have her."

She felt him relax. "I won't let anything happen to you, Polly."

"Not good enough!" Polly sat up and glared at him. "You can't protect me just by saying so. I'll leave now if I think there's any possibility that my staying will result in Lou Jenson, or Victor or Gene, getting Laurel. If it were only my mother... But she'll never leave Lou. Even if she wanted to, he wouldn't let her. And she wants to stay. She's fragile, and so dependent.... You would try to protect Laurel, wouldn't you? You'd take care of her?"

"Of course. I want her with me, Polly."

And— And what? Surely she didn't expect him to take that statement any further. Surely she didn't expect him to say that he wanted her to be with him, too?

No, she didn't expect it. But she *wanted* it. With all her heart.

"Then I'll stay for now," she said, wondering if she should take back the words as soon as she spoke them. She felt corraled. Hobbled.

Yet the relieved look that lightened the shadows on Reeve's beloved face was worth those words...for now. "Good." His grin made him appear years younger. "It'll work out. You'll see."

She wanted to believe him. But that was another reason she should leave right away, she told herself after Reeve departed a few minutes later. Staying would result in her getting hurt.

She had cared once for Carl, and look what he had turned out to be.

She was not equating Reeve with Carl. Not Reeve, who had taken such extraordinary care of them. But there could be no future between them. She had learned, so miserably, that beneath even an ostensibly perfect surface lurked heartache. And Reeve would always believe she would run away if things got difficult.

Maybe she would.

What should she do? What *could* she do?

For the moment, she would do as she had told Reeve. She would stay. For now.

"ARE YOU THE ONE that Crackauer person is after?" asked Frannie Meltzer the next afternoon. Still in her nurse's uniform, she sat on a reproduction of a tufted Victorian chair, in her aunt Esther's furniture-crowded living room, running a comb through her short platinum hair.

Startled, Polly asked, "What do you mean?" She had come with Laurel at Esther's call. Esther was walking Laurel around her house, trying to get her to take her afternoon nap.

"Just putting two and two together," Frannie replied. "I called my aunt when you didn't show up at work. She said you weren't sick, but she saw suitcases when she went up to watch Laurel. The only new powder in the mix around here is that investigator guy. Are you that Catherine he's looking for?"

"I...I'd rather not say," Polly said nervously. She wanted to trust Frannie, but the more people who knew her identity, the more likely it was she'd be given away to Crackauer.

"Good enough," Frannie said. "I take it you don't want to answer any other questions, either."

Gnawing at her lower lip, Polly nodded.

"Too bad. I'm curious about what happened to that

woman's husband. If you're her, you don't appear to have been kidnapped, so—''

Polly felt the blood leave her face. ''I can't discuss it.''

''Never mind.'' Frannie shrugged. ''I can handle my curiosity when I have to. Anyway, that Crackauer won't be around long.''

''Really?'' It was Polly's turn to be curious.

''He cornered me late this morning. He'd talked with some nurses in maternity, a few doctors. None came up with anyone fitting the description of the woman he was after, even when he said his employer had promised a lot of money for the best lead.''

Polly couldn't help her hopeful smile. ''With an incentive like money I'd imagine people would be eager to point a finger at anyone.''

''Some places, maybe,'' said Esther, who had entered the room with an alert Laurel on her shoulder.

Frannie nodded. ''No one at Selborn Community liked the guy. Word was passed around that he was a flake and should be humored but given not a hint of anything helpful. Far as I could tell, that's just what everyone did.''

''Thank you!'' Polly exclaimed.

''Not me,'' Frannie said. ''Thank Reeve. Everyone at the center thinks the world of him. A hint from him is like a command from anyone else.''

Reeve. He was coming through for her. Polly wanted to hug him.

Frannie and Esther both wore knowing smiles. Polly felt herself redden. ''Looks like Laurel's settling down,'' she said hurriedly. ''I'll take her up to our apartment for her nap.'' She held out her arms for her daughter.

"Everything will be fine, Polly," Esther said. "Wait and see."

But Polly did not believe in fairy tales and happy endings. Not anymore.

It would be too easy to expect that Crackauer would leave and there would be no more reasons to worry.

Much too easy.

THAT EVENING, Polly heard a knock at her door. Despite her usual fleeting panic, she got her breathing quickly under control. It had to be one of her friends: Esther or Frannie...or Reeve.

"Who is it?" she called, holding a squirming, fussing Laurel tightly, in case she needed to protect the baby.

It was Reeve. He came in bearing boxes of Chinese food. "I brought dinner. It's a special occasion." His pleased smile made her insides glow.

"Really? Why?" With a kiss, Polly deposited Laurel in her playpen. The baby let out a screech of protest but didn't cry.

Reeve deposited the food on the kitchen table. The delicious aroma of garlic and spices filled the tiny room.

"We're celebrating your safety," Reeve replied with a smile toward Laurel as he removed his jacket. "I've reason to believe Crackauer left today."

Polly clutched his arm, feeling taut, hard muscles beneath the sleeve of his brown-and-gold sweater. "How do you know?"

"I didn't see him around the center after this morning. I'd noticed him taking notes on a Peak Inn pad, so I called there. Sure enough, they'd had a guest named Crackauer. He checked out this afternoon."

"That's wonderful!" She laughed as he picked her up

and whirled her around the tiny kitchen. She reveled in the feel of his heated, hard body against her.

But she knew better than to relax completely at Reeve's news. Crackauer might just have moved to another hotel. Or he might have found out everything he needed to, and left to report to her family. Still, she wouldn't spoil Reeve's good mood.

Later, after they ate, Polly sat pressed against Reeve's side on the threadbare living room sofa, her head nestled against his shoulder. She had turned on the news, just in case. The newscasters were discussing the next impending storm, a big one. Lots of snow was expected.

"Polly?" Reeve's voice was uncharacteristically steely, and she pulled away, her heart pounding.

"Yes?" Nervously, she wondered what he intended to say.

He turned to look at her. His late-day shadow, the hollows of his cheeks and the bleakness in his eyes erased his usual youthful appearance. What was wrong?

"You were right," he said. "How can I expect you to tell me everything if I don't reciprocate?"

A warm and mushy protectiveness settled around Polly's heart as she relaxed a little. Was he about to tell what had really happened to his wife and child? "You should tell me only what you want to, Reeve. What you feel you can." She left the rest of the thought unspoken: just as she would tell him only what she felt *she* could. She reached out and stroked the stubble along his cheek.

He grabbed her hand and kissed the palm. A wave of desire washed through her, and she could see, by the hooding of his eyes, that he had noticed. He smiled wanly. "There's nothing secret about my life—at least nothing I want to keep from you."

She wanted to protest; she wasn't keeping things from

him simply because she wanted to have secrets from him. But she did not want to break the mood. "Then tell me," she said gently. "Please." She muted the television.

He pulled her against him, wrapping his strong arms about her so tightly that she felt nearly crushed. But the gesture was to comfort him, not her, and so she did not protest.

"There's a snowstorm coming. They always make me crazy now, ever since…" he paused. "You know I was married and that my wife left me." His words weren't a question, but she nodded against his chin. "We had a daughter, Cindy. She was nearly two. I'd met Annette in Vail, skiing one winter. She was from Virginia, a schoolteacher, but her heart wasn't in it. When she realized I was a doctor, and that I had started a medical center, she was impressed. She was beautiful, and one thing led to another. She visited me here in Selborn Peak, and I could tell she didn't care for the town, but I had been bowled over. We married, and she started a campaign right away to get me to move to Virginia— or, at worst, Denver." He stopped speaking, and Polly moved in his arms to look at his face. His expression was hard, and he seemed to stare at the wooden wainscoting along the wall.

"But you wanted to stay here," she prompted softly.

He nodded. "She'd known where I lived, what I did, before we married. She spoke of leaving, and I'd talk her into waiting, promising things would get better. Then she got pregnant, and I thought things *did* get better. But as soon as Cindy was born, she began using her as leverage, threatening to take my daughter and move away. I wasn't very wise, and things were hectic at the center. I tried humoring her, hoping she would come around. I was stupid enough to think she cared for me as much as I cared for her, and that somehow she'd change. She did stay for nearly two years. But then one night, with no warning, she left.''

Polly held him close as he related the rest of the story: his anger at finding the note. His fear when he tried to follow in one of the worst blizzards in years.

''I think the snow finally made her decide to go,'' he said wearily, his voice cracking. ''She knew Selborn Peak would be cut off from the rest of civilization, perhaps for days. I suppose she thought she could make it before the roads became impassable. The snow fell too hard to leave tire tracks visible on the interstate…but I saw the newly broken section of guardrail not far out of town. When I arrived at the scene the night you had your accident, I relived it all—finding the car, looking inside at an unconscious woman. Only my wife had already had her baby. Annette was dead…and so was Cindy.''

''Oh, Reeve!'' Polly cried. ''I'm so sorry.''

''I died a little myself that night, Polly.'' Reeve's voice was muffled against her neck. ''That's why, if you leave…'' His voice trailed off.

She wanted to reassure him. To vow to stay forever. But he knew better. And so did she.

''If I have to go,'' she whispered, ''I'll at least tell you.'' Surely that was a promise she could keep.

Chapter Eleven

Reeve regretted later having said so much. He knew Polly's fear, her vulnerable state, and how in her mind she was already miles away from Selborn Peak. He hadn't originally intended to tell his story, but had felt compelled to when he'd heard about the approaching snowstorm.

On some level, he hoped it would make her want to stay. But that made him furious with himself. If she remained, he wanted it to be because she wanted to, not because she felt sorry for him.

That night, he enjoyed the small domesticity of helping to bathe Laurel, patting on sweet smelling baby powder, dressing her and putting her to bed. It no longer hurt so deeply to remember performing the same little chores for Cindy.

Later, Polly and he watched more television. Now he understood her fixation on national news. He had become that way himself.

"Oh, no!" Polly exclaimed five minutes into the eleven o'clock news. "That's my stepbrother Gene."

They turned up the sound. "We're happy to say that one of the last tips we received seems true," he was saying. The guy, too slick-looking, nevertheless appeared emotional. He even seemed to be crying, as he swiped at his eyes. "We think we know where Catherine and the baby are. We're making one more appeal for the kidnapper to let them go before we close in. That way things will go easier on him. We just want her to come home."

"How can they think they have a viable tip?" Reeve asked, confused. "If they know you're here, they'd know there is no kidnapper."

"They haven't found me!" Polly sounded elated. She explained the code she and her stepbrothers had used. This time Gene had said everything in reverse of what he had meant. "I know they could be using the code to fool me, but there's no reason for this message if they've actually found me. They're asking me once more to just come home." She gave Reeve a big kiss on the cheek, then laughed. "Crackauer didn't recognize me. Everything is going to be okay."

That kiss led to another, which, to Polly's delight, led to a wonderful evening of passion.

WHEN ALICIA CALLED the following morning, Polly readily agreed to have lunch with her. They met at a coffee shop, where Alicia had arranged for them to have a booth in the rear. Polly put Laurel's car seat on the sturdy plastic bench beside her.

After they both had ordered sandwiches, Alicia, dressed in a smart gold blouse and flowing skirt, apologized. "I know Reeve cares for you. I'm sorry I butted in at first. It's just that I've wanted him since we were both about six years old."

Polly glanced down at herself. She had put on a dress today—a dark red one in which she felt at least passable, if not glamorous. Hardly a femme fatale, though somehow Polly had gotten Reeve's attention over the poised and pretty Alicia.

"It was one of the saddest days in my life," Alicia continued, "when he and his family moved away. I was so happy when he returned to start the medical center. I thought it was kismet—until he brought back Annette."

Polly couldn't help asking, "What was she like?"

"Difficult but pretty, and I could tell how much Reeve cared about her. Still, I knew it wouldn't work. She never seemed at home, and she treated Selborn Peak natives as though we were backwater hicks."

Alicia paused as the waitress brought them water.

"I kept scolding myself for my antipathy. I thought it was sour grapes, since I didn't wind up with Reeve. Then she ran out on him."

Polly felt again her horror and sympathy as Reeve had described the scene. She sucked in her lips, then said, "He told me all about that."

Alicia's perfectly made up blue eyes widened. "Really?" She took a deep breath. "You actually must be helping him get over it. He never speaks of the accident to anyone."

"It could be because I went through something similar."

"Don't apologize. I thought his losing Annette was our big second chance—but then he met you. It's all right. I've come to accept that he just doesn't feel that way about me. Probably didn't when we were six, either. And it's been convenient for me to think myself in love with someone unattainable."

The waitress served their sandwiches. Polly took a big bite of her BLT but nearly choked as Alicia began speaking again. "You know I saw those flyers that were sent to the medical center."

Polly nodded, putting her sandwich back on her plate.

"I spoke with Crackauer," Alicia continued. "He promised me an exclusive story if I come up with anything that helps him find Catherine Calvert Elkins. I suspect I could give him a big lead. A very big lead."

Panic made Polly lose her appetite completely. She tried to make her face appear untroubled but was certain she failed.

Alicia patted her arm. "You look as though that sandwich is full of worms." She laughed. "Sorry. I shouldn't torture you. But I did think I recognized you from those first news stories, though I wasn't sure. And I have something to say and wanted to make my point clear. You don't have to worry—probably. First, I suspect I'm the thousandth reporter Crackauer has promised an exclusive to. And then there's Reeve. He said things aren't what they seem. I may be staking my career on this, but I'll leave it alone, at least for now. I'm working on that other big story, anyway, for a Denver TV station. And I still care about Reeve, even if I'll never have him. For his sake, I'll keep quiet. But let me warn you, Polly or whoever you are. Don't hurt him, or you'll answer to me."

IGNORING THE BITTER WIND that slapped her smarting cheeks, Polly trudged through the half inch of gleaming white snow that had fallen while Alicia and she were eating. Hurt Reeve? She would just as soon go over another cliff in her car. Without Laurel, of course.

If she had a car. Despite all the ministrations of the dedicated mechanic, hers had been a total loss. Which didn't matter; in Selborn Peak she was able to walk everywhere she wanted to go.

Hurt Reeve? She certainly didn't want to. She cared

for him. A lot. She might even have fallen in love with him.

And now, for the first time, she dared to believe she might be able to remain here. She had been lucky; Crackauer was gone.

If she were a little luckier, he would tell her family to write off this tiny town because it did not hide the woman and baby they sought. He would say that not even a nosy reporter, tempted by an exclusive, had had information to sell to him.

Oh, please, let him believe that was so! Polly crossed her fingers as well as she could in her thick leather gloves.

As she made her way toward Selborn Community Medical Center, she inhaled the icy, crisp air, which smelled of fresh snow. The sky was gray, threatening more precipitation, but for the moment the weather was clear. She could not see much of the towering Rockies above Selborn Peak, though, as they were blanketed in low-hanging mist.

She shivered a little in her borrowed parka, glad Laurel was with Esther, and hurried down the silent, nearly empty streets. When she reached the center, its warmth once more enveloped her. She felt as though she had come home.

"Polly," called a familiar, deep voice that was even more welcome than a roaring fire.

"Reeve," she breathed as he strode down the hall of the center as confidently as if he owned the place. Which he did. He wore a long-sleeved lab jacket over his dark trousers. She did so like him in white.

She liked him even better in nothing....

She felt her face redden as he reached her and took

her gloved hands in his bare ones. "Brr," he said with a smile.

"Oh, Polly, glad you're here." Clifford's nasal voice interrupted. "I want to show you the checks we just received from a few of your accounts."

"Really? Then more are starting to come through?" Polly grinned first at Reeve's proud smile, then at Clifford.

"Yes. Come on, I'll show you."

"I'll come, too," Reeve said, more to Polly than to the administrator.

As Polly and Reeve followed Clifford to his office, her boots squeaked on the clean hospital floors.

"Not everyone is paying," Clifford said cautiously. The man was still not quick with compliments, but his scowl wasn't as pronounced as usual. "We're far from the collection amount the board really wanted," he continued ungraciously.

"Not enough to buy the rescue helicopter and let my committee off the hook?" Though Reeve sounded disappointed, he smiled at her so she knew he was teasing Clifford.

Still, Polly felt sympathetic. She knew, in this remote area, how much a helicopter would mean to this facility. They could rescue people more easily, sweep them away to Denver.

Save lives. Make Reeve's dream for the place even more of a reality.

But although his committee liked Polly's fund-raising ideas, they were abysmally slow to act upon them.

"At this rate, we'll never get that helicopter," Clifford said with an irritated shake of his head. When they reached his office, he sat down at his perfectly organized desk. He handed Polly a folder filled with opened envelopes. "See if you can get people to pay more each month."

"I'm working with them." She peered inside some of the envelopes. "There are checks in each one," she marveled to Reeve, and he squeezed her shoulder. To Clifford, she said, "I really think I'm getting them each to pay as much as they can."

Clifford made a noise that might have indicated concession. "In any event some of the worst have started to cough up. That's good." He peered up at her over his dark-rimmed glasses, and she knew she had been dismissed. She nearly laughed aloud. Clifford was Clifford. She was almost becoming fond of him.

Or maybe her feeling of well-being was strong enough to encompass even him.

She accompanied Reeve back to his office. "Can you come in?" he asked.

"For a minute."

His waiting room was crammed full, as usual. She followed him into his cluttered office. He shut the door behind them. "Polly," he said huskily, and gathered her tightly into his arms. She lifted her face, and he obliged with a kiss that heated her down to her heavy-socks-clad toes. "How was lunch with Alicia?" He pulled slightly away. "I warned her to be on good behavior."

"She behaved fine," Polly said with a laugh. "So did I. Now we've called a truce, we might even become friends." *As long as I don't hurt you,* she thought, looking into eyes that gazed at her hungrily. A lightning bolt of desire shot through her.

Hurt him? Not if she could help it. Not now and not ever.

"I've got to get to those patients," Reeve said regretfully. "Can I bring dinner to your place tonight?"

"Just bring yourself," Polly said. "I'll cook."

REEVE NUZZLED Polly's neck as they sat together on her sofa late that evening, after they had played with Laurel and put her to bed.

Polly had cooked him an outstanding meal of chicken and dumplings. His Polly: sweet, sexy and smart, and an excellent cook, too. Reeve felt a rumble of contentment start deeper inside him than his well-fed stomach.

Or was that rumble a sign of another hunger yet to be appeased?

"That's my stepfather!" Polly's sudden pull away from him brought him out of his reverie. She grabbed for the remote control device and turned on the sound. Her breathing was ragged, and fear shadowed her lovely features.

Damn the man for having this effect on her. Reeve held her close, feeling her tremble. He glared at the small screen. Reeve had seen her stepfather on newscasts before, but he always stayed in the background. Now the thin, silver-haired man with a weak chin and too-friendly eyes was being interviewed.

"I don't have much to add to what my sons have been saying," he said with a sad shake of his head. "We're losing hope of getting my stepdaughter back unscathed, but we're willing to forgive the kidnapper anything. Give him anything. The police are closing in, but we don't want it to be too late," He looked straight at the camera. "Catherine, if you're able to see this, just know your mother misses you. We'll bring you home if we can, you and your baby. Everything will be as wonderful as before. We promise."

He did not touch his eye, though Polly had said he knew of his children's "code." That indicated he meant what he said—if anyone could believe this man. Polly's friend had disappeared after crossing Jenson. Polly's father had been murdered, and possibly other people had been destroyed as well. Reeve doubted that Jenson's word stood for much.

But Polly relaxed in Reeve's arms. "It's going to be all right," she murmured. "I believe they're finally conceding they can't find me and appealing to me once more to come home."

He held his breath. "And you? If they're willing to make amends, do you intend to go back to them?"

"And run out on you?" She nestled close to him, kissing his Adam's apple, then tucking her head beneath his chin. "Well, Dr. Snyder, if I decide to go back home and leave all this behind, you'll be the first to know."

"Promise?" he asked huskily as he began to run his hand up under her sweater. Her bare skin was warm and smooth, and he wanted to feel more of it. Against more of him. He kissed her harder.

Her whispered reply, "I promise," vibrated against his lips. Her tongue slipped inside as his hands grew even busier.

THE NEXT DAY, Polly could hardly wait to go to the center to see Reeve. Their night had been wonderful, filled with passion and the promise of more to come.

"Someday," Reeve had said as he had put on his jacket to leave, "I won't have to go home. Better yet, you'll be living with me."

Polly had silenced him with a kiss. His words had stopped short of a proposal, thank heavens. Perhaps they were more of a proposition, although Polly did not intend to live with any man without being married to him—it would set a terrible example for Laurel.

In any event, Polly doubted she would marry again. Not even Reeve. She believed she knew him. She was beginning to love him with all her heart. But she still could not trust with her mind.

She busily went about making her phone calls in the morning. People still hung up on her, but she was able to be persistent, despite all the obstacles the job presented. Then there were the accounts who were truly repentant and willing to try to pay, if only just a little every month.

Those were the people Polly understood. They were the ones whom she could help, and who could help her make a success of her new career.

She was finally beginning to do things on her own— and doing a good job of it.

A peep from Laurel brought Polly to her side. "Hi, sweetheart," she said. Laurel gave her a big, toothless smile, and Polly, laughing, picked up her daughter and hugged her.

Esther arrived on time, bringing a fresh loaf of bread and her usual cheerfulness, and Polly greeted her landlady warmly. "Just go about your business," Esther said as she shooed Polly out the door into the brisk wintry air. "Laurel and I will get along fine, like always."

The only thing that marred the perfection of the day was Polly's stop at Reeve's office at lunchtime. As usual, his waiting room brimmed with eager patients.

"He's going to be late," Donna said with a shake of her head. "He had a persistent pharmaceuticals salesman stop by this morning. Anyhow, he told me to tell you to go to the cafeteria without him. He'll meet you there."

"Fine." Polly didn't allow herself to feel too disappointed. She had been with Reeve less than half a day earlier—for several glorious hours. She would continue to bask in the memory until she saw him again. And he would show up before long.

She went obediently to the cafeteria. She wasn't due in her cubicle outside Clifford's office for another forty-five minutes.

Polly took a cup of coffee into a corner that wasn't too crowded; she would wait for Reeve before eating. She proceeded to finish her notes on the delinquent patients she had called that morning.

"Mind if I join you?"

Polly looked up. It was Frannie, wearing a black cardigan over her nurse's uniform.

"Please do!" Polly was happy for the company, though Frannie said she could only stay for a minute.

"Just on my break," she said. She pushed her hand through her short platinum hair and grinned at Polly. "I hear things are hot and heavy between Reeve and you."

Polly felt heat rise up her face. "What gives you that idea?"

"Aunt Esther keeps track of the comings and goings in her neighborhood. And there have been a whole lot of visits by Dr. Snyder lately. *Long* visits." Frannie held up her pudgy hand. "Now, don't get all embarrassed on me. You know that was exactly what Esther and I wanted. For both of you. So, are you making plans for the future yet?"

Polly shook her head, wanting to feel irritation at Frannie, but amused instead. "We take one day at a time."

"I'm going to have to light a fire under Reeve," Frannie grumbled as she stood.

"Please don't," Polly protested. "Things are fine."

"Really?" Frannie's dark eyebrows lifted, and then

she winked. "Well, maybe I'd better just let nature take its course." She picked up her coffee cup. "Got to run."

Polly smiled to herself, watching Frannie hustle away. Light a fire under Reeve? They already ignited together like a forest fire.

The cafeteria was becoming more crowded. If Reeve didn't arrive soon, Polly would feel uncomfortable holding a table. Still, she had work to do. She returned to her papers, which she spread back out on the table.

A sharp and sardonic masculine voice interrupted her thoughts a short while later. "Hello, Catherine."

Catherine? She looked up with a start—and gasped.

"Victor!" she exclaimed, rising to face her stepbrother.

Chapter Twelve

"H-how did you find me?" Polly stammered, looking up into Victor's dark eyes. His thin-lipped smile was snide. She recalled that look only too well. He'd gotten it each time he'd pulled a nasty trick on her when they were kids.

She hadn't seen it for years. Clearly, he had saved it just for her, as he had their code. She hoped he did not see her shudder.

"Your friend Dr. Snyder told me where you were." Victor wore a brown leather jacket, obviously expensive, unbuttoned over his designer shirt and trousers. And there Polly sat in her borrowed green sweats.

"Reeve? Yes, he'll be joining me for a late lunch any minute." Polly looked around, desperately willing Reeve to walk in. Instead, she saw Alicia, who glanced toward her.

Please, come here, Polly begged silently. Instead, Alicia headed toward the food service area.

"What I meant," Victor continued in a low voice so no one else could hear, "was not that he told me you were here in the cafeteria, though actually he did. But he also let me know you were in this charming little town—Selborn Peak, Colorado.'' The name rolled off his tongue as though he touted Paris or Rome.

Polly's blood froze as much as if she had walked outside in the snow without a jacket. "What do you mean?" she whispered.

"He said he wanted a rescue helicopter for his dear, remote little medical center. Dad had promised a reward to whoever provided information that helped us find you. A helicopter wasn't out of line."

The helicopter? Reeve wanted it, sure, but had he revealed her location in order to get one? Reeve wouldn't...would he?

But how did Victor know the center needed a helicopter? And that Reeve was involved?

She felt Reeve's name rush to her lips, but she swallowed it. He would have an explanation. But where was he?

Victor looked around the crowded cafeteria, his straight, Jenson-family nose wrinkled in obvious distaste. "Let's take a walk. You don't want anyone to overhear us, do you?"

"No." But she did not intend to leave this large room full of people. She did not want to be alone with Victor. She rose slowly, gathering papers and her coffee cup. She dropped some files to buy time and bent to pick them up. Victor grabbed them.

He glanced at them, then thrust them at her. "Your exciting work as a bill collector, I believe." His bark of a laugh was ugly. "Catherine Calvert Elkins, stepdaughter of North Calvert's most powerful man, married to an up-and-coming attorney...reduced to begging for money. How droll."

"It's not begging," she said firmly, despising the quaver in her voice.

He looked her up and down. "I don't like your hair short and curly. And you dyed it black—not your color, Catherine. Maybe deep chestnut, but not black. And you're too thin after having the baby." He paused, then grinned at her again. "And how is little Laurel?"

He knew about the baby! Of course he did; Polly—Catherine—had been pregnant. But how could he know Laurel's name?

He knew about her job, too. What else did he know?

"My baby is fine." Polly kept her voice level.

"I can't wait to see her. Why don't we go get her now?"

"That won't be possible, Victor," Polly said airily. "I'm sorry you don't think much of my job, but nevertheless I have work to do. Nice to have seen you, but you might as well go home." She turned her back and walked as nonchalantly as she could toward where she had seen Alicia, skirting the tables filled with seated hospital workers and patients' families. She had an idea. She didn't know if it would work, but—

Victor caught up and grabbed her shoulder. She nearly gagged on the cloying scent of his men's cologne. "Oh, it'll be more than possible for me to see little Laurel," he growled into her ear. "I'm to bring her home, you see. Her dad wants her."

Polly turned toward him, her eyes wide with shock. "C-Carl?" She could barely say his name. "But he's—"

"Alive, Catherine," Victor interrupted. "No thanks to you. I'm here to bring his daughter home. Preferably his wife, too. I'm leaving tonight. Are you coming?"

Polly sagged against the closest empty table. She felt dizzy, claustrophobic, as though everything were closing in on her. "No. Yes. I have to think about it."

Carl was alive. She was still married. Victor had found her. He planned to take Laurel, whether she went home or not.

And Reeve. Oh, no—Reeve! What would he think of her now?

But had he told Victor where to find her?

"Hide and seek is over, Catherine. You've lost. Time to go home."

"I haven't betrayed the family," she said desperately, "and I promise—"

"Go ahead and tell. Who'll believe a woman crazy enough to shoot her husband and run away while eight months' pregnant? And now she's in the throes of post-partum depression, doesn't know what she's saying." He pulled a set of keys from his pocket and tossed them into the air nonchalantly, catching them again. "Your hormones are off-kilter, poor kid. You may never recover. Looks like funny farm time to me. Just like your mother."

"Mama? What did Lou do to her?" Polly's dismay was rampant. Had Lou, after all the veiled threats he had made over the years, hospitalized her mother?

"What do you care? That woman suffered because of you, Catherine. And you never even called."

They stood in a brightly lighted hospital cafeteria as people with trays passed by chattering. A couple of orderlies in green uniforms sat down at a table nearby. Polly heard them talking about their dates for the weekend. The place smelled of the usual tasty fare. It all seemed so normal.

And Polly's life was crumbling around her.

"Is everything all right, Polly?" Alicia stood directly in front of her, a tray in her hand, a frown on her striking face. Her usual tote bag was over her shoulder.

"N-no. I'm feeling ill. Would you come to the rest room with me?"

"Of course." Alicia set her tray on an empty table.

"Now, wait a minute," Victor demanded, but Polly ignored him. In a daze, she headed for the rest room, grateful that Alicia took her arm and walked beside her.

As the large white door shut behind them, Polly sagged against a sink.

"What's wrong?" Alicia demanded. "Is that your ex-husband? Did he hurt you?"

"No," Polly said. "But I need your help. And in exchange I'll give you an exclusive story."

"What kind of story?" Alicia sounded suspicious.

"Pulitzer material," Polly said, needing to tantalize the reporter, for the favor she was about to ask was a big one. "It involves an old New England family, political corruption...murder."

"Murder? Really? Do you have proof?"

Maybe, though she doubted the flimsy piece of evidence she had would be enough. But she did not reveal her doubts to Alicia. "Of course." Polly hesitated. "The other side of the story is that I'm crazy," she said, "That's what Victor will tell you. Maybe he's right."

She had to be crazy to believe that Reeve might have betrayed her...didn't she?

Oh, Reeve...

Alicia stared at her, appearing to consider the possibility of her madness. "Was that man with you Victor?"

Polly nodded. "He's my stepbrother."

"Just what is it you want me to do?" Alicia asked.

Polly told her.

"What about Reeve?" Alicia asked when she was done.

"What about Reeve?" Polly repeated lightly, praying

that the heartache she felt did not come through in her voice. "I'm not leaving without saying goodbye. You'll tell him for me." She did not have time to wait and tell him now.

Especially because he might try to stop her. To turn her over to Victor…?

"Now, are we ready?" Polly did not want to give Alicia time to change her mind about helping.

"Sure."

"SO YOU'RE VICTOR JENSON?" Alicia said a minute later, right outside the rest room door. She had a pad of paper and pen in her hand, her tape recorder on the table. "I've seen you on the national news. I'm a reporter. May I interview you for the local paper? I understand you're looking for a kidnap victim. Now, what's her name and—"

Polly heard Victor growl something as she hurried past. She saw him try to follow, but Alicia blocked his path. He grabbed the reporter by the arm, just as a couple of interns walked by. "Hey," one of them said.

That was all Polly saw. She had to hurry. She just prayed that Alicia would keep Victor occupied long enough.

Knowing how tenacious Alicia was, she believed it was possible.

ALICIA'S SPORTS UTILITY vehicle skidded as Polly pulled it into Esther's driveway. Not good, she thought. She needed to go as quickly as possible, but she had to remain safe.

She jumped out of the vehicle and hurried up the stairs to her apartment. Not bothering to knock on the door, she opened it with a key. Her hands were shaking, but somehow she got the door open. "Esther, it's me," she called.

Silence. "Esther?" Polly's heart rate sped up. Where was Esther?

Even more important, where was Laurel? Polly hadn't considered the possibility that Victor would have taken her…but he seemed to know everything about them. Might he have come here before going to the hospital?

Grabbing the rail to keep from falling down the steps, Polly rushed to Esther's house. She knocked frantically on the door.

Nothing.

"Laurel!" she sobbed. What was she going to do—

And then the draperies at the front window moved. "Esther?" Polly cried.

The door was pulled open. "Good thing it's you," boomed Esther's voice. "I brought Laurel down here earlier. There was a strange man walking around my property. He seemed interested in the garage. I called the police, but he was gone before they got here. My locks are better than yours, so I—"

"Thank heavens you did!" Polly gave the large woman a big hug. "Is Laurel all right?"

"Sure. I have her in the bedroom, and—"

"Esther, I have to leave. I don't have time to explain, but it has to do with the man you saw."

The older woman didn't argue. "Just tell me what I can do," she said.

Polly ran back up to her apartment. She grabbed a suitcase from the closet. It was already full of baby things and a few of her own. She had packed it so she would be ready, just in case…. It included the single most important thing she would need to keep Laurel and her safe—maybe. Though she had kept it with her all this time, it might do her no good at all.

She threw some more necessities into the bag. Five minutes later, she was back in Esther's house. As Polly requested, Esther handed her a wad of cash, and Polly wrote her a check for the balance of the money she had earned at Selborn Community.

"You told Dr. Reeve you're leaving?" Esther asked.

"Alicia's going to tell him for me." And if Alicia played her cards right, she would wind up with Reeve.

Polly wished she could meet with him once more. See the expression on his face when she asked if he had betrayed her. Would it be anger because she knew? Or shock at her unwarranted allegation?

The latter, she prayed. For no matter what, she did not want to believe he had turned her over to her stepfather, in exchange for money.

But that was what Victor had told her. And who else would have had all the information her stepbrother now knew?

"I'll call to apologize when I get settled somewhere," she told Esther. "If I tell him now, he might try to stop me."

Esther had bundled Laurel into her snowsuit. Polly strapped her into the borrowed car seat fastened onto the vehicle's rear seat. She would leave it in Denver, with Alicia's sports utility vehicle. She would call to let Alicia know where.

She would also call Reeve to say goodbye. She owed him that, at least. And once she was on her way, he would not be able to stop her.

No matter how foolishly, she would want to return to him....

A storm was approaching. The sky was churning into

a deep and menacing gray, and a light snow had begun to fall. Damn! Polly wished she would not have to navigate in the dark among the mountains when the weather threatened to get worse. But she had no choice. And darkness might provide additional cover.

In minutes, she was on her way. She only hoped that the ruse had worked. Alicia had promised to keep Victor there as long as possible. She had used her cell phone to call a friend from the local TV station, who would bring a camera crew. Maybe they'd put together a news conference to keep Victor occupied.

Alicia had told her a back way out of Selborn Peak, a route that was a favorite of locals, since few tourists used it. Even if Victor figured out that she was driving away from town, he would assume she'd taken the interstate.

Maybe, just maybe, she would make good her escape.

SO FAR SO GOOD, Polly thought twenty minutes later. She drove slowly through the blinding snow and glanced frequently into the rearview mirror. There were few cars on this out-of-the-way road. No one appeared to be following her.

Could it actually have worked? Could she really have slipped out of town, and away from Victor, so easily?

No, not easily. The narrow road was icy and treacherous as it wound through the Rockies. She couldn't drive faster even if she weren't watching for pursuers.

She glanced in the rearview mirror at Laurel. The baby was awake, punching the air and making little sounds that were happy melodies to a mother's ears. Polly smiled. "We're going to be fine," she told her daughter. "You'll see."

Easy enough to convince the baby, she thought. Not so easy to convince herself.

She squinted through the windshield as large flakes fluttered about, illuminated like a million falling feathers in her headlights.

This drive reminded her of the night she had arrived in Selborn Peak, nearly three months earlier. She had learned then how much she hated driving in thunderstorms. Now she was learning to hate snow squalls even more. This was the first time she had left town since then. And that night—that horrible, rainy night—she had had an accident....

But she had been exhausted. Now, she could not recall ever feeling more wide awake.

Reeve had come to her rescue then. Oh, how she wished he could save her now.

He couldn't have betrayed her. Not Reeve!

She looked into her rearview mirror as bright headlights approached quickly. How could anyone feel confident enough on the slippery road to drive that fast? she wondered. She slowed even more and pulled as much to the right as she could, ready to let the car pass.

As she expected, it began to pull around her, but its speed reduced as it reached her side. She glanced toward it—and into Victor's grinning face.

"No!" Polly screamed as he turned his wheel toward her. She pushed on her accelerator, trying to get away, even as his bumper made contact with her car. She turned her own wheel. The vehicle began to spin. She slammed on her brakes and heard the squeal of her tires. Weren't these supposed to be antilock brakes?

The car didn't slow. There was a guardrail beside her—no, in front of her. Too close, too—

"I'm sorry," she screamed. "Laurel! Reeve."

And then the car headed off the road toward the jagged mountain rocks.

Chapter Thirteen

Polly was running away, damn her! She had broken her promise and hadn't even let him know she was leaving.

Why, then, Reeve asked himself, was he going after her? Especially on a night like this, when snow had begun to fall in thick, white sheets. When water had frozen beneath the snow, forming ice on the curving mountain roads.

Because she was in danger. Because this was a night that reminded him of another perilous night long ago. Because Polly had a crazy family who killed people—and might even kill her.

And because he loved—

No. He would not let his mind veer in that direction. Even if he had been foolish enough to consider it before, he wouldn't now. Never again.

His heart thudded hard against his rib cage as he tried to make his way along the treacherous two-lane highway. He leaned forward in the seat of his Volvo, straining to watch the road through headlights that shone into the snow and reflected brutally back again. The air conditioner was on, the better to keep his windows from fogging. He shivered despite his heavy clothes, the thick gloves that gripped the steering wheel.

The rhythmic beat of the windshield wiper snapped back and forth over the steady rush of air inside. Otherwise, he was surrounded by the silence of the empty road.

"Thanks, Alicia," Reeve muttered aloud. When he had finally reached the cafeteria to join Polly, Alicia had come over to him; Polly had delegated her to tell Reeve she'd had to depart in a hurry. One of her stepbrothers had appeared in town, and Alicia had lent Polly her sports utility vehicle to make an escape.

What Polly didn't know was that Alicia had told Victor how to find her. From what Reeve gathered, Alicia had staged a mock interview of Victor. He had given her an earful, all right—he had told Alicia a plausible story of Polly's congenital madness, describing in gory detail Catherine Calvert Elkins's pattern of pathological lies and mutilated pets, insane acts that had culminated in the attempted murder of her husband.

Attempted murder. That implied Polly's husband was still alive.

There would be time enough to deal with that bit of pernicious information when Reeve was sure Polly was all right.

Victor had promised Alicia an exclusive if she would tell the distraught man how to find his poor, psychotic sister and the baby she might harm, not to mention herself.

"She'd told me her brother would say she was crazy, Reeve," Alicia had related. "She didn't say how convincing he would be. He promised me details for a story, too. That wasn't important, but the baby was."

Of course a story would be important to Alicia. But Reeve didn't believe she would knowingly put a woman and infant in danger to get it. Still, Alicia had told Victor the direction Polly had taken, the description and license number of the car she had lent to her. Only after Alicia had finished had she had second thoughts and told Reeve.

"I'd thought it would be better for you to have her out of your life," she'd cried. "Maybe that was even why I told her brother how to find her. But I didn't mean to hurt you or her. Or the baby. Oh, Reeve, what should I do now?"

"I'll handle it," he'd said calmly. Why bother expressing his anger toward her? He was even angrier with himself for having let his heart get involved.

"I'll just make sure you're all right, Polly Black—or Catherine Elkins, whatever you're calling yourself today." He spoke aloud in the car to calm his nerves. "Laurel, too. Especially the baby. Then I'll go have a good, stiff drink and forget you ever came to Selborn Peak."

It would be as easy as that.

Right.

He strained to see the sparse road signs along the highway in the driving snow. How far could Polly have gotten?

Maybe Victor Jenson had not followed.

Maybe Polly had left early enough that she would make it to the next town with no trouble.

Sure, and maybe his Volvo would sprout a rotor and turn into a rescue helicopter.

Tension made his shoulders ache, his eyes smart. He blinked frequently—which was why he almost missed seeing the shape on the shoulder of the road. It was covered in white, resting against a guardrail: a car, large and boxy. A sports utility vehicle.

"Polly!" Reeve pulled his car off the road. Should he call for help now?

No, first he would need to see if it was Polly. Maybe the car was abandoned. Maybe she had gone with her stepbrother.

He wrenched open his car door, and the freezing wind hit him in the face, smashing snow against his exposed skin. He bent his head against the force and proceeded as quickly as he could toward the vehicle. As he reached it, he realized the front end had been crushed. He pulled open the door.

"Polly!"

She lay across the seat, unconscious.

Quickly, he checked her over. Her skin was cold. There was a large lump at the side of her head. She had hit it on something—the steering wheel? He didn't want to move her without the equipment of an EMT, in case there were more injuries than apparent.

But where was Laurel? There wasn't even a car seat in the vehicle. Maybe Polly hadn't been leaving, after all. She wouldn't go without taking her baby.

Unless... "Victor Jenson, you son of a—" Reeve spat.

He would see to the baby later. Right now, he had to make certain Polly was all right.

He reached into his pocket for his cell phone.

POLLY'S EYELIDS WERE heavy. She struggled to open them. They fluttered first. With concentrated effort, she managed to raise them just a little.

She saw only a blur of white. "Welcome back, Polly," said a deep, soothing voice. A familiar male voice—the voice she loved.

Except...why did she feel so hollow inside?

"Reeve," she whispered. She opened her eyes more fully.

There he was, dressed in the white lab jacket in which he looked so wonderful. It set off the breadth of his shoulders, the ginger shade of his hair.

She smiled at him lovingly…and he scowled in return.

Her heart plummeted. Had she imagined what there was between them? "Reeve?" Her voice was weak, and she lay in a hospital bed, as she had the first time she remembered seeing him. "How did I get here?"

It came back to her then: her flight, the icy road… Victor. He had found her, thanks to Reeve. Reeve had sold her out. For a helicopter.

Then Victor had forced her off the road, and— "Laurel! Reeve, is she all right?" Despite herself, she reached out her hand toward him.

"I'm sure she's fine, Polly." His voice was a monotone, and he did not touch her.

"Wh-where is she? Can I see her?"

Frannie Meltzer rushed forward. She had been standing behind Reeve. "She wasn't there when Reeve found you," the nurse blurted, the features on her round face distorted as though she was about to cry. "He thinks your brother took her."

"Victor?" Polly's whisper came out as a frantic croak.

"Say the word and I'll go after them." Ricky Edwards, in his green orderly uniform, was in the room, too. The thin young man's sad eyes looked angry. "I've got a car now, since I wrecked my cycle. I'll catch the bastard."

"No, Ricky. But thanks. I'll take care of it." Polly sat up and tried to swing her legs over the side of the bed, but the room whirled around her. "Oh," she said, holding her head.

"Stay still," Reeve said firmly. "I've called the police."

"Oh, Reeve." Polly began to weep. She wanted him to take her into his arms. To lend her strength so she could garner some of her own.

But not now. Not this man. It might be because of him that Victor had Laurel.

"Everything will be fine," Reeve said. His voice was distant. So was he. He did not approach any closer to the bed.

He was mad at her. It was defensiveness, of course. Why should *he* be upset? He had been the one to betray *her.*

She knew one reason he could be angry. She had been running away. She hadn't warned him first, as she had said she would. He surely should have realized it was an emergency, that she had fled for her life—and Laurel's. Perhaps her flight had reminded him of his wife. But under these circumstances, she could not cater to his feelings.

"I'm sorry," she said coolly. "I had to leave. I had to try to get away without Victor following, and I didn't have time to say goodbye. Of course, I didn't know then that you knew Victor so well."

"We'll leave you lovebirds alone." Frannie waved her hand as though erasing herself from the picture. "Come on, Ricky."

In moments, only Reeve was left in the room with her. "What do you mean, that I know Victor?"

"He said he'd told you that my stepfather would pay for your rescue helicopter if you'd tell him how to find me."

"You believed him." Reeve's voice was icy.

"What else could I think? He did know where I was."

"There were other possibilities. Was your stepbrother using his code as he lied to you?"

"He was lying?" For a moment, Polly doubted herself. But how else could Victor have known?

"And you were leaving without telling me."

"I asked Alicia to let you know," Polly said, now on the defensive. "And I'd have called you from Denver when I got there."

"It's all right." Reeve's tone was heavy with resignation. "I understand from Alicia that your husband is still alive. You certainly didn't owe me anything—except maybe an explanation."

"I would have. I didn't know until..." A thought struck her. She would need every bit of ammunition she could amass now to get her baby back, however flimsy it might be. "Is my suitcase here, Reeve? Was it in the car with me?"

He shook his head. "There wasn't anything but your purse in the vehicle when I found you."

"Oh, no," she whispered hoarsely. Her father's letter was in Victor's hands. It had only been a photocopy, but she had kept it with her, hopeful it would do her some good someday.

She had considered making more copies, but since she was on the run, she'd had no place to keep them. In any event, her only copy was gone now, along with Laurel.

Reeve interrupted her thoughts. "I'll leave you to rest. I'm sure the police will be by soon to talk to you." He turned and left the room.

Her world had shattered about her. Her family knew where she was. Carl was alive. Victor might even have assumed she would die out there in the car, in the snow-storm. He had Laurel.

And Reeve had betrayed her. Hadn't he?

In any event, he now hated her.

Burying her head in the starkly white pillow that smelled of bleach, Polly wept.

A RINGING SOUND WOKE Polly from a troubled sleep. She blinked. She was in a hospital room…. The Medical Center… Victor! Laurel!

She sat up with a cry that turned into a groan. Her head ached.

Where was Reeve? He had been here and…they had fought. He was gone. She had lost him.

The ringing continued. It was the phone on the white stand beside the bed. She reached for it, ignoring the pain her movement caused.

"Hello, Catherine," said the falsely cheerful voice at the other end. Polly heard a baby's angry cries in the background.

"What's wrong with Laurel, Victor?" Polly demanded.

"Who knows? Mother can't figure it out, either. Your sweet little baby is driving Mother crazy, Catherine. You don't want that, do you?"

"Mother? Where is she? Where are you?" Polly's head pounded as she glanced at a clock on the wall. It had only been a few hours since Victor had stolen Laurel. He could not have gotten the baby all the way back to Connecticut. That meant he had brought her mother out here. She wasn't hospitalized, after all. Yet another lie.

"We're in a safe place," he said. "Wouldn't you like to join us?"

"Kidnapping is against the law, Victor. I already told the police that you took my baby." Fortunately, they had not stayed long, for she had desperately needed to rest. "Tell me where you are, and I'll come get Laurel. I won't press charges if you just give her back safe and sound." And just maybe she could rescue her mother, too.

Her separation from Laurel had already cost Polly much more than she wanted Victor to know. Her arms felt empty. Her breasts, however, had been full, so full…. She'd had to request a shot. There would be no more nursing of her baby.

Fortunately, Laurel was used to a bottle, so she would not starve. Polly only prayed that her family treated the baby right.

"Of course you won't press charges." Victor's tone had turned ugly. "I have the baby's father's permission. We're going to get custody of Laurel since her mother is clearly incompetent, shooting her husband, then running away."

"Is Carl with you, too? Let me speak to him." What could she say? Apologize for having tried to kill him?

He had tried to kill her first…but it would just be his word against hers. And he had the upper hand. Her family would back him. And he had Laurel.

Polly was still married. Any hope, no matter how slim it had been, for a life with Reeve here in Selborn Peak was now shattered. But it had been anyway, with Reeve's possible betrayal and her attempt to flee.

Now she would have to go home to Carl. She would divorce him, certainly—but she had no doubt the fight to keep Laurel would be horrendous.

She would not wish that on Reeve. She would not even want him in the picture; her relationship with him, as tenuous as it had been, might work against her being able to keep her daughter. But, oh, how she would miss him!

"Carl can't come to the phone now," Victor said. "Neither can Mother. Just say the magic words, little sis, and I'll let you know where to find us. But you have to use the right words."

Polly's heart sank. "What words?" She suspected she knew.

"How about, 'I'm sorry, Victor. I'm ready to come home and be a good girl.' But don't say them unless you mean them."

"If I do, what then?"

"Then we'll go home, one happy family, all together again."

"And if I don't?" Polly bit her lower lip, waiting for the answer.

"Well, first there's poor Laurel, with her unfit mother. We'll have no trouble getting custody. Then there's Mother. All the excitement of having her son-in-law shot, her crazy daughter running away to give birth— it's just been too much for her. She's finally gone over the edge."

"Victor! Mother has always been good to Gene and you. You and Lou have made threats like this forever, but—"

"But now we mean them. Oh, and then there's that letter your poor father allegedly wrote before he died, accusing *my* father of murder. More likely, your fickle friend Warren forged John Calvert's signature."

Polly knew better. The letter was from her father. It was genuine. But if Victor had discovered her only copy, her leverage was gone.

Her fears were realized with his next words. "I found

a copy in your suitcase under some diapers, of all things. Of course, I destroyed it. So, what do you say, Catherrine? Make it quick, sis, my ear's tired of having this phone connected to it.''

Polly took a deep breath. She smiled grimly and touched the corner of her eye. ''I'm sorry, Victor,'' she said. ''I'm ready to come home and be a good girl.''

REEVE FELT DRAWN to Polly's hospital room like a magnet.

He should stay away from her, he knew. Far away.

She was still married. She had tried to flee. And she believed he had given away her location in order to get the coveted rescue helicopter for the medical center.

Damn it! How could she believe something so callous about him?

Still, her baby had been taken by her family. She no doubt felt distraught. All alone. She would need a friend.

Standing in the hallway outside her room, he laughed—a bitter, self-mocking bark. A friend. That was all he could ever be to her now. And imagine him, Reeve Snyder, wanting to be friends with a runaway wife.

He knocked on the door. ''Come in,'' came a muffled voice.

''What do you think you're doing?'' he demanded. Polly stood, hanging on to the bed. She looked haggard in her abbreviated hospital gown, ready to keel over if he simply blew in her direction. Her dark curls were disheveled, as though she had just awakened from a sound sleep. But in her hands she clasped the clothes she had worn when she had been brought in.

''I'm going to find Laurel.'' Her voice was weak, but her tone allowed for no contradiction. She slipped her jeans on over her shapely legs, and he could see the effort it took.

"The authorities are working on finding her. You need rest." He used his best firm but distant doctor's voice—despite the fact that what he wanted was to hold her in his arms.

"The authorities don't know where Victor has taken her. I do. Or at least I have a way to find her." Turning her back, she removed the gown. He clenched a fist as he glimpsed the soft skin of her back before she raised her arms and pulled her sweater over her head. He wanted to touch that sweet, enticing flesh—but he never would again.

Her words echoed in his mind. "You know where Laurel is? How? Where?"

"I heard from Victor. We made a deal." Pulling down her black sweater, she turned to face him. Her gray eyes looked as bleak and despairing as he felt, but her small chin was raised resolutely.

"What deal?"

"I go home with him, and I get to keep my daughter. Plus, my mother stays out of the rest home." Turning toward the closet that held her coat, she took a few steps, then stumbled. He rushed to catch her. She felt small and vulnerable in his arms. He held her tightly, but she struggled. "Please, Reeve," she begged. "Don't make this harder than it already is."

"You're in no condition to do it alone. I'm coming, too."

"No," she insisted.

"Polly, no matter what you believe, I did not tell Victor where to find you. I know who did...but it wasn't me."

Her expression grew confused. "You know… Was it Alicia?"

"Never mind."

But Polly's eyes told him that she was mulling over this new information. "It was Alicia, wasn't it? But why…well, it doesn't matter. Reeve, you can't come. Victor was very specific. Crackauer is picking me up, and I'm to go with him alone. Besides…" She hesitated. "They'll only ruin your life, too, if you try to help me." Her full lower lip trembled as she looked up at him. He wanted to touch it. To kiss it.

Ruin his life? Those miserable sons of guns who were her family had already ruined the chance at happiness he had thought he'd found with her. Her stepbrothers…her husband. What more could they do to him?

"I'm coming," he insisted. "I'll follow in a separate car, and I'll try to be discreet. But if you don't agree, I'll call the police. They'll tail you anyway."

"But what would that do to Laurel…my mother? Please, Reeve."

She must have seen in his eyes that he was intractable, for she dropped her head in acquiescence. "Just promise," she murmured, "that you won't interfere. I'm doing what I must. And I have to do it myself. I *will* do it myself."

"I know you can do it," Reeve said, admiring her courage despite himself. "But you've got to accept help."

"I would if I could," Polly replied. "But I'm afraid no one can help us now."

Chapter Fourteen

Polly made her way out the door to the medical center's nearly empty parking lot. Darkness had already begun to fall, and the sodium lights cast a glow made all the more eerie by the swirl of the newly falling snow.

Every inch of Polly still ached. The pain, and the unsureness of her step in the miserable weather, slowed her considerably, but she could not let either stop her.

An ambulance was parked nearby on the driveway. The cold seemed even more intense than it had been when she'd attempted her mad flight the day before. She breathed shallowly, for she felt as though anything deeper would freeze her lungs.

Above, the craggy white peaks, nearly invisible in the vanishing daylight, shimmered as low-hanging clouds dropped another layer of snow upon them. The hazy mountains seemed stalwart, immutable. She stared at them for a moment, willing them to impart to her the quiet strength that she needed.

A white sedan pulled up to the curb just as Polly reached it. The car's headlights reflected the glistening snowflakes that swirled everywhere. She peered inside. Crackauer stared back. He used a control button to roll down the window. His voice from inside the car was muffled. "Get in, Mrs. Elkins. Or should I call you Ms. Black?"

Polly shrugged beneath the oversize black lamb's wool coat that Alicia Frost had lent to her, insisting it was perfect for Polly to flee in. Alicia had come to visit, and to apologize, just before Polly left. "I don't care what you call me, Mr. Crackauer. Just tell me where my family is holding Laurel."

That was part of the plan she had devised with Reeve. If possible, she was to get a location from Crackauer, then repeat it aloud. Reeve waited to hear it, inside the parked ambulance. He would follow, anyway, in his Volvo, but it would help for him to know where they were going, just in case he lost Crackauer's car—entirely possible as the weather grew worse.

"You'll see where they are when we're there. Now, get in."

How had Polly ever considered Crackauer ordinary looking? Today he appeared to be the personification of malevolence. His features hadn't changed; he still had a nose that was too large. His mouth was perhaps a bit narrow, his face fleshy, with a hint of jowls. The expression in his light eyes appeared neutral, nonthreatening. But something indefinable about him made her shudder to the depths of her soul.

Maybe it was that he was too cool, given the circumstances. He held her future in his leather-gloved hands, and that did not seem to bother him in the least.

That, more than anything, made her determined to follow Reeve's instructions.

"No, Mr. Crackauer, I won't get in until you tell me exactly where we're going. I need to know where Laurel is, and that she's safe, before I join you."

"She's fine. She's with your family, as if you didn't

know, and they're taking good care of her." He no longer sounded quite so composed. Somehow that made Polly feel better.

"Are they near here?" she pressed. "Otherwise, how will we get to them in this weather?"

"I got a call from them on my car phone. I'm to pick you up tonight and we'll stay somewhere on the way."

Polly's heart fell. She would not see Laurel for hours. As long as her baby was safe, though, she could deal with it.

But she couldn't deal with being with Crackauer that long.

She stole a glance toward the back of the ambulance. The double rear doors were slightly ajar, the better for Reeve to listen. The knowledge that he was right there, if she needed him, bolstered her courage.

"I'm hardly going to spend the night anywhere with you, Mr. Crackauer. Just pick me up here tomorrow morning. And I'm not going anywhere with you unless I know where Laurel is."

She pivoted as though she were returning to the center. When her back was to him, she closed her eyes, as a pain that had nothing to do with her physical condition surged through her. What if he called her bluff, drove away and didn't come back? What if, due to this foolishness, she never saw Laurel again?

As though Reeve had called to her, she glanced toward where he waited. Through the snow, in the crack between the double rear doors, she saw a thumb pointed upward.

That made her smile despite herself.

"Wait!" Crackauer's voice was a shout. A car door slammed nearly simultaneously. By the time Polly turned, Crackauer was beside her. He hadn't bothered to put a jacket over his black sweatshirt and baggy khaki pants. She hadn't realized from the suit he had worn before just how barrel-chested and burly he was. He shivered slightly in the cold as he towered over her, clearly attempting to intimidate her.

What was worse, he was succeeding. Recollections of the years she had spent heeding orders given to her by others flowed through her. She could not give in to him. Not now.

"You tell me right now where my daughter is," she demanded. "Or you can tell my family you failed. I am not, repeat not, going with you otherwise."

The man scowled at her for a moment, fury radiating from him. "It doesn't matter where she is," he finally barked. "You'll be in hell before you see her again." He grabbed her arm and began to drag her toward the car.

He was too large, too strong to resist. "No!" she cried, trying to tear at the fingers wrapped about her like choking tentacles. But in moments, he had the car door open and was attempting to thrust her in.

"No!" echoed another voice.

"Hey!" yelled Crackauer. She looked up to see Reeve's arm go around the investigator's thick neck, but Crackauer did not let her go. He jabbed his elbow into Reeve's ribs. Fortunately, Reeve's leather jacket was thick, and the blow seemed not to affect him. Polly used the opportunity to dig the heel of her boot into Crackauer's instep. Thankfully, he was wearing athletic shoes instead of something more substantial. He shouted and let Polly go.

Reeve still had him about the neck. He pulled his arm tighter, as though cutting off Crackauer's air. "Now, answer the lady," he growled. "Where is her daughter?"

Polly had never dreamed that Reeve, the compassionate and caring doctor, could behave this way. But he'd said that he was wild once, had learned to control it in the army.

She had no doubt that he knew what he was doing— and that he was brave and strong enough to succeed.

"Let...me...go. Can't...talk."

"Oh, you'll talk right now, or you'll never talk again. I'm a doctor, remember? I know just how to ruin a larynx this way—that's voice box to you, Crackauer."

"Don't know," Crackauer gasped. "Have the phone number—to call tomorrow when I've succeeded."

Fortunately, the parking lot remained empty. Because of the weather? Polly didn't know. Nor did she know what they would do if someone came. "Please, Reeve," Polly whispered urgently. "We have to hurry."

"You heard Ms. Black," Reeve hissed. "Tell me where that phone number is, and make it quick!"

But Crackauer didn't respond. Instead, he writhed and attempted to grab Reeve.

"Damn!" Reeve said. As the investigator gagged and fought, Reeve managed to wrestle him to the ground, his arm still around the older man's neck. Once Crackauer was down, Reeve straddled his chest, fighting until he was able to kneel on the investigator's arms to control him. Reeve put both hands around Crackauer's throat, which he seemed to both squeeze and massage at the same time. In seconds, the investigator was unconscious.

"Did you kill him?" Polly asked, frightened more for Reeve and the possible consequences than for the horrible man on the ground.

"No—just a little trick with his carotid artery and jugular vein. I always wanted to try that." Reeve's grin was almost mischievous, but then he turned serious.

"We still need to know where to go. Let's look in the car for that phone number."

Polly slid inside. The interior was nearly immaculate, and when she opened the glove compartment and saw the papers there, she realized it was a rental.

"I don't see anything," she called to Reeve, desperation in her voice.

"Let me try...." Reeve knelt over Crackauer. Polly watched him check the investigator's neck for a pulse. Apparently satisfied, he dug into the pockets of Crackauer's jeans. After searching the man's wallet, he cried in triumph, "Here! This has to be it."

As he stood, Ricky Edwards ran from the center. "I saw you out here, Dr. Snyder. Is everything all right?"

"Now it is," Reeve said. "This man was bothering Polly."

Ricky appeared as though he wanted to kick the fallen man, whose body was beginning to collect a thin layer of snow.

"Grab a gurney and get him inside to emergency," Reeve said, stepping in front of the young man. "I'll take care of him."

"ARE YOU SURE you won't be in trouble with the police?"

Reeve enjoyed the worried tone in Polly's voice—even though her concern was valid. He took his eyes from the treacherous, snow-covered road just long enough to glance at her. Her lovely face gleamed palely in the shadowed interior of the Volvo.

"Everything should be all right. After all, I've given instructions that they're to be notified of Crackauer's possible involvement in Laurel's kidnapping the moment he starts to wake up. The thing is, with the IV I've given him, that's not likely to be until sometime tomorrow.''

"Did you need, medically, to keep him asleep that long?''

Reeve smiled grimly. ''The police aren't likely to get involved in a medical judgment call. And I doubt Crackauer is going to be in any position to sue me for medical malpractice.''

Polly hesitated, then said in a small voice, ''He seemed to say… Do you think my family told him to kill me?''

Damn her family! But Reeve replied gently, ''He may have misunderstood. Most likely, he was overstepping his bounds.''

"I really appreciate all you're doing for me, Reeve.''

Whatever feelings he wanted from her, indebtedness wasn't one of them. ''I'm doing it for myself,'' he contradicted. ''My life here was routine and boring till the night I found you off the road—the first time. Now just look at all the excitement I've got!''

Polly's grin was rueful. ''Glad to be of service.'' She was quiet for a moment, then asked, ''How long is the snow supposed to last?''

"Do you mean, when can we go after Laurel?''

"Yes.''

"Much as I hate to grant Crackauer credit for any sense, he was right about one thing—we can't drive to Denver tonight.''

While he had gotten Crackauer stabilized, Polly had called the phone number in his wallet. It belonged to the Brown Palace Hotel in Denver. The reception desk confirmed they had guests named Jenson, but would not reveal the room number. Polly told him she had not asked to speak with them; she had not wanted to reveal that Crackauer's plans had been changed.

"The prediction is that this won't last more than another couple of hours. Road crews will be out bright and early, so with luck we'll be on our way to Denver by nine in the morning."

"You don't have to go with me," she began.

Reeve inhaled deeply, keeping himself from saying something he would regret. "We've been through this, Polly. I know you prefer to do things for yourself. *I* prefer to help. And right now, my preferences take priority. It's my car, after all."

He glanced at her. The exasperation in the way she shook her head was contradicted by the tenderness in her smile—a look that did more toward toasting his toes than the excellent heating system in his car.

They reached his street, which was less than a mile from the medical center. Usually, it took only five minutes to drive up the slopes to his home, but as treacherous as the roads were this night, he had taken his time. They had left the hospital more than twenty minutes earlier. He pulled into his driveway, turned off the ignition and looked over at her.

"Let's go inside," he said. "You've already shown that you can cook a mean meal, but let me demonstrate to you what a master physician-chef can do."

"THAT WAS DELICIOUS," Polly said, pushing back from Reeve's spacious wooden table awhile later. This was the first time she had visited his home. His kitchen was a cook's dream, large, with lots of counter space in golden tile that complemented the Mexican tile floor. The cabinets were tall and deep, of the same rich oak that was used through the rest of the modern-style house built into the mountainside.

With its capacious, open rooms replete with vaulted and beamed ceilings, the place suited Reeve, being masculine yet comfortable.

And the dinner he cooked *had* been delicious. Somehow, he had put together a spicy mulligatawny stew in hardly any time, and he had done it from scratch.

He had changed into jeans, and a sweater in deep shades of green and brown that went wonderfully with his gingery hair. He had given her the task of peeling and slicing potatoes. She had enjoyed working beside him, watching his sure and fluid motions as he cooked with seemingly as much skill as he doctored.

The problem was that she had no appetite. She kept thinking about Laurel and what tomorrow would bring. Would they even be able to find her sweet baby? What if her family left the hotel before Reeve and she arrived? And what about Carl?

When they were done eating, she helped with the dishes. "I suppose you didn't eat much because you didn't want to admit I was the better cook." Reeve's smile softened his words, and she forced herself to grin back. She appreciated his efforts to cheer her.

"Oh, your skills are certainly adequate," she said lightly.

"Adequate! One of these days we'll have a contest. Maybe we'll wait till Laurel is old enough to judge."

"Sure," she said, knowing her tone sounded dejected. That presupposed they found Laurel and Polly was able to get her back.

"It'll be all right, Polly." She heard Reeve's words, but her tears began to flow nevertheless.

In a moment, she was in his arms. She rested her

cheek against his strong chest, let him enfold her in his comforting clasp.

But it was more than comfort she felt as his hands rubbed her back. Startled, she looked into his eyes and saw her own swiftly ignited desire mirrored there. His reaction stoked the simmering fires within her.

"Reeve?" The word came out as a question.

"Polly, I brought you here because we needed somewhere safe to stay tonight." His voice was hoarse, and his hands had begun to stroke not only the innocent contours of her back, but the erotic curve of her buttocks. "But I want you."

She remained still for a moment. This could be their last time, their very last—

She stepped back as sanity returned. "I can't!" she cried. "Reeve, it doesn't matter what I'd like. I'm not— I mean, Victor said… I'm still married. Carl is alive."

Not giving him time to respond, she turned and hurried into the guest bedroom Reeve had designated for her—knowing there was no way she would sleep tonight.

Not when Laurel was not with her. Not with what was waiting for her tomorrow.

And not with all the yearnings inside that she felt for the giving, generous and utterly sensuous man whose bedroom was just down the hall. Who would be sleeping nearby, yet as far away as if he were in another country.

He had wanted assurances she would not run away from him. She almost wished she had provided them— for now she couldn't.

She was married. And if the only way she could keep Laurel was to stay with Carl, she would have no choice.

She had made love with Reeve before—glorious, fiery love—but she had still been married. If she had known, she would have abstained, no matter how much she had desired to be with him.

She knew now. And no matter what she wanted from life, what she craved most—Reeve might no longer be part of it.

She had learned one thing, though. A person could be self-sufficient, do things on her own, yet still accept the help of people who cared about her.

Particularly a very special person, about whom she cared deeply...

That wasn't dependency. It was intelligence, to take assistance when it was offered.

It was a lesson she would remember forever. For memories might be all she would have left of Reeve— the man she loved.

REEVE DID NOT EVEN TRY to go to bed for a long time that night. Instead, he remained in his office, going over patient charts, medical journals, anything to keep his mind off Polly.

More than once, he nearly went to her. So what if her husband was still alive? Surely she would retrieve her daughter and stay in Selborn Peak, where she had begun a new existence, under a new name. Begun a new life.

She would divorce her husband. She had to.

And if she didn't?

With a groan, Reeve slammed the book he had been holding down on his desk. The sound reverberated through his high-ceilinged office.

Maybe, just maybe, he had become close enough to Polly that she no longer wished to run away from him.

But all the wishes in the world—his and hers—might not be strong enough to keep her with him.

Chapter Fifteen

Of course the Brown Palace Hotel would be top of the line, for her family to stay here, Polly thought. Denver's grandest traditional establishment, Reeve had called it.

Polly's body still ached from her latest accident and her head still spun. Nevertheless, she walked resolutely along the carpeting of the top floor toward the suite with the number Victor had given when they'd called from the lobby minutes earlier. She ignored the stunning atrium open to the lobby nine stories below.

Reeve's stride beside her along the open corridor was composed and determined. He wore a brown leather jacket over corduroy trousers, and his tall, muscular presence gave her comfort—though she knew he could do nothing to help her.

He did not touch her, not even in reassurance. Oh, how she wanted him to—no matter how fruitless it would be.

He had made phone calls before they left. Crackauer, he informed her, had not yet awakened. Then Reeve had driven them to Denver. The ride had seemed to take forever, though the snowstorm had stopped as promised and the roads were cleared. Polly almost wished it had lasted even longer; it was probably the last time she would ever be alone with Reeve. Not that they spoke much. There was nothing left to say.

After all that had happened in the last couple of days, she was certain Reeve hadn't betrayed her to Victor. After all, Victor would have done his research, learned that she saw a lot of Reeve. He would have wanted to drive a wedge between them.

But it didn't matter, anyway; there was no greater wedge than the fact that she was still married.

Reeve and she reached the door and Polly stopped. "Thanks for the ride, Reeve," she whispered, "and everything else. But you should go now."

His nostrils flared. "I'm not leaving."

"But..." She didn't have the energy to argue; she had to save it for the fight to come. "Okay," she said defeatedly. She knocked.

In moments, the door was pulled open. "Ah, little sis," boomed Victor's despised voice. He stepped aside for her to enter, though she did not move. "It's even more pleasant to see you than it was to hear from you. We expected Mr. Crackauer to let us know he'd picked you up and that you were on the way."

"Or was he supposed to call after he dropped her off—someplace where she would never be found?" Reeve said.

Polly bit her bottom lip, waiting for Victor's reply. But her stepbrother only frowned as he seemed for the first time to notice who had accompanied her. "You must be the renowned Dr. Snyder." His look hardened. "That's a nasty accusation, Dr. Snyder."

"It's a nasty situation all around, Mr. Jenson."

"Not at all. It's a family reunion. You'd better leave. Now that Catherine has returned, we've private family matters to discuss."

Reeve, taller than Victor, glared down at her stepbrother. "I'll hang around to see how things go."

"Suit yourself." Victor shrugged his shoulders beneath his white silk shirt. They were narrower shoulders than Reeve's. Shoulders that no one would dare to lean on for comfort. "You didn't tell me, Catherine, just where our Mr. Crackauer is."

"He wasn't feeling well, so he sent me instead." Reeve's cool stare dared Victor to contradict him. "And just when was he supposed to arrive with…Catherine? Or news of her?"

"Anytime today. Why don't you both come in?" Victor turned his back and walked away.

As Reeve strode into the room after him, Polly saw him flex his hands as though preventing them from becoming fists. She appreciated his protectiveness. It was his nature. But she prayed that somehow *she* could protect *him* from this group of jackals that was her family.

The suite was lavishly decorated, with ornate antique furniture and sweeping draperies. On the opulently upholstered sofa sat her mother, holding Laurel. Polly dashed forward. "Mother! Are you all right? How is Laurel?" She held out her arms, but her mother turned away as though shielding the baby. Laurel began to cry.

"I'm taking care of you now," her mother crooned to the infant in her lap. Despite Polly's worries for her, Ava Calvert Jenson looked no worse than the last time she had seen her, though the wrinkles about her eyes appeared more pronounced. Her hair was the same shining, moderate brown, styled conservatively. She wore an attractive poppy-colored dress.

Polly knelt by the sofa and touched her mother's thin arm. At least Laurel had quieted; she seemed content sucking on the bottle Ava held.

"I missed you, Mama," Polly said. Ava's expression was watchful as she regarded her daughter. "I did what I did because I had to, for the baby. I'm sorry if it hurt you. I'll explain everything as soon as I can. Please, trust me."

"Why should she trust a daughter who shot her husband?"

Polly looked up. Her stepfather entered the room from an open doorway. He looked as dapper as ever; he even wore a dark mayoral suit, as though he had expected company. He was followed by her other stepbrother, Gene, a younger version of Victor.

"Who didn't even call to let her own mother know she was alive and well," Lou continued as he advanced toward Polly. "Just ran away from home like some immature child instead of an adult, married woman with a child of her own to think of. Your poor mother. I'm worried she'll never recuperate."

Shuddering, Polly took a breath and made herself rise to her full height. Her stepfather stopped his approach so close that he nearly touched her. Although it was late morning, she smelled wine on his breath.

She wanted to shrink back but didn't. The only way she could survive this was to be strong.

She pulled her coat tightly around her and dug her hands into its deep pockets. "You're right," she said. Lou Jenson smiled. He had always been kindest when she agreed with him. "I shouldn't have run. I've learned my lesson—you can't flee from problems. They always catch up." She dared a glance at Reeve, who leaned nonchalantly against the wall across the room. His half smile was approving, and it bolstered her self-confidence. "So, I'm ready to go home with you and take care of Mother. I'll face Carl, too. Is he here?"

"Carl?" Her mother spoke in a monotone. "He's dead. You knew that, Catherine. You shot him."

Polly felt the blood drain from her face. She had certainly thought she had killed Carl, but Victor had said—

"I told Catherine that Carl was still alive," Victor stated with a careless shrug. "I figured she'd think it easier to come home if she didn't have to deal with a murder charge."

"He…he is dead, then?" she asked her mother. Ava was the only one of the family she dared to trust.

Ava nodded, her eyes still firmly watching her daughter.

Polly could not dredge up remorse that Carl was gone. Instead, she recalled how he had taunted her that last night. Had threatened her, and then, when she refused to promise to be an obedient wife and daughter once more, had aimed the gun at her. She had been pregnant. She had been scared. She had only tried to save her baby.

Polly glanced at Reeve. His golden-brown eyes shone, as though he were suddenly filled with renewed hope. She had not absconded with another man's child. She was not a married woman.

But neither was she free to be with the man she loved. She looked quickly away.

"Yes, your husband is dead," Lou said. He took a seat beside his wife on the carved sofa and fondled Laurel's hair.

Polly tried not to wince; her sweet, innocent daughter was being touched by this man who had wreaked such havoc on so many lives. He had killed her father and probably Warren. Perhaps others as well. He had killed her mother's spirit, had tried to kill her own. But what could she do?

"Sit, everyone." As Lou gestured around the room,

the large diamond on his right hand sparkled in the light from the crystal lamp on the end table. "You, too, Dr. Snyder, if you won't leave. We've got to discuss the future. Catherine's...and little Laurel's." He took the baby from his wife. Laurel let out an angry squawk when she no longer had the bottle in her mouth, but Lou positioned it so she was eating once more.

Polly had to hold herself carefully in check to avoid running over and snatching her baby. Acting on impulse would gain her nothing. She had to be alert, watchful...wise.

"It's warm in here, Catherine," Lou said. "Wouldn't you like to take off your coat?"

She shook her head. "No, thanks. I'm still feeling chilled after my little...accident the other night. I'd imagine I spoiled your plans by not dying then." She glared at Victor. His smile did not change—but he did not deny her accusation.

"Don't be absurd," Lou said. Polly sat on the chair that he designated. She would not defy her stepfather—in that.

Reeve did not sit. Instead, he took a position behind her. Though he did not touch her, she could feel the heat from one of his large hands as it rested on the back of her chair near her neck. She wanted to rub against it for strength, but instead sat up, straight and ladylike, just as she had been taught in the proper finishing school to which she had been sent before entering college.

"Gene, Victor, how about pouring everyone something to drink."

Her stepbrothers hastened to do as their father directed. Polly almost laughed at how those two men jumped when their father, the mayor, snapped his fingers. They had probably not had an original thought between them.

All of the terrible things that had been done in the past years had been effected, directly or indirectly, by Lou Jenson.

Polly politely took the glass of orange juice that Gene handed her. He gave her as evil a wink as Victor ever had. She shuddered, and he smiled at her obvious discomfort. He knew what Lou had in store for her, and he loved it.

Polly wanted to grab Laurel and bolt. But too much depended upon her behavior: her mother's future. Laurel's. Hers. Perhaps even Reeve's.

Lou looked not at Polly, but over her shoulder. "Dr. Snyder, I really think this would be a good time for you to leave. You can see that no one has hurt either Catherine or the baby. No one will. But we have private—"

"Family matters to discuss," interrupted Reeve. "I know. But I'm not leaving until I know exactly what you have planned for...Catherine."

She felt his fingertips as he touched her gently. *Thank you,* she wanted to say. But she remained still.

"A lot depends on Catherine herself." Lou sat back on the sofa and rearranged Laurel so he could casually cross his legs. "We'd hate to have her brought to trial for murdering her husband. I'm not even certain that I can prevent it. I'm the mayor of North Calvert, not God."

Oh, but he liked to pretend he was God, Polly thought. And she was sure now how he was going to play it. Maybe he had intended that Crackauer kill her, and maybe not. In any event, he was a master at improvisation. There would be no evidence to convict her of

Carl's death if she became her old obedient self once
more. If she didn't…

"It was self-defense," Reeve said. She loved how he
stuck up for her even in the face of her cruel family.
She would remember it always—even when they were
irrevocably parted. Her hands began to shake.

"Catherine *said* it was self-defense," Lou stated.
"But Gene and Victor heard her arguing with Carl earlier. Threatening him if he didn't let her leave town for
a while—to visit an old school friend, wasn't it?"

"That's not the way it was at all," Polly hissed
through her teeth. "And you know it."

"Who, us?" Victor, who had taken a seat on a stiff
wooden chair between his father and Gene, took a long
sip of wine. Then he deliberately reached up and stroked
the side of his right eye. He was about to lie—to control
her. "I know you killed him, Catherine. I even saw you
with the gun afterward, and I knew you'd bought one,
had been practicing at a shooting range. I'd hate to testify in court, but if I had to—"

"I don't even know how to fire a gun!" Polly exclaimed. Her shooting of Carl had been entirely acci-
dental. She wanted so much to be strong, but how could
she win? Victor would have someone ready to testify
that she'd bought a gun from him, someone else prepared to state that he'd seen her firing it. She made herself calm down. "So to prevent this story from coming
out," she said softly, "what would I have to do?"

"Come home," Lou said, giving Laurel back to her
grandmother. Ava took the baby, but her attention remained on her husband. Her gaze moved up and down,
as though she were studying a total stranger.

Oh, Mama, Polly thought. Had her mind snapped under all the pressure? But her eyes were clear and fo-

cused. There was something else in her expression. Something strange. But Polly hadn't time to dwell on it. She turned back to her stepfather.

Still seated, he reached out as if he would hug Polly. "We missed you. Your mother needs you. I was afraid she would have one of her spells and never come out of it. With you home, perhaps she will be better. And we could be certain, if you lived with us, that you would be a good and competent mother to dear little Laurel, instead of a murderess with a temper that could not be controlled. That's all we ask of you, Catherine. Just come on home."

And be subjugated. Lose her autonomy, her self-respect—so hard won with her small but successful job at the medical center.

Live with the fact that her family was a bunch of murdering criminals—and that they would have access to her beloved daughter.

Live without the ability even to call Reeve...

How could she fight this?

The horrifying answer was she wasn't sure she could. But she had a secret arsenal....

"All right." She kept her voice firm and resolute. "If I must, to protect my mother and daughter, I'll go with you. But don't expect me to be the person you knew before. I won't run away again, but don't expect me to obey your every command. You killed my father and my friend Warren, and now you've tried to kill me. That was what Victor wanted the other night, and when he didn't succeed, you sent Crackauer to do it. Right?"

"You see what kind of irrational behavior my stepdaughter is capable of?" Lou had stood and faced Reeve man to man, as though asking for Reeve's understanding. The pained expression on his sophisticatedly handsome face appeared almost genuine. "She makes these unprovable accusations all the time. And yet she was the one who killed her husband."

There was silence after those words, and they seemed to hang in the air. Why didn't Reeve contradict them? Had his belief in her innocence died, now that he knew Carl was truly dead, too?

"You know, Dr. Snyder, that we offered a reward for whoever restored Catherine to her family. We're willing to award your medical center that helicopter you've been saving for." Victor grinned slyly at Polly. He was obviously trying once again to drive a wedge between them. Instead, he had eliminated one altogether. He wouldn't be offering to pay for a helicopter now if Reeve had already sold her out.

"We'll live without it," Reeve said pleasantly. Oh, how Polly wanted to hug him then, in apology and gratitude. And more. But she remained still.

"Have you thought about your hospital's reputation?" Lou Jenson asked. "In a small town like your Selborn Peak, it probably would not do a doctor any good to be thought of as being...close to a murderess."

"Well," said the deep, resonant voice she loved, "we have an interesting situation here. You, Mr. Jenson, have said that Polly killed her husband. Right?"

Lou, still standing near Reeve, nodded, his dark eyebrows raised as though in dismay at the very thought.

"Gene and Victor heard her arguing, and Victor caught her essentially in the act of murder. Isn't that so?"

Her stepbrothers, seated beside one another, gave similar malicious smiles as they acknowledged what he said.

"On the other hand, Pol—er, Catherine, believes that Lou killed her real father and her friend Warren. Not only that, but she is certain that you sent her husband to silence her. Only problem was, he was silenced instead. Do you deny any of this?''

"We deny it all, of course," growled Victor.

"That's too bad," Reeve said. "It's what's going to come out in the news—along with the recent threats to Catherine's life."

Lou Jenson frowned furiously. "What do you mean?"

Reeve moved from behind Polly to take a seat on the antique chair between Gene and her. He crossed one muscular leg casually over the other and straightened his dark corduroy trousers. "It's like this, Victor, I believe you met Alicia Frost, the reporter. She said you promised her a story."

"Right," he drawled. "She was most helpful in tracking down Catherine after she tried to run away again. I figured I could come up with some little story to appease her."

"Interesting," Reeve said. "But it won't be quite as you intended. Before we left Selborn Peak, I told Alicia all I knew about this whole sordid situation, which was a lot, after I finally got the story from Polly. I figured some investigative reporting would help protect Polly and her mother and daughter from further harm. Even me, if you got it into your heads that I was a threat. More deaths or disappearances might seem a little suspicious, don't you think? Particularly when reported on national news. If I know Alicia, she's already hot on the trail, and on my advice she's making sure plenty of people know what she's doing and why—a little protection for her, too."

"You're lying," Victor said, waving his arm as though erasing the thought. "You didn't tell that reporter anything."

Reeve gave a lazy grin that made Polly's spirits soar. He hadn't said anything when Alicia had visited her the last time in the hospital. But he had been on the phone a long time this morning before they left.

"You don't see me touching my eyelid, do you?" Reeve asked. "Oh, yes, Polly told me about your little code, as well as everything else. And now Alicia knows about it, too."

Victor's glare at Polly was furious. Oh, yes, their silly, insidious code was supposed to be secret. Sacred. Polly couldn't be happier now that she had shared it with Reeve.

"That woman wouldn't dare report anything about us without proof," Gene interjected as he stood and poured himself another glass of wine. "We'd slap a defamation lawsuit on her so fast that her head would spin."

"Isn't truth a defense in a defamation lawsuit?" Polly asked innocently. She yearned to give Reeve a big, grateful kiss. His plan seemed so simple...yet it just might work! "I heard that from you as I was growing up, when you dug up dirt on political enemies."

"You'll never prove anything."

"But it'll make an interesting story," Reeve said. "And from what Polly told me, the last thing you want in your lives is scandal. Notoriety wreaks havoc on rising political careers, doesn't it?"

"What do you want, Snyder?" barked Lou Jenson. "A little extra money besides the helicopter?"

"What I want is freedom for Polly and her daughter. And her mother, for that matter."

"Look, you son of a—"

"Shush, Lou," Ava Jenson interrupted her husband. Polly glanced at her mother, who remained on the sofa with Laurel in her arms. Polly started. Ava had an uncharacteristically aware grin on her face. What did it mean?

Her mother rose. She handed Laurel to Polly, who gratefully accepted the return of her daughter. "Oh, this has been enlightening. I like your new young man, Catherine. He's brave. He inspires courage in other people, too. I think it's time I have my say."

Polly stared. Was this her mother? Ava Calvert Jenson suddenly appeared to have grown several inches. She stood straight and tall, her regal chin raised. Her eyes, gray like Polly's own, blazed. Polly recalled that expression on her mother's face: proud and self-assured. But she hadn't seen it for—how long? Since her childhood?

Since before her father had died?

"Sit down, Ava." Though his tone was gentle, there was no mistaking the command in Lou Jenson's voice.

"Oh, I don't think so, Lou."

"You don't want to get overexcited. Remember what Dr. Milton said."

"Dr. Milton," said Ava Jenson, "is a self-important quack whom you employed to keep me drugged and docile. But I've grown quite tired of that, as I'm sure you've noticed."

"He has said more than once that you belong in a rest home," Lou snapped. "I've protected you, but—"

Ava laughed. "You've protected me? You've done nothing but attempt to destroy me from the minute we were married."

"No, even before that, Mother," Polly contradicted, hope bubbling up inside her. Where was the timid, ill woman of the last years? *Gone,* she prayed.

"Right. Before that. You murdered my John—because he stood in the way of your political power. I didn't want to believe it until Warren came to me with the letter my poor, dear first husband had written.''

"A forgery," Lou growled, taking a step toward his wife. Reeve reached out to keep him back.

"No, I recognized his writing. In fact, Warren gave me the original of the letter before he…disappeared. I have it hidden safely away. I have some thoughts on where poor Warren might be, too—not so safely hidden away. In fact, like Catherine, I'm sure one of you killed him.''

"Who did it, Lou?" Polly demanded. "Did you murder Warren, like you did my father?"

"You can't prove anything." Lou's voice had turned airy, and he waved one hand unconcernedly as he took his seat once more. He hadn't admitted to the murders. But he hadn't denied them, either. "No one can authenticate that letter, and everyone will know your mother's claims are just the ravings of a woman who's been long suspected in Calvert of being near lunacy."

"She's not, you know," Polly insisted.

"No, I'm not," Ava agreed. "Not now. I was certainly foolish, marrying Lou so soon after John died, simply because I didn't care what happened to me. He married me for John's name, for political power… Who knows why? Not for love, but that didn't matter to me. I didn't care about much of anything until you, Catherine, and your baby were put into danger. That was why they wanted Laurel here, you know. They thought they could calm me down once more if I had charge of your little one. But I knew why they sent that investigator after you, and it wasn't just to have a little chat. I was so worried…."

Holding Laurel carefully at her side, Polly hugged her mother.

"Lunacy!" interrupted Lou Jenson. "We'll have her put away so fast for this—"

"No you won't!" Polly reacted to the shadow of fear that crossed her mother's face. "You'll be fine, Mama," she promised. "They can't touch you now. We'll have you examined by experts—you know some good psychiatrists, don't you, Reeve?"

"Of course," he replied. "And I have a feeling that they'll find you're just fine, Mrs. Jenson."

"Call me Ava," Polly's mother said, with a relieved smile. "I won't be Mrs. Jenson much longer, if I have anything to say about it."

"Now, Ava..." For the first time, Lou Jenson appeared alarmed. He rose and approached his wife, but she stood her ground, even as Reeve placed himself in front of her.

"You've come to think of me as a nonentity for so long, a blob of mud beneath your oh, so powerful mayoral boots, that you forget I still have eyes and ears. My eyes saw John's note. My ears heard you discuss what really happened to Carl."

Hoisting a fussing Laurel to her shoulder, Polly asked, "What do you mean, Mother?" She stood and began swaying back and forth to soothe the baby.

"They knew you were upset about Warren's disappearance, so Lou told Carl to put the fear of God into you so you'd keep your mouth shut. He didn't really mean that Carl should hurt you, though. They didn't want you dead...then. When you shot him in self-defense and left, Carl called our house. He was far from dead when Lou, Victor and Gene got to your place. But they were angry, first that he had attacked you with a gun, and second because you'd gotten away and might talk. So they finished the job you'd accidentally started."

"One of them killed Carl?" Polly stared at her mother, hope making her knees weak.

Ava nodded. "I haven't quite been able to figure out which, though I suspect Victor, with his temper. Carl was found with two bullet holes in him, not one. And after you were endangered, you and your baby, I knew I couldn't be an ostrich any longer. I even threw away my tranquilizers."

"So Victor killed Carl?" Still dazed, Polly nevertheless needed to ask the question. "He left me to die in the snow after stealing Laurel...but with Carl he actually pulled the trigger?"

For the first time, her elder stepbrother appeared nonplussed. He rose from his chair. "I only meant to scare—"

"I'll make sure you're both locked up for insanity," Lou growled, then reiterated yet again, "You can't prove any of this."

"The original of John Calvert's letter might help," Reeve said. "Maybe it *can* be authenticated. If not, it's at least enough to get an investigation started. It'll all make an interesting news story." He rose and held out his hand to Polly. "Now," he said, "I don't think I have any further interest in your personal family discussion. Neither does Polly, I suspect. Or Ava, for that matter. Are you two and Laurel coming with me?"

"Absolutely," Polly said with a grin.

"Just let me get my coat," said Ava.

"Oh, I don't think so." Victor sounded blasé as he rose from his chair—but he had a gun leveled directly at Polly.

"I have a few choices here," he said. "I could shoot Dr. Snyder and Mother, then tell the authorities that poor Catherine totally lost her mind and killed them both. Or

I could go for Catherine and her doctor, and let it be known that Mother was the crazy one. Or—''

''What about fingerprints and evidence about who fired?'' Polly demanded boldly, though her heart pounded. Either way, Reeve would be killed; they could not afford to have him, an obviously sane outsider, survive.

She could not let him die. She should never have allowed him to get involved. She moved to plant herself in front of him. But she still had Laurel. She turned sideways so that any bullet would hit her, not the baby.

Reeve grabbed her upper arms and slowly thrust her to the side. Their eyes met. Once again, just as she intended to protect him, he was trying to protect Laurel and her.

She felt the tremulousness of her brief, loving smile replaced immediately by fear. If they could get out of this alive, together...

''You watch too much television, little sis,'' Victor responded with a laugh. ''Maybe that's why you've gone crazy. In any event, we can make the evidence work in our favor. Don't worry about that.''

''I'm not worried,'' Polly lied boldly. But she was terrified. How could she protect Laurel? Reeve? Her mother?

She glanced at Ava. Poor Mama, standing beside Victor, was blinking reddened eyes. She looked confused once more, opening and closing her hands. The excitement had been too much for her; she was folding herself back inside the shell she had used for protection for so long.

''Let them go, Jenson,'' Reeve demanded. ''You can't kill us all and expect that whatever cockamamie story you concoct will get you off free. Besides, Alicia knows what's going on, and her story will contradict any lies you tell. It's over."

"For you, it is." Victor sneered, raising the gun and aiming. "Now, give me the baby, Catherine."

"No, Victor." Ava's voice was weak, but she stumbled toward her stepson.

Startled, Victor glanced at Ava. His momentary distraction was enough. Reeve lunged at him.

For long, terrifying moments, the two men fought over the gun, turning slowly as, in a macabre dance of destruction, they struggled together.

Lou and Gene Jenson stood nearby, obviously looking for a way to intervene. But they didn't dare get any closer as Reeve fought to keep the gun, still clutched in Victor's hand, pointed downward as he attempted to wrest it away.

Polly froze. The circumstances reminded her vividly of another situation, only weeks earlier, when she had tried to save her own life, and her baby's, by grabbing her husband's gun.

It had gone off. It had killed Carl. No, wounded him. She hadn't, after all, killed him. But who would be shot here?

Not Reeve. *Oh, Lord, please protect him,* Polly begged silently as she curled herself defensively about her infant.

With a final burst of energy, Reeve grabbed Victor's hand and slammed it against the wall. Victor shrieked in pain, dropping the gun. All four men lunged for it....

But Reeve was the one who stepped back, pointing the weapon at the Jensons.

"Now, Polly," he said without looking at her, "it's time to call the police." The handsome, youthful features she had come to love so well were a frozen mask of determination.

She had no doubt he would shoot these men to protect her, her baby, her mother.

And she had never loved him more.

She tried to maneuver around the group to get to the phone, but Lou took a step forward, his hands raised placatingly. Reeve steadied the gun as he aimed toward the older man.

Lou was the one to back down. He shrugged. "All right," he said defiantly. "Go and tell your sordid little lies. Our lawyers will enjoy turning the tables on you. It'll be your word against ours."

"Oh, I don't think so," Polly said. She moved Laurel onto her left hip, then reached down into the deep pocket of the coat she had borrowed from Alicia.

The coat was not all she had borrowed.

Triumphantly, she drew out Alicia's small tape recorder and showed it to Lou, Victor and Gene. Despite his distance from her, Lou's hand went out as though he meant to grab it. An angry noise issued from Victor's mouth. Gene just shook his head.

Polly could recall no stunning admissions they had made on tape. But they hadn't denied much, either. The recording would definitely be of use to Alicia—and for protection.

Polly watched as Reeve held the gun on the three men while she called the police.

MUCH LATER, as Polly carried Laurel into the hallway, she allowed herself to relax. It was over. With luck, she would never again have to watch behind her. The police had taken Lou, Victor and Gene into custody.

Reeve and Ava were with her. Polly waited until the

four of them were ensconced safely in the elevator before leaning on Reeve. He took her into his arms.

"I love you," he whispered into her ear as he hugged Laurel and her gently.

A warmth like none she had ever felt before spiraled through Polly at his welcome words. "I love you, too," she said.

She glanced up to find her mother regarding them, her brows raised in amusement.

"Do you think," Polly asked Reeve, "that there's a place at Selborn Peak for three generations of displaced Calvert women?"

"With me," Reeve said. "Definitely with me."

Chapter Sixteen

Polly turned on the news and sat on an overstuffed sofa in the Selborn Community Medical Center lounge. Familiar faces confronted her, as she knew they would.

After more than a year since the ordeal in the hotel room, seeing her former family, even in person, no longer bothered her. At least not as much as it once had. But she much preferred the distance of watching them on television.

"The Connecticut Supreme Court has denied the appeals of former North Calvert mayor Lou Jenson and his son Victor on their murder convictions. In a bizarre conspiracy that lasted for decades, Lou was found by the lower court to have murdered the former mayor of the small town, John Calvert, and, fifteen years later, District Attorney Warren Daucher, who had unearthed evidence in Calvert's death. Daucher's body was found after a tip from Lou Jenson's former wife, Ava.

"Lou's son Victor was found guilty of having murdered his brother-in-law, Carl Elkins, and was also an accessory in Warren's killing. Another son, Gene, was convicted of being an accessory in the recent murders. And in another twist, a private investigator, Al Crackauer, testified, in exchange for limited immunity, about a conspiracy to kidnap and murder Lou Jenson's step-daughter, Catherine Calvert Elkins.

"The Elkinses are suspected in other disappearances that occurred in the small town of North Calvert over the last fifteen years, as well as extortion and bribery, but the investigation into these matters continues."

Alicia continued to probe for answers, Polly knew, keeping the detectives on the case vigilant. Though she did not appear on newscasts, Alicia had gained national recognition for her coverage of the story about North Calvert, Connecticut's, flawed first family. She had moved to Denver to further her career as an investigative reporter and seemed to thrive on it. Polly was happy for her.

The sofa sank beside Polly as someone else sat down. A strong, comforting arm drew her close. "Why did I know I would find you here?" Reeve asked.

"You know how I feel about the news," his wife replied.

"I'll have to ask your obstetrician whether hearing such stuff is good for the baby." Reeve tenderly patted the growing bulge at Polly's abdomen.

"Our son won't understand."

"Or daughter," Reeve added.

"Or daughter," Polly agreed with a smile. "I was just going to the child care center to see Laurel. Want to join me?"

"Sure."

On the way, Polly peered into her new office, small but a step up from her cubicle. She was glad she'd stopped in. There was a voice mail message from her friend Lorelei, who was coming to Selborn Peak for a long-delayed visit—her first after she had been maid of honor at Polly's and Reeve's wedding.

"Will you still arrive next Tuesday?" Polly asked, returning the call immediately.

"Absolutely," Lorelei replied. "Now, don't have that new baby till I get there. I want to help usher her into the world."

"Or him." Polly smiled at Reeve, who hovered nearby.

After Polly hung up, they walked slowly down the hospital corridor together, arm in arm. Polly looked up at her husband's face. He bent down, and his lips met hers tenderly. "I love you, Polly Snyder," he whispered.

She had changed her first name, legally, to Polly. Her last name, too, had been changed when she married Reeve.

When they finally reached the child care center, noise blasted through the walls, but Reeve pushed open the door anyway and they both went in.

The brightly painted room, with shiny linoleum floors and dozens of tiny plastic tables and chairs strewn around, was an utter mess, with toys and games tossed everywhere. It was a normal day, Polly thought.

Unsurprisingly, their eighteen-month-old daughter, Laurel, was at the center of the chaos. "Mine!" she exclaimed when she saw her mother. She was beautiful and perfect and growing rapidly. In tiny blue jeans and a red knit top, she toddled toward Polly and Reeve, holding an unfamiliar-looking rag doll.

"I don't think so, honey," Polly said.

"It is hers," confirmed Ava Calvert. Polly's newly divorced mother was a full-time employee at the child care facility. She was almost always bright and animated these days. She claimed that the dark days of her years of confusion and subjugation were already fading into an ugly memory.

"Ricky brought the doll for Laurel today to keep her occupied," said Esther Meltzer, who also worked there. She was Ava's landlady; Ava had moved into Polly's old apartment.

"How is our orderly-in-chief doing with the puppet theater he's building for the kids?" Polly asked.

"Here I am," cried Ricky from behind a large wooden structure in one corner. "I'll have it done in a few days." He had spent a lot of time in the child care facility recently; he was dating one of the college student volunteers. He had been working long, hard hours and had made headway in paying down his debt to the medical center. Soon he would start classes in a local community college. Polly was proud of him.

"Is everything under control?" she asked as she always did. In addition to her other duties as head of the hospital's accounts receivables, she was the chief administrator of the child care facility. Plus she had a responsible position as cochair of the center's fund-raising committee.

One day, she thought, after Reeve's tenure was up, she might even run for city council.

"Everything's fine," her mother and Esther both assured her.

A little while later, in the hall once more, Polly grasped her husband's handsome face in her hands. "Come here, you." She stroked his slightly shadowed cheeks with her thumbs, then gave him another kiss, harder than the one they'd shared before. "I needed that for fortification. It's a rough day—Clifford's on the warpath. He thinks I'm being too soft on slow payers again."

"Good old Clifford," Reeve responded with irony.

The hospital administrator had been the one, in

exchange for promises of funds for the rescue helicopter, to deliver to Crackauer a lot of the information Victor had used against Polly. When he had realized his mistake, his apologies had been effusive—for Clifford. Reeve had wanted to fire him, but Polly had interceded. Hopefully, he had learned his lesson.

"Anyway, Clifford's right this time. You're always too soft on slow payers." Reeve's reminder was tender. The love shining in his golden eyes weakened her knees and filled her with the desire that grew with every moment she spent with this man. If only they could get home early tonight…

Bringing herself back to reality, she sighed and responded, "Almost everyone pays this way… eventually."

They walked together once more until they reached the door to the outdoor garden between the medical center and the office building. Reeve pushed it open.

"I hope your day's not too rough," Reeve said with a laugh. "It—" His voice was drowned out by the sound of the emergency helicopter that was just landing on the medical center's roof.

With Reeve's support, Polly had taken charge of the "Lifesaver Walkway" fund-raising effort, and Selborn Community, with Alicia's excellent stories as publicity, had finally been able to afford the helicopter a few months earlier. Polly was delighted she had been able to assist, particularly when one of the first transported patients had been Ernie Pride, the man instrumental in getting Reeve to Polly's side to rescue her in the first place. Ernie was recovering well from his heart attack.

Until the sound of the helicopter died, Polly studied the new terra-cotta tilework of the walkway. She pointed with pride to a large one in a prominent position in a corner, which was inscribed, In Honor of the Wedding of Dr. and Mrs. Reeve Snyder. In a conspiracy spearheaded by Frannie Meltzer and her aunt Esther, all their friends had contributed to the commemorative tile.

Without a word, Reeve drew her onto their tile and kissed her soundly once more.

When he released her, he looked toward the hospital roof, then back down at Polly. With one eyebrow raised, he asked, "With Clifford getting tough on you, do you ever feel like just getting into that helicopter and flying away?"

He was teasing. For he knew her answer, now and forever.

"And run away from you, my love?" she replied. She nestled into the haven of his arms, her mouth nearly touching his. "Never again."